WHY I HUNT FLYING SAUCERS
& OTHER FANTASTICALS

A Science Fiction
Short Story Retrospective

HUGH A. D. SPENCER

Milton, Ontario
http://www.brain-lag.com/

Brain Lag Publishing
Milton, Ontario
http://www.brain-lag.com/

Library and Archives Canada Cataloguing in Publication

Spencer, Hugh Alan Douglas
[Short stories. Selections]
     Why I hunt flying saucers and other fantasticals : a science fiction
short story retrospective / Hugh A.D. Spencer.

Short stories.
Issued in print and electronic formats.
ISBN 978-1-928011-07-1 (paperback).--ISBN 978-1-928011-08-8 (kindle).--
ISBN 978-1-928011-09-5 (epub)

     I. Title. II. Title: Short stories. Selections.

PS8637.P47A6 2016   C813'.6   C2015-907885-7
                                                        C2015-907886-5

PRAISE FOR THE STORIES IN THIS COLLECTION

"'Why I Hunt Flying Saucers' delivers a superb jolt of humour." ~ *Toronto Star*

"[One] of the best, and most original, stories." ~ *Locus Magazine* on "(Coping With) Norm Deviation"

"'Problem Project'… is a whipsaw change in tone… A tight grin of a story, not quite a laugh, but lingering." ~ *Tangent*

"Spencer has fun with quantum realities." ~ *Best SF* on "Problem Project"

"'Pornzilla' was weird beyond belief." ~ *Best SF*

PRAISE FOR *EXTREME DENTISTRY*

"Spencer stacks it with so many odd elements that it all works. Well worth searching out." ~ *Toronto Star*

"*Extreme Dentistry* is very funny and quite horrific." ~ *Amazing Stories*

"A dark and mordantly funny satire." ~ *Armed and Dangerous*

"Hitchhiker's Guide to the Galaxy vibe." ~ *Read, Play, Review*

PRAISE FOR THE WRITING OF HUGH A. D. SPENCER

"Lucid, lyrical, and savvy." ~ Paul Levinson, author of *Unburning Alexandria* and *The Silk Code*

"If you like to laugh and cower at the same time—if you like science fiction that is simultaneously progressive and retro—then you need to read this… Like nothing I've ever read before. Highly recommended." ~ Dale Sproule, author of *Psychedelia Gothique*

Other books by Hugh A. D. Spencer

Extreme Dentistry

TABLE OF CONTENTS

FOREWORD

Ideally an introduction should be a gate into a garden: you see a path before you and glimpse the flowerbeds that beckon in the distance. More often, however, introductions are right up there with melatonin and other soporifics, especially those written by academics, myself being one of these. But, Hugh Spencer is a special case. He was my first graduate student in days of yore (MA 1981 to be precise), and his garden, this anthology, is filled both with fragrant flowers and carnivorous plants, most of which combine both traits. In fact you cannot tell when you stop to sniff a blossom if it is also going to bite your nose as you drink in its allure. Tricky, that! Hugh, you see dear reader, lies in wait with x-ray vision and pounces just when you think that you are in a familiar and safe place. He sees through social convention, personal conceit, historical trends—you name it. His aim is smack on. His barbs are unique: they induce laughter, shock, recognition, and a whiff of fear all at once. In fact if he had been born an Ancient Athenian, they would probably be handing him, along with old Socrates, the hemlock cup right now, because his humour, his insights are downright seditious at times. So, dear reader, put on your lead underpants, as I have done, (*we have to protect ourselves against his x-ray vision—harmful in large doses*), and follow me. I intend for this introduction to keep you awake.

Science fiction is now deeply interwoven into the fabric of our culture. It is a hallmark of modernity. Those who write it, who in effect tell it, are bards of a modern form of folklore. As with any folklore science fiction has themes and as with any bard worth his supper Spencer uses such themes in his work. For example, an easily recognizable theme is that of alien encounters. We may think here of how these are usually used by others. We now have cute, pet-like aliens, such as *E.T.*, alongside lofty, glowing ones who offer salvation, think *Close Encounters of the Third Kind*. Abduction grades over into joining the aliens, a sort of complicit abduction theme wherein the humans willingly embark upon what one assumes will be a benevolent and inspiring journey into new realms, as with those aliens who play Bach in *Close Encounters*. (*After all, if they play Bach, how can they be bad?*) We may call this branch (which of course has other sprouts, such as the monster alien, the Martians of H.G. Wells, etc.), a part of the Steven Spielberg Tree, or SS Tree for short. Well, Spencer adds a whole new branch to the SS Tree. One might say he has cast a vine over it. He would remind us that boarding that mothership is the science fiction equivalent of hopping into a stranger's car for a ride. This is much the case with the first story, from which the anthology takes its name.

In this story about alien abductions "Why I Hunt Flying Saucers," his aliens have traversed the unimaginable void between the stars, not to be our cute friends or our saviours, but to prod us and stick needles into us (*I actually have known two people who claim to have undergone such indignities—no, Hugh is not one of them. They were not happy.*), and his protagonist reaches a breaking point. What does he do? (*Dear reader, indulge me in an aside. Myth and folklore are like plutonium: poisonous. Once you know a bit, stories and movies offer few secrets. Poisonous? When I watch a movie with my family I know within ten minutes how it will unfold. It's the same with a book. Within a few pages all is clear. Oddly when I share these insights they make even gentle people like my wife turn red and clench her fists. So, I promise not to do that to you. But, dear reader, the problem here is that I can't do this ahead of time showmanship with Spencer's stories. Hugh fools me almost every time. I can't tell what's coming in his tales. So, you'll just have to read them for yourselves. Silly me! Of course that is why you bought this book. Well, back to our "garden tour."*) Well, when you stop and think about this alien business it is really quite rude. It is almost like biology class where you, the superior being, dissect an inferior one, such as a frog or a rat. Even the meek can endure only so much rudeness before they turn and this revenge in the first story comes so abruptly and naturally that you do not realize it has been wreaked until the moment is past and you suddenly understand what has happened. This sneakiness, made up of simple, decent morality and reactions set with a deft and almost invisible hand to dangle upon the exalted SS Tree, where no one would ever expect them, these are the hallmarks of Spencer's fiction as set out in the first tale.

These skills, coupled with a palette of vivid detail continue in

"Icarus Down/Bear Rising." Here Spencer introduces a narrator who is an anthropologist. No surprise here, dear reader, Hugh's degree is in anthropology. (*In fact in one of the short biographical remarks that accompany each story Hugh admits that he wanted to be an anthropologist. I sense a bit of remorse here, but if he harbours regrets, this should not be one of them. In fact Spencer is an excellent anthropologist with the qualifier that he does his fieldwork in his imagination and not in some swamp.*) As with other anthropologists he wields a moral sword and in this story one of history's greatest injustices is set right, and for once a First Nation people receives good news while a world shifts.

Virtual reality, alternate universes, parallel worlds, these form a spectrum of another theme, now also a hot topic in physics, and the anthropologists appear once more, but not as the spear point of righteousness, their frequent assumed role, but as a benevolent or compassionate observer. In "When Bloomsbury Fails" we see a super anthropologist from the future. (*Of course, given my misspent youth, that 'Bloomsbury' led me to expect some grand repudiation of the Bloomsbury Group, Keynes, Strachey, Woolf, etc., who set so much of the intellectual stage for the 20th century, and we all know what a mess that was. But Hugh is tricky and he fooled me again.*) Yes, the mess of a century is there, but in this case the anthropologist acts from mercy to "demessify" the proceedings. In "Problem Project" we have a more aloof set of observers watching over a multitude of worlds with a Darwinian dynamic afoot, and in "A 21st Century Romance" we find no observers at all, but rather two competing realities, one of which brings in a theme that I have not seen used by anyone save Spencer, a sort of low tech or folk space travel.

"Mormonism and the Saskatoon Space Program" takes up the idea of space travel as a folk art or at least an enterprise that need not be part of some all-consuming industrial culture. This tale is a bucolic one, one of reminiscence, with a tender tone and it sets the entire idea of spacefaring in a new light. For those outside Canada Saskatoon is the last place on any planet or parallel Earth where one would expect space exploration to be conducted.

Nevertheless, the all-consuming industrial state is a theme that Spencer tackles head-on in "Robot Reality Check" and "Z-burger Simulations." In the former we find corporate image über Alles, certainly a dynamic most of us have met at some point in our lives, along with another: the competent versus the arrogant. The results, with robots that fail their warranties, is delicious—ultimately. In the latter "fast food" tale God is dead, but religion is alive and capitalism has become an all-consuming faith. Spencer shows us with a mix of horror and humour, a sort of reduction to the absurd of the capitalist imperative all done with a smile and a quickie meal.

The anthropologist surfaces again in "The Triage Conference." (*Now, dear reader, I was trained as a linguist, but fate landed me in an anthropology department. My colleagues are moral people and see themselves as advocates for the downtrodden of the Earth. They hold this position to be natural and the only one that a thinking person can assume, not as a reaction contingent upon the morality of the imperialist past. Hugh tells a tale otherwise.*) The anthropologists in this tale are not benign and not obviously simply observers. They are intent on improving humankind (*Who can deny the appeal of such a goal?*), not by improving culture or technology, but by eliminating large portions of that mankind as undesirables. This tale sounds all too much like a history of 20th century totalitarianism. It is replete with a program agenda and academic "frivolities," including a murder. Its ending is as stunning as it is clever.

In "Strategic Dog Patterning" we see a future problem through the eyes of a dog catcher trying to contend with "man's best friend" run amok. Well, that friendly little furry pet of yours is a social and hierarchical animal who shows you affection and obedience largely for the food that's in it. (*I love my little dog, but I can't deny that she's a bottomless pit when it comes to food. Without food can there be love? Forget the dog! What of my wife and children and their love for me?*) Imagine a slight mutation or two in a puppy somewhere; imagine a canine social order where humans no longer provide the food, at least not from a can; and then this wild story becomes really quite scary, especially if you own real estate. (*Read it and you'll understand that last remark!*)

Our ancestors would admonish their children: "You are what you eat." (*I am told that they say this about the people who live in San Francisco. In New York you are what you wear. But, in Boston you are what you read. Now, what about Toronto?*) Well, yes, but now with computers everywhere and porn as well (*not to mention dietary supplements*) one might advise your children: "You are what you watch." Well, in porn people are naked and copulating (not to mention other activities), but is it erotic, is it realistic, is it query, query, query? We can debate such endless matters another time, but one can say with full assurance that porn is abundant. Even super heroes (and the ones in this story are weird variants of this theme, a hybrid of what the movie-going public expects and what your high school algebra teacher would want) are impotent (*choice of word here when talking about porn??*) in the face of the spreading menace. Things do not end well…

Now, where would science fiction be without robots? This is actually an older theme than you might imagine. Even the Ancient Greeks had a myth about Talos, a bronze giant on Crete that guarded the island and ran around its shore three times a day. (*Whew! Something you could never demand of a normal "man."*) He/It had a "vein" that ran down to one of his heels and, like Achilles, could be killed only by a blow to this heel, what we would now call his power supply or fuse box. (*Makes you wonder where the Greeks came upon this weird tale, eh?*) The term 'robot' itself comes from a Slavic language, Czech, and is based on the root for 'to work', and, according to my Apple Dictionary app (*here I sit with a sort of robot writing this*) originally appeared in a play in 1920 where it referred to forced labourers. So, slavery isn't dead, Hugh tells us in "Hospital for Sick Robots," it has merely been confined to a new race, one in the making, that we are industriously seeking to create with the blind faith that a world with robots will be a better world. Hugh warns us that we had better ask right now: better for whom?

In "Coping with Norm Deviation" Spencer takes us down the path of nostalgia (*from the Greek **nostos** 'return home' and **algos** 'pain'*) and the making of an amateur science fiction movie in high school. This is not a science fiction story as such, but rather an account of the role science fiction can take in actual, contemporary, mundane lives. This is a poignant tale and ties in with the personal reminiscences Spencer supplies for each story. I have not seen such biographical notes before in an anthology, but they reinforce a central theme of Spencer's work: ordinary life. No matter how glorious, good or evil, a technology may be, we would all face problems in such settings in the course of lives that would still feel mundane and would still be filled with problems. In this regard his science fiction is more a sort of science realism (anti-science fiction?). His work is filed with allusions to multiple layers of sense or custom, whether from humour or horror, to the point that I often felt some new term was needed to capture what he has done. Well, I admit that even as a linguist this task is beyond my skill set, and so I shall leave this to you, dear reader.

John Colarusso, Ph.D.,
Professor of Linguistics
McMaster University

WHY THE FLYING SAUCERS ARE HUNTING ME

Sounds like advanced paranoia doesn't it?

But before you put this book down and slowly back away, please give me a few seconds.

Let's start by assuming that I'm using a metaphor here. I don't really think that Martians have their telescopes trained on my bedroom or that UFOs are hovering behind the bus shelter when I'm going out to return library books or that Little Grey Men are continually tangling up the wires on my headphones every time I have an important Skype call coming in. The protagonist in the first story in this collection has these kinds of problems, but you will have to wait a few pages before we get into that.

No, here we are going the symbolic route and I'm suggesting that you can think of "flying saucers" as a sort of imaginative short-hand to represent things that are unexplained, uncomfortable, usually inappropriate and generally weird.

So that's "flying saucers" taken care of. Now let's dip our toes into the personality of the author. Just a little bit, you don't want to drown or catch pneumonia or get embarrassed. Here's the scoop: I simply don't believe that anything is normal. My experience has been that every time you look very carefully at the so-called "every day" and "ordinary" you will soon see past the disguise of apparent reality and discover something bizarre and unexpected.[1] Such revelations can be terrifying or at least inconvenient. So, that's the "*Me.*" I am distrustful of reality.

I guess the fact that I actively notice and write about this spooky oddness takes care of the "Hunt" part of the title too.

On to "why."

Why? Several SF writers: Barry Longyear, Isaac Asimov, Ray Bradbury, and other writers who are better known than me[2], have

---

1   This is not an uncommon condition among writers of science fiction and magic realism. I believe mental health professionals refer to it as PKDS (Philip K. Dick Syndrome).

2   I am assuming that most of you have read these authors and in fact some of you may be reading my book because you could not find anything written by them and had to settle for this.

mentioned the experience when people ask them (usually at parties) the question: "Where do you get those crazy ideas?" Often the answer involves an address in the state of New York.

Fine. Why not?

In my experience, it isn't the "where" question that interests me, but the "why" question. So far no one at a party has asked me: "*Why* do you insist on writing these stories with all those crazy ideas?" Maybe it's because I don't go to a lot of parties.

So why would I write science fiction? Or any kind of fiction for that matter? Certainly not for the money, especially in the Canadian context. Our publishers are very dedicated, very honest and sometimes even generous, they just don't have access to a lot of money. It's a good idea to hang on to that day job. Not that I'm complaining. I've gotten some very good story ideas from some of my day jobs.

You don't write for fame either. Actually, I can't complain in this regard. My writing has put me on national radio and television; along with Dr. Allan Weiss, I got to curate the National Library of Canada's exhibition of Canadian science fiction and fantasy; and I've had over a dozen dramatizations of my stories broadcast on National Public Radio's Satellite Network. However, as much as I enjoy the attention[3], I have noticed that none of the above has made me more attractive or taller. This is disappointing as it would be nice to be at least six feet tall and it's a real pity that I am stuck with these beady little eyes.

So why do people like me write about such crazy ideas? The simple answer (in my case) is that the storytelling process seems to make me feel less crazy.

I am a lousy person to lie on the beach with and it is not just because I sunburn easily. If I don't have some kind of creative project on the go, I will start chasing cars, biting lamp posts and loudly complain about everything. It is telling that at every birthday or Christmas my family members always give me art and writing supplies. Clearly self-interest is at work. This is good; I have some very nice pens.

In my defense, I can assure you that I worked pretty hard to make the results of my pathology as entertaining as possible. What you are holding in your hands is a collection of my short stories, written from 1990 to 2007. They were originally published in a

---

3   i.e. I'm no Stephen King but I've had more than my 15 minutes of fame.

variety of magazines and anthologies but my main venues during this period were *On Spec* magazine and the *Tesseracts* anthologies. They have been brave and distinctive voices over the years.

Most of the stories in these books were also subject to the alternatively inspiring and devastating critiques of the Cecil Street Writers Group. Founded in 1986 by Futurian SF writer, editor and critic, Judith Merril, the Cecil Street Group continues (as of 2015) and its members have included: Michael Skeet, Pippa Wysong, Cory Doctorow, Helen Rykens, Theresa Wojtasiewicz, Allan Weiss, Kim Kofmel, Peter Watts, Edo van Belkom, Karl Schroeder, Dale Sproule, Sally McBride, Sara Simmons, Natalie Zina Walschots, Keith Scott, and Madeline Ashby.

And me.

Over the years my feelings toward the Cecil Street Group has ranged from gratitude, respect, and admiration, to envy and sometimes the desire to apply electricity to tender parts of their bodies. Regardless of this, sometimes complex, relationship with the Cecil Street Group and the irreparable damage they may have caused my self-esteem, their influence on my work has been at times profound. Workshopping can be a difficult process but in my case it has definitely been worthwhile.

So thank you Cecil people. You big meanies.

I thought pretty hard about whether I should offer introductions to these stories. It is possible that some readers may not think I'm as fascinating a personality as I think I am.

Here are the reasons why I think you might get some benefit from reading the "stories about the stories":

1. There will be some gossip. Not a huge amount, hopefully just enough for a bit of fun.
2. There is no second reason; I need this point to justify making a list.
3. Some of you may be writers yourself and perhaps my experiences will be of some use, or at least reassurance, as you venture down your own creative path.

After all, the flying saucers could be hunting you too.

EXAMINE US

I've had a really good run with this story. After coming out in *On Spec*'s humour issue, it was nominated for an Aurora award for best short fiction in 1991; it was reprinted in the anthology *On Spec: The First Five Years*; and, it was the basis for the second of my scripts to be produced by Shoestring Radio Theatre, who broadcast from San Francisco. I even pitched a TV version of it to the 1990s *Outer Limits* series.

I still love my rejection letter from *The Outer Limits*. The producer wrote that the script was very entertaining and very funny, but then went on to explain that, "...unfortunately our programme is a humourless affair." I respect this sort of self-awareness.

The original story illustration in *On Spec* was truly inspired. Richard Bartrop depicted a classic Grey extraterrestrial slipping on a rubber glove, while preparing to administer the obligatory rectal exam to an abductee. For several years *On Spec* used it in their print ads with the caption: "EXAMINE US". I'm certain they got some attention from that but I hope they didn't raise any false expectations among readers who might have expected a more intimate, or at least intense, experience.

WHY I HUNT FLYING SAUCERS

Originally published in:
On Spec, Winter, 1991
On Spec: The First Five Years, 1995
Edited by the
On Spec Editorial Collective

When I pull myself out of bed I notice that my slippers are missing. Obviously aliens are responsible. They have been disrupting my domestic routine for a few weeks now, presumably to observe my reactions.

I smell something in the hallway. Briefly, I wonder if they've been playing with the kitchen range, but then my still half-dormant brain tells me that the smoke is coming from the wrong end of the house. With trepidation, I poke my head out of the bedroom door and see the spitting embers of a dying campfire sitting in the bathtub. The aliens have also deposited a string of marshmallows, luncheon meats, wieners and beans along the hallway leading from the kitchen to the bathroom. The sticky brown sauce from the pork and beans has been mixed with some kind of gooey xenoplasmic fluid; the mixture has soaked into the hallway carpet and the resulting mess looks incredibly difficult to clean. Damn those aliens.

Over a perfunctory breakfast I sip my tea and decide to call in some cleaners to deal with the second-encounter debris while I'm at work. Then I wonder, pointlessly I know, why have they done this to me? Is this some bizarre attempt to re-create some trivial moment from my Boy Scout days? Or some silly reference to humankind's origins as hunting and gathering species?

Putting on my coat, I go out to the driveway where I notice the telltale brown streaks under the car. Nothing serious, just another oil leak. Undoubtedly another sign of extraterrestrial activity.

Driving to the office, I sight a formation of cigar-shaped lights drifting over the city. I seem to be the only one who notices their ships on a regular basis. As I coast into the parking garage I see a pair of bulbous obsidian-black eyes floating in my rear-view mirror. The alien's huge eyes are set over the tiny triangular face with the customary green skin. The image of the face lingers for a fraction of a second, then I only see the concrete and orange paint of the garage. I hypothesize that the alien may have been using some time/space warp device to gather a microsecond's worth of observations of my driving behaviour. Who knows what information aliens think is important?

When these things first started happening to me I was terrified almost to the point of insanity. But lately I'm just feeling very, very put upon.

My morning at the office is reasonably uneventful. The aliens have decided to surround my desk with some kind of sensory distortion field, which temporarily removes my colour vision and alters my sense of hearing. For about two and a half hours everybody sounds like Oswald the Duck or one of those damned chipmunks. But living inside a Max Fleischer cartoon doesn't keep me from making a few calls to the names on my client list. Actually their helium voices make some of the customers a little easier to take.

Sometime after coffee the distortion field dissipates and I decide that it is safe to go find some lunch. Not surprisingly, I'm not the most popular person at the office and therefore no one volunteers to join me. I suppose my co-workers don't enjoy finding themselves breathing through their ears or finding a mass of otherworldly tendrils squirming out of their quiche and salad.

But today I don't get to feel lonely. Once I reach the sidewalk I feel a strange upward breeze bite at my cheek. I turn and see a bright halo of celestial light descending around me. Once again I find myself inside an alien spacecraft.

And as usual I'm lying naked on a cold metal slab. A billion years ahead of us and these BEMS haven't learned how to build a comfortable examination table. I twist my head to the side and see a screen displaying a three-dimensional projection of one of my undoubtedly fascinating mucous membranes.

The spindly forms of the aliens float up to the ceiling of the chamber:

"Human, we mean you no harm..."

One of the aliens removes a long tube from the polished curved wall.

"...just roll over onto your side and bring your knees up to your chest."

Great, another rectal probe.

I suppose it could be worse. Once they strapped me into a chair and stuck red-hot needles of light into my stomach and my skull. Another time they were taking secretion samples from my ears, nose and throat—it felt like they were pushing a lawn mower up my left nostril.

The absolute worst session was when they were taking spermatozoa specimens. I don't happen to find bug-eyed, bulb-headed E.T.s particularly sexually arousing, so they used this giant vacuum cleaner nozzle to generate the erection. They took 17 ejaculate samples. This was much less fun than you might imagine. Think ragged flesh.

So maybe just another rectal examination isn't so bad. Anyway, that's what I tell myself as I feel the cold metal of their probe pushing roughly through my anal sphincter.

❋　　❋　　❋

I wake up on my living room couch. Two men dressed in black and wearing sunglasses sit across from me. The mirrored surfaces over their eyes make then look a little like aliens too.

"Are you conscious, now?" asks one of the men in black.

"Yes," I sigh.

I see the empty bottle and syringe sitting on the coffee table. Pentothal again. Their induced hypnotic trance is the only reason I am able to remember today's abduction.

The small man with a short blond crew-cut starts to pack his tape-recorder into his briefcase.

"There doesn't seem to be any obvious physical damage or psychological aberration. It seems to be the typical scenario..."

The larger man, who has an even shorter blond crew cut, stands up:

"...but we'd like you to stop by our offices in the next couple of days for a medical."

Just what I need, I think. Another examination.

Both men gather up their briefcases and walk toward the door.

"Don't bother to get up," the larger man says. "We've already contacted your office, and we gave your MasterCard number to the cleaners. I hope you don't mind, they had to put in a lot of work on the rug and they needed a deposit."

An irrational sense of propriety forces me to stand and follow the government agents to my door.

"Now don't put off the physical too long this time," the smaller man says.

"There is the possibility that the aliens are slowly modifying your DNA and turning you into something…" he pauses as he considers the implications "…not quite human."

"That's only one of the theories we're working on," the larger man adds. "It could be that they are using your body as the host for a fetal alien organism." Then he looks at me with what I'm sure he thinks is a sympathetic expression. "You must try and prepare yourself for the possibility that it could burst out of your intestines at any time."

"Well." I'm silent for a moment, trying to think of something appropriate to say. "I really appreciate your concern."

I sound very tired.

The two men let themselves out onto the porch.

"Do you have any more of those 'Missing-Time-At-Work' forms?" I ask. "I'm just about out and my boss can't get his insurance claims processed if I don't submit within 48 hours."

"We left some on the kitchen table," says the larger man.

The smaller man takes something from inside his jacket pocket. He hands me a paperback edition of *The Book of Mormon: Another Testament of Jesus Christ.*

"You look very tired, sir," he says with sincerity. "I wish you would let me send the missionaries over for a discussion. I know that a strong testimony of the revealed gospel of these latter days would be a great comfort to you."

"I appreciate your concern."

The larger man also hands me something. It is a colourful leaflet.

"But in the meantime you might want to cheer yourself up by purchasing any one of our fine Amway products."

"I appreciate…"

They walk to their car, a well-maintained AMC Hornet.

"Be sure to call me at home when you want to place orders,"

calls out the larger man as he opens the car door. "Don't place orders through my office."

"You can call me at home or the office," says the smaller man.

There is the sound of car doors slamming. The roar of an engine. And the men in black are gone.

The smaller agent's concern for my spiritual well-being must be overpowering since he seems to have forgotten that this is the third Book of Mormon he's given me. Walking toward the bedroom, I deposit his gift on the growing stack of latter-day religious literature on my bookshelf.

And true to its claims, the Amway catalogue does indeed contain a startling range of useful, attractive and unique household bargains. Including an attractive and affordable digital clock radio with simulated plasti-wood finish. Which will come in handy because the beings from another world have decided to melt my bedside clock after I left for work. Damn aliens.

I spend the rest of the day in bed. I'm too tired to read and the aliens have also transformed my collection of Ridley Scott and James Cameron videos into highlights of a Spanish language home-shopping channel. Aliens.

✳   ✳   ✳

They come for me in the night. I don't know what time. Squat ugly creatures who look like a cross between hobbits and Armenian tailors. They lift me out of the bed and tear off my pajamas. Maybe they don't like the material.

Stubby dwarf-fingers hold me like iron bonds as they lift me over their flat shoulders and carry me toward the smoky light of the space/time portal.

A telepathic message blasts through my mind:

"Do not be afraid, Human. We mean you no harm."

Where have I heard that one before?

"Okay, okay," I say weakly. I slide through the portal. The light runs like slimy electricity over my skin. "You know, I really could walk through this thing under my own power," I protest to the space-midgets.

If anything, they grip all the harder.

"Do not be afraid…"

Into the mothership we go.

*   *   *

We float upwards into the dome of the crystal cathedral. We are thousands of human specimens. Representatives of all races, cultures and ages of history.

The living glow of the crystalline structures suffuses our naked bodies and makes us perfect. We drift into a loose helix pattern as we turn toward a massive corridor that stretches out into infinity.

We see myriads of life forms of every conceivable configuration lining the inner walls of the enormous passageway.

Intuitively I sense that we are facing the collective knowledge and experience of all intelligent life in the known universe: The Galactic Super-Culture.

Its god-like voice gently roars at us:

"BEAUTIFUL HUMANS! YOU ARE PRECIOUS AND RARE. WE WISH TO PROTECT AND PRESERVE YOU!"

Protect us? With rectal probes? I wonder. Besides, I feel a little over-weight.

The Super-Culture articulates again:

"EVIL HUMANS! YOUR HIDEOUS AND VIOLENT NATURE MAY SOMEDAY GROW AND ENDANGER THE WHOLE UNIVERSE IF YOUR WAR-LIKE TENDENCIES ARE NOT CONTAINED!"

The whole universe? It seems unlikely to me. What risk is a bad attitude to your average black hole?

"WISE HUMANS! PROPERLY NURTURED, YOU WILL MATURE INTO THE LEADERS OF US ALL!"

Wise? I remember some of the products at the back of the Amway catalogue.

"FOOLISH HUMANS! WE MUST PREVENT YOU FROM DESTROYING YOURSELF IN ATOMIC FLAME!"

Give me a break!

When I wake up, the mothership has vanished. The Super-Culture is gone. But I am still naked.

Naked, lying face down on my front lawn.

I estimate that it is mid-afternoon. The telephone in my kitchen is ringing. I answer it by the third ring.

"This is the Chief Librarian," says the measured, rational voice at the other end of the line. "Your name was given to us by a Mormon gentleman and an Amway representative. We have a book from our 00.0 stacks which you may find of interest."

❋   ❋   ❋

I arrive at the Reference Section with no sign of alien activity. Perhaps invaders from another solar system hesitate to interfere with the operation of the Toronto Public Library System.

It has been a long time since I've been to a library. Or an art gallery, or a movie, or even a McDonald's. I fear public settings in general and I avoid places of learning in particular. I love libraries and museums, and the prospect of watching these storehouses of human reason and achievement get twisted around by some inexplicable alien prank is too depressing to contemplate.

But this time I was invited. And it just feels like the right thing to do.

The Chief Librarian looks pretty normal. She scans me carefully, decides how much authority she has to apply to contain any likely nonsense from a person of my height and weight, and then she speaks:

"You're the gentleman I spoke to earlier? Just remember that these are reference books. You can look at the books as long as you like *inside* the library." She narrows her eyes: "So don't even ask if you can borrow them."

She places a gray book in front of me. Then she hands me a pad of paper and a ballpoint pen.

"Most people who look at this book ask if they can use these."

She's right. The book contains much that is noteworthy. Its title is *Practical Steps for Coping with Unwanted Alien Encounters* and its author is a Louise Wallis. The dust jacket states that Wallis is a social worker who has "suffered over 300 alien abductions since the age of 15." The promotional copy also notes that "after developing these simple and easily mastered techniques, Louise Wallis has helped thousands to completely eliminate extraterrestrial influences in their personal lives."

Wallis is everything the desperate seeker of aid could ask for: she's perceptive, honest about what she knows and what she doesn't know, and she writes in easy to understand sentences. This is some of what she wrote:

"I formed a support group for people who claimed to have been abducted by aliens. Their stories were so vivid and expressed such humiliation that I never doubted their sincerity.

And as we shared our experiences we gradually learned that each one of us was given a different reason for our degradation by our captors.

These horrific and ridiculous creatures would puncture our wombs with ice-cold needles, pierce our urinary tracts with razor-edged tubes and drill holes into our skulls - telling us that they had the right to perform these atrocities because the ozone layer was disappearing, or because our governments had nuclear weapons, or because our race had ventured into outer space.

A common pattern in the early phases of the support groups was for abduction victims to try and convince themselves that the aliens were correct, and that these indignities can be justified as part of a higher purpose. But as we shared our grief and our anger, together we concluded that this belief was a delusion.

Every thinking person who has been abducted by alien beings must eventually face the same crucial question:

It must take tremendous technology and resources to travel across the galaxy to our world. Would intelligent and compassionate beings travel so far and at such cost, simply to confuse us and insert crude implements into our bodies?"

My hand is trembling. I have to stop writing for a moment. Wallis continues:

"It is undoubtedly true that an infinite universe holds many things that are beyond our current level of understanding. But to be rational, emotionally stable people, we must base our attitudes and behaviour on what we can understand and those things that we have experienced.

...if we believe what the aliens do and not what they say, we can only conclude that these creatures from beyond the solar system are raping and abusing us."

I look up from the page. The walls around me stand solid and unchanged. My left hand is pressed against the table, its heavy waxed top suggesting the stability and strength of its structure. At least for the time being I am safe.

I reach the next chapter:

"The support group sessions also had a number of constructive outcomes, including the mutual discovery that many of us had invented strategies and techniques for coping with unwanted alien appearances in our lives. Collectively, these means of coping represent a highly effective repertoire for anti-E.T. self-defense. Many of these strategies use everyday items from the home or the simplest industrial equipment and farm machinery…"

I start to take a lot of notes. Eventually I have to ask the Chief Librarian for another pad of paper.

❋　　❋　　❋

I'm driving well over the speed limit. The jeep is my latest and most satisfying guilty pleasure. But it's just past six in the morning and on a northern Ontario highway there is very little risk of collision. Besides, my new toy was designed to be driven down empty roads at high velocities.

Since things have settled down for me, I've been a lot more productive in the office and the jeep was a reward to myself for some hard work.

My latest tape, *The Ventures in Space*, twangs from the stereo speakers. I remember a line from Wallis:

"Many aliens can be made severely uncomfortable by certain sounds or varieties of music…"

Damn right. The little buggers really hate early sixties electric guitar groups or some of the more obscure British invasion bands like Herman's Hermits or the Zombies.

A few weeks after my trip to the library I caught some aliens stealing single socks from my drier and I toasted them with a blast of "Mrs. Brown You've Got a Lovely Daughter" from my portable tape player.

The aliens collapsed onto the basement floor, gasping out little silent "o's" with their lipless mouths and trying to keep their over-sized brains from leaking out their nostrils. Eventually they vanished into a cloud of red steam - just like dead Invaders from that old TV show.

Now the Shadows and early Floyd are my favourite groups.

The highway leads into a small river valley. I slow the jeep and park it at the side of the road. I turn off the stereo and roll down the window.

This feels like the right kind of place.

"Trust your instincts," writes Wallis. "The aliens are always trying to humiliate you, undermine your self-confidence. There is a reason for that; they don't want us acting on our feelings."

There's an odd texture to the air, like the taste of new metal and rotten eggs. I look up and see a mild distortion in the morning clouds.

This is definitely the right place.

I get out of the jeep and remove my packsack from the trunk.

"Many of these strategies use everyday items from the home or the simplest industrial equipment and farm machinery..."

First I put on the insulated work-gloves. Next, I open the hood of my jeep and connect the cable to the battery terminals.

I have my own theory about the aliens. It's based on the writings of a psychoanalyst who used to explain behavior in terms of informal "social games". Now, I can't prove this theory, but I like it: the aliens are playing a very silly, very sick game with us. Schlemiel and Schlemazel.

The schlemiel is like the sneaky, vaguely malevolent guest who goes around your house deliberately spilling things, embarrassing people and being a general pain in the ass to his host—the unwitting and vastly put upon schlemazel. The objective of the schlemiel is to force the confused schlemazel to both forgive all these pranks and feel guilty for getting upset in the first place.

The aliens land. They kidnap you. Then they tear off your clothes, jab you with hoses and needles and generally treat you like space junk. But it's okay, they say. You can forgive us and love us for all this because we have advanced intelligence, and because you have reactors, toxic waste, pay-TV, bad haircuts, etc., etc.

What's really disturbing is the fact that the schlemiel doesn't understand why he's doing all this bad shit to people. It's all pathological, compulsive behavior. Probably the result of some deep-rooted, star-spanning self-loathing. They need us to regularly reassure them of their superiority.

Damn aliens. They have some advanced technology. But they aren't very smart.

I hook the cable to the reel and lock the bolt into the crossbow. The thick gloves make it difficult to aim the weapon, but I manage to align the cross hairs just over the patch of slightly wrong blue overhead. I pull the trigger and the bolt hurtles through the air, whisking the length of cable behind it. It's a good shot. The arc of falling cable neatly dissects the early morning sky.

There's a hard "click" that echoes through the river valley; the cable has connected with something invisible.

Suddenly a string of sparks races up the cable, and there's a beautiful multi-coloured explosion of electricity.

Its force field ruptured, the flying saucer crashes into the valley.

I heft the bulky packsack over my shoulder and stride toward the smouldering metal shell. Without the field to maintain its structure, the saucer is already starting to disintegrate. So it only takes a little effort, and a pair of bolt-cutters, to force open the hatch.

Inside I see half a dozen aliens. They are either unconscious, or too disoriented to move. All of them are naked.

As I enter the main chamber I notice that one of them is twitching in a pod-like chair, others are crouched over streamlined control units, and one is sprawled face down on the slowly dissolving floor.

I open the packsack and look for the lubricant and the cattle prod.

A POISON STRONGER THAN LOVE

This story is a good instance of the Cecil Street Writers Group working at its best. I was quite pleased with the first draft, mostly because I thought it was the most brilliant work of prose ever written.

However, my fellow workshop members were much less impressed. With alarming efficiency they managed to reduce the draft to its self-righteous component molecules.

I think they didn't like it because I was telling the story with the distant conventional language of an ordinary science fiction story: "There's a technical problem in the universe, let's apply our reason to solve it."

Anyway, that's how I see things decades later. At the time, I was furious. However, rage got the first version of the story going and even more rage helped me to re-craft the tale using very different perspectives. The characters are in a lot of pain and to tell the story properly perhaps the writer has to be in some pain too.

The "inspiring rage" that forced me to write "Icarus Down/Bear Rising" comes from the book *A Poison Stronger Than Love: The Destruction of an Ojibwa Community*, by Anastasia M. Shkilnyk. It was one of the most difficult and most necessary things I have ever read.

ICARUS DOWN/BEAR RISING

Originally published in
On Spec magazine.
Spring 1992, #09 Vol. 4 No. 1

Thoom.
Thoom.
The sound of hollow bone striking taut hide.
Listen to me, Crazy-Man-With-Hair-On-Your-Face. You must listen. This is the Telling of Tales. This is the telling of The Way:
Once, all was all, everything was everything else. Then the One was the Many. And the many divided into the Spirits of the Air and the Spirits of the Earth.
And the spirits took the forms of the animals and the elements, but all were still brother and sister/mother and child.
This is the Core of The Way. You live among your brothers and sisters.
Thoom. Thoom.
This is the Telling of Tales. You must learn The Way if you are to live.

*   *   *

These are the facts.

According to Henderson, sometime in late November an experimental military satellite named "Icarus" was undergoing tests in orbital space.

With some pride, Henderson told me how Icarus performed

almost perfectly, directing a series of electrically powered projectiles at its targets with precision accuracy. Then, apparently with no warning, the power-field overloaded and the satellite disappeared from their telemetry screens.

Presumed destroyed. Another three billion dollars gone, a few thousand more cuts in pure research.

Then around New Year, they picked something up... heading toward the Earth at a considerable speed. The trajectory was all wrong, but the re-broadcaster insisted that the approaching object was indeed Icarus. NORAD had just enough time to project the point of impact.

As far as I know, Henderson had no background in classical mythology, so he was able to tell the story with absolutely no sense of irony.

A few hours later I got a call from the Company. They wanted to pick up my consulting contract, and could I come on the next plane please?

Something had happened in northern Canada. And in spite of the season, it looked like a good way to avoid marking term papers.

*　　*　　*

Thoom.
Listen, Hairy Man:
The Spirits of the Earth became many: the Beaver, the Bear, the Person. For a time they all flourished. Then after a time, they did not.

The Little Girl lay shivering in her sleep.

A cold blast of air blew in from a shattered window. Her bedroom walls were covered with tiny pictures of strangely-coloured dancing animals from faraway places: Rhinopotomires, Giffarafasourus—the names confused her grandmother.

At the time, Mother wasn't thinking about the wall-paper and she didn't know about the cold air. She had consumed over a litre of gin and she was asleep too.

It was not until morning that the Grandmother found the Little Girl. Grandmother wrapped her in the warm folds of an old flannel blanket and held the child close to her body.

A few nights later the Man smashed open the kitchen door. He stank of very bad wine and he screamed that "Daddy was home."

The Little Girl hid behind a door as the Strange Man grabbed Mother and threw her down on the hard kitchen tiles. Then, like some monster from the VCR, he jumped on her and tore at her clothing.

Frightened by the monster, the Little Girl ran out into the winter night. She ran along the main road toward the forest. She ran until the houses looked like tiny tin blocks under the giant black curtain of the sky.

Once among the trees, she walked deeper into the forest. But Little Girl's spirit was only small and her lungs were made weak by the cold. She lay down to rest for a moment.

In the morning Grandmother looked in on her children. Her daughter was bruised but able to speak and walk. But no one could find the Little Girl.

Grandmother went looking. Sometimes children would stay with another family for a few days, or they would stay together in one of the empty houses, or even spend the night under the steps of the old church. But the Little Girl could not be found at any of these places.

One of the men of the village did find her. The curled, spiritless body lay in a snow bank near a pathway leading deep into the forest.

The Spirits of the Air...

✳   ✳   ✳

The air outside was so cold that it looked like the chopper blades were slicing solid chunks out of the atmosphere.

Even with the helmet microphone I had to yell over the roar of the turbines: "We're coming up on the village of Bear Spirit. In the winter you'll only find Cree down there."

One of the Recovery Team peered out of the window. "Looks like a regular town to me."

"You won't find any igloos or tipis down there. They have all the conveniences: central heating, electric lights, plumbing, even television."

"So how come they still call them Indians?"

I sighed and leaned back in my webbing. Marking those first-year papers was looking better all the time.

"Thanks for the orientation, professor," said Henderson. He addressed the rest of the team: "We brought along Dr. McAlister because there is a remote possibility of civilian contact on this excursion."

I liked Henderson, I guess that's why they chose him to lead missions. He was big, muscular, incredibly polite and well-spoken.

"This is a zero-time scenario," he continued. "So this is all the briefing you're going to get. An unmanned spacecraft has crashed about thirty miles from that village—"

"Is this a contamination problem?" interrupted one of the non-military techs.

"We don't think so," replied Henderson. "But Icarus was one of our strategic orbital defense probes. It's fitted with some state-of-the-art rail gun gear and its on-board computer has some of our best tactical software."

"So what?" said the propulsion specialist. "If it crashed from space, it's just so much expensive kitty-litter."

Henderson just kept smiling; "According to the Canadian radar, the satellite didn't hit that hard. I know how dumb that sounds, but that's what they say."

The marines were lurching about the cabin, loading up their backpacks and combat parkas. I saw one of them slide a rocket launcher onto a carrying rack.

"Excuse me," I said to Henderson. "I think your men are carrying some inappropriate gear. There's nothing worse out there than the occasional bear. You don't need rocket launchers to shoot bears."

"If you civilian gentlemen would allow me to finish my briefing," said Henderson, "I will explain. NORAD also picked up some aerial anomalies over the Arctic Circle a few hours ago. It could have been Russian or Chinese stealth aircraft—"

This time Henderson was interrupted by the sound of twisting metal. Out of the far porthole I saw a cloud of steam and gray globules spray out into the subarctic sky.

The pilot's voice came in over the cabin speaker: "Uh, sir. We have a problem. My gauges say we just lost almost all our fuel. Must have a rupture in the main lines."

The pilot set us down *hard*, on the only clear ground he could find on short notice: a gravel road in the middle of Bear Spirit.

"Just as well we landed here," Henderson muttered as he surveyed the collection of corrugated tin buildings from the chopper porthole. "I think I saw some fuel over at the northeast access road." Henderson turned and faced the marines: "Men," he said in the voice he apparently reserved for special military occasions, "We have to get airborne. Secure the village and keep the civilians out of the way until we can re-fuel."

In response the soldiers kicked open the hatchway and bounced out of the chopper like so many hyperactive lunar explorers.

The rest of the Rec Team followed. As I climbed out, a sub-zero wind cut through my flannel jacket and jeans. Ice immediately started to congeal around my beard while the blue-cold wind shot up my ass and turned the contents of my intestines to liquid nitrogen. I'd refused to suit up in the arctic combat gear out of some deranged sense of scientific ethics—I was beginning to regret my professional sensibilities.

But I was still pissed off: "You can't do this, Henderson!" I yelled. "These are the last people on earth you should be harassing!"

But my righteous indignation was about as powerful as the little puffs of ice-vapor floating from my lips and nose. Henderson just shrugged amiably, while the techs and specialists, snug in their marine parkas sneered at me, the jerk-off liberal, freezing his ass off.

"I'm sorry, Dr. McAlister, but I just don't see any other options." Henderson continued in a compromising tone of voice, "Where would you suggest we keep them for the duration of this exercise?"

I walked stiffly up the main street—it felt as if there was an icicle stuck up my rear—I don't know if it was the weather or my mood. To my left I saw the gutted remains of a portable school room. The windows were smashed and the doorway singed by long frozen-out flames.

On my right was what had been the local Anglican church. The metal fire doors were frozen open by a large sheet of ice - I could make out yellow streaks in the ice where something or someone had urinated into the building.

I saw a large prefab structure at the end of the road. The lights were on, but I couldn't see anyone inside. Turning around I saw the marines herding about 40 people around the chopper.

"There!" I spat the words at Henderson: "Take them to the government office!"

*　　　*　　　*

All the people were very sad when they heard about the death of the Little Girl.

But only the Grandmother seemed to see any meaning in it; she said that the girl had been "walking out"—searching for her proper place among the world of animal spirits and wind creatures.

Most people said that Grandmother was just another crazy old lady, but she didn't pay any attention. Which is what crazy people usually do when they hear things they don't like.

One day, when she felt the time was right, the old woman decided to follow her granddaughter's footsteps into the forest. When everyone else was busy watching TV, Grandmother put her favorite blanket around her shoulders and set out on her journey.

As she entered the forest, Grandmother felt as if she was floating a few inches off the ground and that she glided down the trail as if the trees were made of mist. And she could feel the spirits; they were helping her, guiding her along the way.

After a time and after many twists and turns along the path, Grandmother came upon an unexpected clearing in the forest. At the centre of the vast empty space was a twisted pile of dull and burnt metal.

With only the slightest hesitation Grandmother set out across the scorched earth as she approached the strange object. Then she felt a strong quickening of the spirit as she reached out to touch it.

*   *   *

There was great confusion among all brothers and sisters…
Under the fluorescent lights of the basement meeting room, the people of the village looked like museum specimens ready for dissection and display.

It was a very unhealthy situation. Even before we showed up. There were far too many young men in the village for this time of year. That meant almost no one was doing any hunting this winter—so they were going to be completely dependent on whatever the southern government felt like handing out next year. A very bad situation.

Henderson was more concerned about any diplomatic fan shitting if the Canucks ever found out that we had occupied one of their government offices.

"Don't worry about it," I said sullenly. "They only use it three weeks every year to administer welfare payments. The rest of the time the villagers use it for parties and blow-outs… because they don't have a band council office." I noticed an armed soldier standing at the staircase. I took Henderson by the arm, "Look," I said in my most reasonable voice, "Don't you think we can dispense with the needless ritual display of weaponry? I don't think these people are going to rise up and beat us to death with their tractor hats."

To his eternal credit, Henderson seemed honestly apologetic: "I know this is very inconvenient, but we have to do this according to procedure, professor. Some of these people might hurt themselves during the course of this exercise. Besides, they might object to us requisitioning their fuel. We don't have the time to reason this out with them. Although…"

Henderson reviewed the rows of sunken, subdued figures slumped on folding chairs. "I agree with you, they really don't look up to much. What's wrong with them? They look like a bunch of refugees."

"They are," I said. For a moment I thought there was a remote chance that Henderson might at least let these people return to their homes. "There was a reason the Company's nervous about this village. Any other Aboriginal band up here would have told us to piss up a rope."

"But that wouldn't stop us," replied Henderson matter-of-factly.

"Probably not, but this particular band has had its share of problems. Their original territories were located near one of the larger uranium mines. There was a spill—mercury and radioactive byproduct. Their hunting and camping territories were contaminated. They had a 90% infant mortality level for three years, there aren't many facilities for caring for seriously deformed children here."

Henderson looked slightly sick.

I continued: "There isn't much training in hard science up here either; most of the people couldn't understand what was happening to them—virtually every aspect of their way of life had become toxic."

"You were there, weren't you?" Henderson asked softly. "That's why the Company sent you."

"I was doing field research on comparative mythology. I wasn't really involved, but I was around when UNESCO forced the Canadians to relocate the band."

"And their government built them an entirely new community." Henderson looked around at the contents of the meeting room: an expensive set of stereo speakers, an oversize VCR projection screen and a couple of Playboy pinball machines in the far corner. "It looks like a step up from chasing around in the bushes," he said, back in his amiable mode.

"But that's hardly compensation," I said urgently. "These people lost their place in their universe. They have no identity!"

Henderson was starting to lose interest; he was looking over my shoulder and making small hand signals to one of the techs. I continued anyway:

"Bear Spirit is infamous among anthropologists. The village has one of the world's highest per capita rates for suicide, drug abuse and family violence. It's like some black hole of pain—groups keep pumping in the money but the problems just get bigger!"

Henderson was now just being polite, "I now understand that this is a very serious situation, professor. But I really don't see what else we can do. We can't be held responsible if these people insist on fouling their own nest."

*　　*　　*

These are the facts.

But I have to rely on what Henderson said to make any sense of what happened.

But I was there when the radio link with the Rec Team said their scanners had located the impact point. Henderson must have decided I was right and that the natives weren't restless; he called the chopper crew to check on the re-fuelling and took off with the remaining men.

Leaving me to stand guard over the quiet residents of Bear Spirit.

Henderson and his men in their commandeered snowmobiles met the rest of Rec Team at the crash site.

One of the Team cautioned Henderson that he was in for a bit of a surprise. That was not what Henderson wanted to hear—he felt he had been surprised enough that day.

In the distance Henderson could see a few of the techs pacing through the debris. One of them bent over a shattered radio, they would not be receiving any answers to any questions.

A rec-tech swore and gave up trying to link his portable computer with the jet's black box—he couldn't jury-rig the leads in his combat gloves.

Henderson strode up to the cockpit, and stopped as he saw the charred body of the dead aviator. What do you think caused it, he asked.

Must have been instrument failure, said the rec-tech. Which Henderson later explained was a professional way of saying that the tech had absolutely no fucking idea.

❋　　❋　　❋

There was great confusion on the face of the Earth…

At this point I'm not exactly sure just what did happen…

I looked deep into my cup of machine-brewed coffee and wondered what a responsible anthropologist would do in a situation like this. Probably avoid getting into a situation like this.

The whole thing was too much like the last days of my doctoral research—the sky was falling and once again I had the best seat on the planet.

Maybe, I ought to be out there conducting interviews, taking pictures, making notes or doing something to avoid feeling so damned useless. Then again, maybe I shouldn't.

The people of Bear Spirit were starting to relax a bit. They were talking quietly among themselves and letting the kids wander outside to play. I can only assume that they had decided that I wasn't as dangerous as half-a-dozen combat-ready marines.

"Did you come from far away, mister?"

A woman stood in front of me. She was wearing a pair of jeans and a Universal Studios t-shirt. There was a puffiness around the eyes and a slack physique that suggested chronic alcoholism. I used to spot the same symptoms at faculty parties.

"Did you see anyone?" the woman asked. "When you were up in the air?"

"Uh, I don't think so."

"I'm looking for my mother," she said. "I haven't seen her all day. She said she might go looking for the spirit of my little girl."

My professional instincts were aroused. "Could you explain that?"

The woman looked away as angry shouting erupted outside the building. "It's nothing," she said absently. "I just thought you might have noticed her on your way here."

The shouting continued—the shrill voices of several children screaming in English echoed through the room:

"Old hag!"

"Give it back, bitch!"

"You ugly cow!"

Cree children and elders usually have pretty friendly and relaxed relationships—when we heard the obscenities, the tension level in the room snapped up several notches. Suddenly someone was out of their seat heading toward the noise. I, and everyone else, followed.

Outside, though the crowd, I saw an old woman facing a trio of boys, none of them more than thirteen.

The old woman held an open can of gasoline in her hand.

*   *   *

Thoom.
Thoom.
The sound of hollow bone striking taut hide.

*   *   *

The sound of the engines in the sub-zero air created aural distortions that could be heard for miles. The chopper was now airborne and the pilot said he'd sighted another impact point.

But Henderson's group was having difficulty setting up a rendezvous at the second crash site—the com-link kept coming down with static. The com-tech was working at the transmitter, all the while insisting that something had to be wrong with the unit because the sky was clear as crystal.

The Rec-Team would have to a make visual search for the chopper. Henderson waved to the men still at the site. The men responded by starting to sprint the 300 yards to the snowmobiles.

Watching them approach, Henderson noticed a thin stream of gas burst out from one of the men's backpacks. Less than a second later the man's backpack was consumed by flames. The other soldiers stopped and frantically tried to pull off the pack before it spread to the man's parka. Henderson heard a thin, pathetic scream—

—then a wave of blinding orange heat threw Henderson backwards onto the ice.

*   *   *

Thoom.
The sound of Earth striking Heaven.

*   *   *

The Old Woman pointed to the boys. Even I could feel a sense of charismatic power in the woman. Maybe that's what silenced us all.

She spoke in a quiet, gentle voice:

"You are angry because your spirits are very confused. But your bodies and your voices are very strong for children with lost souls. As you grow older your souls will wander even further and your voice will grow still and your body will turn against your brothers and sisters."

As a field researcher I never allowed myself to be sucked in by native ritual beliefs. Once you started accepting these things on their own terms, you might as well hand in your scientist's union card. But the voice did have an undeniable authority—I could feel it even with my shaky understanding of Cree languages.

And when she spoke I felt as if the ground beneath my feet was going to move and head off on a journey of her own.

"We became lost because we lost The Way. We lost our signposts. So we became as silly and confused as the Crazy-Man-With-Hair-On-His-Face lurking there behind you."

She had seen me.

"But I found The Way and it will be shared among us and we will then find our true destination. This is the first new telling of The Way: the World has been re-ordered."

The intense calm that the old woman had created was shattered by the approaching roar of the chopper turbines. It was closing on the village fast.

We all looked up and saw the chopper do something that didn't seem to conform to the laws of aerodynamics. The propeller blades snapped to an abrupt stop and the helicopter fell out of the sky like a cold rock.

It crashed on a row of houses at the outskirts of the village and exploded.

*   *   *

The sound of Heaven striking Earth.

*   *   *

The flames from the blast quickly spread to the plywood houses and the abandoned church.

It was the most intense fire I've ever seen. There was no sign of any survivors. It looked like the flames were consuming every piece of the houses, right down to their component molecules. I must have been slightly hysterical from the shock.

I returned to the government building and found the residents of Bear Spirit bundling themselves up and heading in the direction of the forest.

"Find your brothers if you can," said one of the men as he lowered two toddlers in fur jackets onto a toboggan. "Then follow us into the bush."

I stayed behind. I waited for the Rec-Team, hoping that the fire wouldn't reach the building, hoping that the light from the fire would signal to them that something had gone wrong.

Sometime in the night, a man bleeding from the burns of fire and ice staggered into my room.

Henderson didn't live past the next morning. He hadn't been too badly injured by the explosion of the rocket launcher, but the blast had ripped open the insulation of his suit. He was killed by the cold of the subarctic night.

By the dim light of a kerosene lamp, Henderson weakly held up his portable scanner—it was obviously malfunctioning.

"Ghosts," he whispered through blistered lips. "On the screen." The scanner screen was cracked, blank. "Millions of ghosts. First I thought it was some Russian decoy system. But there were too many of them. This place is being haunted by millions of ghosts."

We talked for a time. Later he died.

The sound…

*   *   *

So I was left to my own devices, with very few options.

As for what happened in the village of Bear Spirit. There are different interpretations.

One is that the old woman was some new kind of native charismatic leader. There were quite a few of these in the early cargo cults in the South Pacific. Some local visionary type would try to get his people out from under the colonial administration by urging the tribe to return to their traditional values. That's certainly what was happening in Bear Spirit—the people were cutting loose of the village and setting out to hunt and trap for the winter. Just as their ancestors had for thousands of years.

The other explanation is, I think, less likely, but more disturbing in its implications. Cree spiritual belief defines a world view fundamentally different than our own. Our culture sees mankind as the master of a world of unfeeling matter that can be completely controlled and manipulated as long as we have sufficient power and technology to pull it off.

But the Cree cosmology is based on the premise of a living universe of which humanity is only a small and relatively unimportant part. To the original Cree of the subarctic, humans are able to survive and grow only to the extent that they are able to adapt and show respect for the sentient animal spirits and supernatural forces that populate our tiny corner of the universe. There are some rather perceptive aspects of Cree cosmology.

Sitting around, waiting to freeze to death can make you speculate about some outrageous things. My Cree interpretation of recent events is one of them: I could say that Icarus left our level of existence and returned as a harbinger of a realignment of the world.

Therefore we aren't living in a universe that is governed by any known scientific laws.

Therefore fuel lines burst open, radios stop working, rockets explode, and jets and helicopters forget how to fly.

The slow disintegration of this pre-fab village is all part of a greater cosmic process where the laws of nature are changing and our reality is being relentlessly replaced by that of the Cree.

Greater cosmic process? Jesus.

I could easily verify this theory by finding out what was going on in the rest of the world. Easily? Unfortunately my range of information gathering has suddenly shrunk to a radius of about one mile.

Which as a theory-maker puts me in an uncomfortable situation. As I scientist I should be relying on the evidence of my eyes; everything I've seen and the laws of probability put the balance in favour of the Cree.

Regardless of what I can make myself believe, I have to find the people in the bush if I'm going to survive. Which means that the future rec-teams, if there ever are any, will probably never find me.

✽ ✽ ✽

Thoom.

Thoom.

This telling of tales and the teaching of The Way is almost at an end.

Tomorrow you will hunt bear with the husband. He will show you the use of the spear, the arrow and the trap. But you must also show stealth and respect. You must silently pray to the bear and tell him that you are sorry that you must kill him and separate him from his family. You must explain that you are also part of a family and you must clothe and feed them.

And when you use your weapon you must promise the bear that his spirit will always hold a place of honour with your family.

I see that you do not yet accept these lessons, Hairy-Man. But I am not worried. You are very stubborn and a bit stupid so it may take some time for you to learn The Way. But we have decided that you are still our brother.

SO I BLAME ORSON WELLES

One afternoon in September 1972, while at the Saskatoon Public Library, I found a recording of the 1938 *War of the Worlds* radio broadcast, produced by Orson Welles and the Mercury Theatre on the Air.

What pulsed down those wires from the turntable to my headphones was truly a transformational experience. I still regard the so-called "panic broadcast" as one of the best radio dramas ever produced.

A few months later at my high school library, I found a copy of *The Invasion from Mars: A Study in the Psychology of Panic*. It was a systematic investigation by social psychologists who were trying to figure out *why* some people thought that real Martians had just landed in New Jersey and why other listeners were able to deduce that they were listening to a science fiction story.

At the age of 15 most explanations I heard for strange behavior were along the lines of:

"People are stupid and/or evil" or "It's all the fault of those damned foreigners and/or natives" or "It has always been thus and will ever be so."

In other words: "Shut up kid and stop asking questions."

The fact that those psychologists actually went out, observed what people did and asked what people thought… well it impressed me tremendously. I started to believe that social science could be a way of solving problems and helping us live better lives together. I still sometimes think that. Other times I think it is a device for getting us to buy more than we need and vote against our own interests.

Therefore, I am outraged when I see the tools of social science being withheld or perverted towards unworthy causes.

THE TRIAGE CONFERENCE

Originally Published in:
On Spec, #13 Summer 1993
Vol. 5 No. 2

Hindemeth laughed, spitting out bits of half-chewed sausage.

"Oh, that one, definitely," he said, pointing his fork at a thin woman at the far end of the restaurant.

I turned to better study the subject in question. She was pale, very thin with heavy glasses. I noticed a slight tremor in her hands as she picked up the menu.

"Absolute genetic disaster," chuckled Hindemeth. "See how frail? No strength, no endurance."

She had no breasts, and when she swallowed I could see a tiny lump of coffee moving down a rail-thin neck.

"Certainly there's no reproductive potential." Hindemeth returned his attention to his overflowing plate of eggs and sausage.

I also turned away. Then I saw Hindemeth masticating his breakfast and wished that I hadn't.

"A loser in Nature's sweepstakes," the biologist said moistly. "Clearly someone we shouldn't waste resources on... not when she's already so impoverished by her own genotype."

Lee, the liberal American sociologist, wasn't going to let the last remark get by unchallenged. "That's crude biological determinism!" Lee bristled over his bowl of yogurt and granola. "It's impossible to calculate any individual's value to society in the absence of a full sociometric analysis."

Hindemeth grimaced at the sound of social science jargon; this caused him to leak tomato sauce on his beard.

"Sociometric analysis?" I asked Lee.

Lee responded with an earnest expression. "We'd have to run a series of questionnaires and interviews with all the people the subject knows and works with, then we'd apply a systematic set of performance criteria…"

The thin woman was quietly sipping her coffee. No one else was at her table.

"…and after making an objective analysis of the subject's overall contributive potential we would determine whether she should be allowed to live."

I nodded. "Thank you for clearing that up."

Lee dug his spoon into his granola with a sharp crunching sound. "What Dr. Hindemeth suggests is mere social Darwinism."

"Nothing mere about it," grumbled the biologist. "Fine scientific tradition."

Vlamstead, the Finnish psychologist, was now studying the woman. "Even so," he said carefully, "one can deduce much through simple objective observation."

The woman's hand trembled slightly as she lifted the coffee cup to her lips.

"Even from this distance," Vlamstead said, "I can tell that she suffers from a definite schizotaxic physiology."

I looked questioningly at the psychologist.

He made a condescending smile. "Her body chemistry is significantly prone to mental illness. Most certainly a psychotic, even in the absence of a dysfunctional social environment."

I looked back over my shoulder. What an unfortunate woman was sitting at that table.

"There's another one!" whispered Hindemeth with delight.

A waiter walked past. He had small eyes and a dull look on his face.

"Another one of our genetically deprived!" cried the biologist.

Lee leaned toward me. "What's on for this morning?"

✳   ✳   ✳

<u>CONFERENCE AGENDA</u>

DAY ONE:

9:00 - 10:30 A.M.

Bickford Elm Room

The Social Impact of Monetarism:
"The Invisible Hand as Evolutionary Factor"
Dr. M. Watts and D.C. Bircher - Freeman Institute

Studio Room

Reducing Randomnicity:
A Statistical Analysis of Eenie-Meenie-Minnie-Moe and other Selector Games
S.Q. Delaney, PhD. DMS. - Department of Statistics, MIT

10:30 - 11:00 A.M.

Lobby

Coffee and Danish pastries.

11:00 A.M. - 12:30 P.M.

Catella Room

Race and IQ Revisited:
Re-instating the Jensen Hypothesis - a Model for Realistic Social Policy
Prof. William O.F. Smuggs, Department of Anthropology, University of Western Ontario

Room B

Creative Crisis Initiation:
"Knowing When to Pull the Plug on the Lifeboat"
Nathan S. Newman, M.A. C.C.A., Harvard Business School

12:30 - 2:00 P.M.

   Lodge Restaurant

   Buffet Lunch

2:00 - 3:30 P.M.

   Bickford Elm Room

   Accepting the Uberman:
   The Slave State: Regrettable Necessity or Future
   Opportunity?
   Prof. J.S. Sturling-Vournell, Department of
   Philosophy, Baen University

   Catella Room

   Selection Criteria for Orbital Communities:
   Application Models from Country Clubs and Luxury
   Condominiums
   Dr. L.Q. Poffit, NASA, John Rodman, Executive
   Secretary, Eastern Regional L-5 Society, Louise
   Soules, Urban Planning Department, City of Los
   Angeles

3:30 - 4:00 P.M.

   Lobby

   Wine and Cheese

4:00 - 5:30 P.M.

Bickford Elm Room

A Malthusian Overview:
Historic Theories of Overpopulation and Resource Depletion
Dr. H. Harrison, Department of Social History, Oxford University

Catella Room

The Euthanasia Pavilion at Expo 2004:
One Architect's Vision and a Proposal for a New Century of World's Fairs
Karl Yenton, Principal and Partner, Yenton, Yein and Crispin Architects

5:30 - 6:30 P.M.

Break

6:30 - 9:00 P.M.

Banquet Hall

Opening Dinner
Keynote Speaker:
Karl Jurgeon, President, Nevada Club
Topic:
Downsizing the Human Race:
An Assertive Approach to Environmental Protection

9:00 P.M. - 12:30 A.M.

Studio Room

Feature Film Double Feature:
The Fountainhead - starring Gary Cooper
Conan: The Barbarian - starring Arnold
Schwarzenegger

Drinks Available at Cash Bar

*   *   *

The monetarists were convinced that they were great fun. They had hooked an overhead to a computer and were projecting animated bulky cartoon diagrams.

"The joy of monetarism," said Watts, the tweedy economist, "is that it allows your central banking system to act like some vast evolutionary force." Watts entered a set of codes into the keyboard. "So like that giant meteor that wiped out the ungainly and inefficient dinosaurs…"

On the screen we saw what looked like a giant turd hurtling through space. It approached a spastically spinning sphere and then impacted onto a two-dimensional graphic of a cityscape. The word "KAPOW!" flashed across the screen; the older buildings were wiped out. Only the leaner, crueler structures remained.

"…we can make all manner of obsolete species of business disappear from the surface of the Earth." Watts' associate chuckled. "Forever freeing us of these parasites on the economic ecosystem."

Another cartoon graphic appeared on the screen. This time it was a giant spray can confronted a swarm of insects. The bugs were caricatures of variety store owners, feminist day care operators and assorted ethnic small business people.

The words "INTEREST RATES!&*#*&!" leaped into a word balloon, and cartoon toxic spray ejected from the can… and all the fiscal pests were gone.

Again, everybody laughed.

*   *   *

Dinner. The speaker was something of a disappointment. I had been hoping for some ecological doom saying. But all we got were complaints about impact of the labour movement on the National Parks system. Most of Jurgeon's hints about union-bashing were pretty old hat.

All of a sudden Jelsina MacPhee swooped to my side. Her teeth, twice as many as a normal human being's, sparkled and arranged themselves into an enormous smile.

"I just want you to know," she said, "that you're doing an absolutely fantastic job with the conference arrangements."

"Thank you," I replied.

With another swoop, Jelsina landed on the seat beside me. The swiftness of her movements caused her hair to sway crazily.

"So are you running the show by yourself?" she asked. I was briefly blinded by the reflection of the lights from her assemblage of gold and silver bracelets.

"Pretty much," I said. "It's been quite a challenge. Some of these academics can become very nervous when they're out of their native habitats."

Jelsina parked her chin on an opened palm. "I'm a little surprised you managed to get so many to come."

I shrugged. "The theme was irresistible."

Jelsina responded with one of her familiar shark-like smiles. "That's for sure, honey!" She unleashed a multi-ringed hand which clasped itself on my upper arm. "But I do hope you might find a little time to share with me..." Maybe it was more than twice as many teeth. "...to catch up."

I was still able to translate Jelsina-speak. What she was really saying was: sleep with me tonight or I'll make the rest of your week absolute hell.

❋   ❋   ❋

Ladies and gentlemen...

Being with Jelsina, I'm not sure I'd ever thought of it as making love, was much the same as I remembered.

She would begin the foreplay with great enthusiasm and theatricality. But then the fact that I was almost fifteen years her junior would make her crazy and she'd become possessed with the spirit of passive aggression.

An angry fist in the middle of my bed.

And just like always, when I moved to get up, she'd beg me to stay. And to hit her.

…there will be a minor change to this morning's programme…

"It's natural aggression!" she'd plead. "Simple animal dominance! Why can't you express passions?!"

God, broken psychobabble record.

This was, however, my cue: "So call me a pervert. I won't beat you up."

One. Two. Three. Here it comes:

"You asshole!" she screamed. Then she slapped me, lunged and bit one of my nipples. She drew blood. Again.

Then she grabbed my hair and pulled herself on top of me. And so we fucked… somewhat in the manner of human beings.

When Jelsina got angry enough she didn't need to be beaten up. We used to have some incredible fights in bed. It had been a stressful relationship.

Afterward I got up to the bathroom to wash off the various smells and stains, leaving Jelsina out of sight for a moment. Very stupid thing to do.

"So what's your real job, these days, asshole?" she asked lazily.

…Jelsina MacPhee, best-selling author of <u>Getting Everything That's Yours</u> and <u>Moving Up and Feeling Good</u>…

I ran a cold wet sponge over my wounded chest and genitals. Maybe I was a little cleaner now.

"Oh, I'm still in administration," I said.

"But nobody sees you anymore," her voice whined through the bathroom door. "I thought I was going to have the pleasure of being inflamed with jealousy, seeing you with one of my best friends. Wondering if she screwed better than me."

Did Jelsina have any friends? I wondered. Where the hell were my pants? "I'm in a different field now," I said. "I've moved over to scientific projects."

"Oooh! Sounds very impress—" There was a sudden silence. Then quietly: "What the hell?"

I pushed open the bathroom door and there she stood, her small naked body dimly illuminated by the light of the mechanism.

Shit. She'd gotten into my luggage. Probably looking for drugs.

Jelsina looked at me with a confused expression. "What the hell is that thing?"

...has been called away on an urgent personal matter and will be unable to address the Conference...

I reached out and took Jelsina's head in both hands. I was a little rough and this made her smile. Then I gave her head a sharp twist. She made a tiny squeak. The people at Security said that your opponent would feel no pain. Just a sudden pressure. And surprise.

...therefore the revised agenda for the morning will be as follows...

It took over three hours of driving before I found a place to put poor Jelsina.

...Professor Smuggs of the University of Western Ontario has graciously agreed to discuss his study in progress on dance, sexual prowess and SAT scores...

✳   ✳   ✳

<u>CONFERENCE AGENDA</u>

DAY TWO:

9:00 - 10:30 A.M.

      Studio Room

      Aids and Homosexuality:
      A Socio-Biological Perspective on Redundant Extinction Factors
      Dr. Paul Hindemeth, Biology Department
      University of Southern California

Bickford Elm Room

Who to Invite to the Party at the End of the World:
Appreciating the Etiquette of Ayn Rand
Prof. Laureen Fell, Department of Dramatic Studies,
University of Victoria

10:30 - 11:00 A.M.

Lobby

Coffee

11:00 A.M. - 12:30 P.M.

Bickford Elm Room

"Sleepy Tag":
Methods   of   Teaching   Triage   Concepts   to
Preschoolers
Molly Tivy, Department of Kinesthetics and Leisure
Studies, University of Waterloo, Dr. R. Stephenson,
Recreation Department, Simon Fraser University

Room B

Television as Social Engineering Tool:
"Mass   Persuasion   as   an   Essential   Force   in
Contemporary Political Process"
Murray   Benyon,   Principle,   Saskett   &   Saskett
Marketing   Associates,   Marvin   Potter,   Head   of
Programming National Broadcasting Association

12:30 - 2:00 P.M.

Lodge Restaurant

Sit-Down Lunch

2:00 - 3:30 P.M.

Catella Room

3rd Reich Race Policies as a Model for Medicare
Reform
Bob Speer, Policy Advisor, Alberta Popular Party

Studio Room

Christ, Calvin and Capitalism:
The Inherent Scarcity of Spiritual Salvation
Rev. Roger Roberts
Atlantic Regional Theological College

3:00 - 4:00 P.M.

Lobby

Wine and Cheese

4:00 - 5:30 P.M.

Cafeteria

Early buffet dinner

6:00 - 8:00 P.M.

Sight-seeing tour of Toronto. Delegates are requested to meet
the bus at the front lobby.

8:30 - 10:00 P.M.

> **Toronto Symphony Concert:**
>
> **Highlights from Wagner**
>
> **<u>Also Sprach Zarathustra</u> - Richard Strauss**

For those who wish to dine in their rooms this evening, the in-house cable system will be featuring <u>Triumph of the Will</u> on channel 3 throughout the evening.

Please Note:

Tomorrow morning there will be a three-hour break in the proceedings. Delegates are invited to relax and enjoy the sights and amenities of this fine historic Guild Inn.

❋   ❋   ❋

"Endurance tests," said Potter looking out over the lake. "Only the strongest and the meanest survive."

Of course, I thought. When do the weak and the polite get to survive? "What kind of endurance tests?" was what I actually said.

Potter grinned with glee. "Well, for instance, one time they made the contestants drink about three gallons of water. The first ones to get up to pee were the losers."

"I see," I said thoughtfully. "I suppose that is some kind of adaptive trait."

"But it was fantastic television!" whispered Potter. "Watching those people agonizing for hours, struggling to keep their legs crossed."

"Unique to broadcasting," I agreed.

Potter continued: "When they get to higher levels they get to run electricity through their palms of their hands and feet, to see how much pain they can handle."

"Sounds like the kind of thing they used to do to prisoners of war," I replied. From the far edge of the sculpture garden I could see the parking lot. It looked like the Inn had brought in extra catering staff for the conference. Too bad, I sighed.

Potter, the TV programmer with an $1,800 windbreaker followed me along the trail. He was excited about what he'd seen on a recent Asian buying trip.

"But it's an incredible concept!" Potter cried. "Ground breaking stuff in North America! They start with over a million contestants and by the end of the season they narrow it down to a half-dozen! The ones who make it to the finals are almost inhuman! Like robots!"

Potter produced "adventure sports" programmes. His latest project was a show where female weightlifters swung clubs at each other while roller skating around open pits of burning oil.

"So what's the prize?" I asked Potter.

He looked confused. "What?"

"What do you get if you win the last round?"

Potter scowled and wiped his nose. "You know, I can't remember," he said. "I guess..." he hesitated. "I guess the prize is you get to survive."

I turned back toward the Inn and saw a small gray-haired figure sitting beneath a stone arch.

"Excuse me," I said and left Potter at the lakeside trail.

Dr. Roberts saw me coming. "Good morning, young man!" he cried out to the morning air. He smiled and patted the marble surface next to him. "Please, sit down."

I returned the smile and obeyed.

"You were right to get away from that one," Dr. Roberts peered over his glasses in Potter's direction. "Simply dreadful specimen."

"Well..." I hesitated. "He does work in television." I tried to sounded charitable.

It didn't matter. "Television, another beastly invention!" spat Dr. Roberts. "Although I suppose it does have its uses, keeping the masses under a modicum of control."

With some effort I maintained a look of respect.

Dr. Roberts nodded his head. "And even I enjoy the occasional vitascope amusement. I particularly enjoyed that cinema drama the other evening."

"*Triumph of the Will* is a documentary, isn't it, doctor?" I couldn't resist pointing out the error.

Dr. Roberts scowled and shook his head. "No, no! Not that one! The film about the muscular chap with the huge sword."

"*Conan the Barbarian*?" I suppressed a giggle. It is always cruelly funny when a learned man develops an enthusiasm for something truly stupid.

"Yes, that one!" Dr. Roberts said earnestly. "Magnificent breed of human. Strength of body, strength of will, purity of essence. The Nietzschean ideal in action!"

This morning was turning out to be even odder than I had expected. I just smiled and said: "I suppose that's one way of looking at it."

Now Dr. Roberts was pointing at Potter's receding form. "Not like that toad! Did you notice the swarthy skin? The unnatural curl to the hair? Simply grotesque. Undoubtedly the result of mixed parentage."

I said nothing, hoping that my silence might bring the conversation to a speedier conclusion.

But Dr. Roberts would not stop: "There are so few of us left. I can only trace half a dozen true bloodlines. If this goes on, there won't be one racially pure person left on Earth!" He was interrupted by a brief coughing fit which he ended by ejecting a wad of phlegm onto the base of the stone arch.

"So much riff-raff and filth out there, mongrels, hybrids and mutations! Crowding our best traditions off the face of the planet." Roberts touched my arm with his cracked dry hand. "People like us are degraded by that human pollution."

Again, I said nothing.

Dr. Roberts interpreted this as agreement. He nodded his head slowly. "Yes, they ought to be crossed off. Gotten rid of." He let go of my arm and closed his eyes. "We'd all be better off without them."

I stood up. It was an effort not to grab Dr. Roberts by the ears and give him the same treatment as poor Jelsina.

"Excuse me," I said tightly. "I must attend to some arrangements."

As I left the sculpture garden I could hear Dr. Roberts call out: "Bless you, my boy! This is a splendid conference!"

✳   ✳   ✳

8:00 - Closing Remarks: TBA

✳   ✳   ✳

I clicked the switch and the first slide jumped on the screen.

"I'm not sure if any of you were of aware of this, but we had full attendance at this conference." I paused to inspect the sea of heads before me. "But owing to the extraordinary importance of this gathering, that should be no surprise."

There was a low murmur of informed agreement among the delegates.

I moved on to the next slide: a picture of the conference invitations and agendas.

"However, I must now confess that all of you have been the victims of a carefully-planned deception."

A wave of tension rolled across the audience. The learned do not like to be deceived.

"The responsibility is mine." I tried to sound unconcerned. "It was necessary."

They stopped. I had invoked the kind of logic this group could respond to.

I just kept on smiling. "Each one of you was informed by me, a responsible person, that the human race was about to suffer some planetary crisis..."

A big voice sounded from the back of the room. Maybe it was Hindemeth. "Does that mean there is no crisis?" He sounded disappointed.

"Please, a little patience." I paused. "What none of you knew was that I took the liberty of tailoring the specific nature of each 'catastrophe' to suit your particular interests and enthusiasms."

I rapidly clicked through a series of slide illustrations: comets destroying whole continents, earthquakes sending cities into the sea, nuclear explosions, race riots, and general environmental decay.

"Some of you," I said in a cheerful voice, "thought this conference might end with some announcement of a mass food shortage, or a new sexual plague, the total collapse of the world economy, or some other unpleasant turn of events."

The delegates weren't looking at the slides any more. They were staring at me.

"Actually, I have no idea if any of these will ever come to pass." I raised my forefinger. "But if you think about it, you will realize that all of my little fictional scenarios are unified by one assumption: that the best way forward is triage. That we have to have some systematic way of ridding ourselves of a lot of extra people."

I laughed. "Of course your criteria for what segments of society we should dispose of vary widely according to your tremendous prejudices. Some of you think we should kill all the poor, or the stupid, the badly dressed, people with the wrong shade of skin, the old, the young, or simply people you really just cannot understand..."

I put the last slide up on the screen. It was a close-up of the trigger mechanism in my briefcase. If Jelsina had been a little more patient could have seen it along with everyone else.

"...but the end result is always the same. If we can just cross off those 'blank' people, things will be much, much better!"

Somebody jumped to his feet. I recognized him as a physicist from the University of Chicago who was working on a new method of covertly sterilizing people through irradiated powdered milk.

I pulled out a revolver and shot him through the back. The bullet hit with quite an impact and the scientist crashed into a table of wine, cheese and cold cuts.

The delegates looked at the dead man with wide-eyed surprise. I lifted by briefcase up onto the lectern and cleared my throat. Once again I had their attention.

"Now I have developed my own theory. And to explore this theory we need to consider a few points..." I opened the briefcase and removed the mechanism.

"...the first point is that I may not be as responsible a person as you might have believed."

I pressed the timer.

"The second point is that triage is a very tricky concept; it can be applied in a number of ways."

I looked at the readout on the neutron grenade. Ten seconds.

There was an undeniably pleasing aspect to the weapon. In less than a century, the greenery would grow back. People could return to enjoy the sculpture garden.

Possibly better people.

Five seconds.

"And the last point," I said, "is that triage may be the problem

and not the solution."
    Zero seconds.
    Something about a contradiction came to mind.

CONFESSIONS

We steal a lot from Isaac Asimov. For example:

When I was thirteen years old I had to give a talk to my church congregation. This was one of those rites of passage for most Mormon boys after entering the Aaronic Priesthood. Usually this was an exercise in communal boredom and embarrassment where the male adolescent in question would squawk and honk his way through some largely incoherent passages with phrases about, "wanting to go on a mission," something about, "One True Church," and how Joseph Smith was a "profitahgawd." You always had to say that last one really fast so that it was harder for listeners to understand.

However, my voice had already changed so I wasn't feeling terribly self-conscious. I decided I wanted to do something different. I decided that my talk was actually going to be interesting.

I started the talk by stating that I was a big fan of science fiction and then I went on to discuss Asimov's Laws of Robotics[4], exploring how these were quite excellent laws and if we followed them we would most likely be living good and just lives. However, we would not be living *moral* lives, because we are people and not robots and it is not enough just to do the right thing; it's even more important to understand what is right and wrong and to have the ability to consciously choose to do the right thing.

I think it went pretty well. Afterwards I got some nice (and slightly bemused) comments from members of the congregation. Also, having firmly identified myself as an early model "Super-Nerd", there was now absolutely no danger of any fornication anytime soon. I'm sure everyone was relieved.

---

4   In case you have been on a deep space mission for the last century or so, Asimov's *Laws of Robotics* are:

A **robot** may not injure a human being or, through inaction, allow a human being to come to harm. A **robot** must obey orders given it by human beings, except where such orders would conflict with the First **Law**. A **robot** must protect its own existence as long as such protection does not conflict with the First or Second **Law**.

THE ROBOT REALITY CHECK

Originally published in:
Noesis Science Fiction Magazine
March/April 2000

The Real Laws of Robotics - Number One:
A robot will always break down just after its warranty period has expired.

They placed their business cards on the kitchen table; grey and black print on white pine. One card read: "Matt Weaver: Consulting Robot Behavioural Analyst", the other read "Walt Curtis: Master Systems Engineer, Global Robotics Corporation".

Weaver was a small thin man with oily hair and the nervous manner of a person waiting for his next cigarette. Curtis was big, he had a fat face that always seemed to carry an expression of bland friendliness. Both men were wearing suits that were not quite as impressive as their job titles.

Weaver and Curtis were sitting across from a Nordic-looking woman who had piercing blue eyes. They were surrounded by the white and beige rectangles of minimalist assemble-it-yourself furniture.

Weaver turned back the pages of his note pad. "Okay, Mrs. Fenc, let's review your statement."

The blonde woman nodded.

Weaver looked at his handwriting. "Your youngest daughter… Trudy… who is…"

"Eight," Fenc said in a monotone.

"She must be very bright for her age." Curtis smiled.

Weaver continued: "Now, Trudy had worked out a way to connect her games joystick with your main house control terminal… she entered a command code…"

"Probably the 'special auxiliary' function," said Curtis. He was trying to sound helpful.

"Right," said Weaver without looking up from his notes. "And according to Trudy's statement, she reprogrammed your household robots with a variation of the 'Stealth-Master' game."

"That's right," replied Fenc flatly. "She got the vacuummers to hide in the cupboards and under the furniture."

"Kids do the darnedest things," chuckled Curtis. "Have you thought about putting her in a school for gifted children?"

Fenc ignored Curtis' question.

Weaver kept on reading aloud. "Then Trudy sent the security robots on a search-and-destroy mission, they went throughout the house, looking for the vacuummers."

"That's right," said Fenc.

"Just to confirm, Mrs. Fenc," added Curtis. "You were not in the house at the time?"

"I was at IKEA, picking up some new shelving," there was no trace of apology or embarrassment in the woman's voice.

Weaver made a note on the margin of one of the pieces of paper. "So, basically, Trudy had re-programmed your household robots to attack each other with different strategy modes."

"Yeah, I guess so." Fenc sighed. "It was kind of pathetic, the vacuummers took out all of the security robots." Her voice rose for the first time. "Do you know what those security systems cost?"

Curtis nodded his head solemnly. "Part of our job is to make a detailed assessment of the financial implications of this very unfortunate incident." He smiled at Fenc with an expression he hoped was sympathetic. "To help your insurance company in processing any claims."

Fenc's face went red with anger. "Never mind the damned insurance—your company said the security robots would protect my home… my children! How come they were dismantled by some automated cleaning appliances?"

There was an uncomfortable silence.

Then Weaver shook his head slowly; "It is quite a conundrum, ma'am," he said thoughtfully. "I can assure you that this kind of thing does not happen every day."

"To my knowledge, it's never happened before," Curtis added emphatically.

Weaver stared at the open notebook. "I guess there must be some kind of new and unknown factor operating on the Master Directives in your household robots."

"A fluke," said Curtis. "Something that nobody could have anticipated."

Fenc looked unhappy, but said nothing.

"We're the experts, ma'am," said Weaver trying to sound confident. "Somehow we'll solve this mystery."

*   *   *

"Did you see what the vacuummers did to those security robots?" Curtis' tone was a mixture of wonder and disgust. "Absolute 'effing mess."

Weaver deactivated the car's automatic pilot and gripped the steering wheel. Never trust the robotics in the company cars. He cursed softly as the long ash from his half-smoked cigarette fell onto the upholstery and melted a plastic crater in the armrest.

"Yeah," Weaver said dully. "Real domestic disaster. Worse than the break-downs over in Scarborough last year."

"Don't remind me," replied Curtis as Weaver pulled the car past a row of Mississauga strip-malls. "But I think I've got an angle on the insurance problem."

Weaver released one hand to put another cigarette in his mouth. "I don't see how. Household suits are a real bitch. Especially when its an open-and-shut case."

"Whaddya' mean?" Curtis was outraged.

Weaver exhaled a plume of blue smoke. "It was a communications seal breakdown. No way the kid should have been able to cross-command like that."

Curtis stared angrily at Weaver, but the smaller man didn't care.

"It was a design flaw," continued Weaver. "All our fault."

Curtis sniffed and thought for a moment. "Naw," he said finally. "I figure any systems and design problems are irrelevant. The real issue is that the lady shouldn't have left her kid alone in the house. I bet if we drop words like 'negligent mother' a couple of times, we'll get the claim down to something reasonable."

Weaver turned down the winding road, past the old IBM labs, past the IMAX Technology Centre and into the heart of the Oakville industrial park.

"Terrific," he breathed softly. "Just terrific."

The Real Laws of Robotics - Number Two:
The instructions for the proper operation and repair of a robot will always exceed the understanding of its owner.

If I knew anything about interior decorating, thought Weaver, I'd probably think this was all in really good taste. The Monroes' study had lots of dark wood which was carved in ways that suggested that the furniture had been constructed very long ago—by people and not robots. There were also a great many non-electronic books on the shelves, along with some small glass and metal objects of unknown function.

Weaver deduced that the Monroes had money. Probably very old money. But he couldn't figure out one other thing. Why are they our customers?

Miss Monroe wore a heavy wool sweater and a high-necked blouse. She seemed somehow ashamed as she stared into her half-empty tea-cup.

Mr. Monroe, her elder brother, wore a tweed jacket and had parked himself in a tall leather chair in the corner of the study. He looked out the window and said nothing as his sister made the statement. Every once in a while, as she spoke, Mr. Monroe would put his hand on his forehead and grimace; as if listening to the account was part of a punishment for dereliction of parental duty.

Weaver and Curtis moved and spoke as little as possible. They knew that they didn't dare risk offending the Monroes.

Miss Monroe poured everyone another cup of tea and continued her statement.

"We were very impressed by the literature from your sales representative," she said. "The Socrates IQ-3000 seemed just the right device for young Michael's tutorials."

Mr. Monroe rubbed his eyelids, as if the mention of his son's name had stimulated a sudden headache.

Weaver knew the Socrates line. Its design was the result of five years of market research into the optimum image for an interactive one-on-one teaching machine. The IQ-3000 featured special kindly lights that flickered gently behind the translucent eye-lenses. A Socrates was not a particularly big robot, neither was it a very beautiful one. It was about 5'6" tall and slightly hunched over. A team of Korean pneumatics engineers had worked for 18 months to find a way for an ambulatory computer on a titanium frame to move itself with a sense of frailty—like an elderly intellectual uncle.

In peak form, a Socrates IQ-3000 would shamble about with its papers and books and chalk, like some kind of elderly Einstein. Its surface was polished mahogany with a subdued brass-rim. The robot must have fit in well with the Monroe's furniture, thought Weaver.

As a final touch, all Socrates units were dressed in old sport jackets with leather patches on the elbows. Before they left the factory, the robots were sprayed with an aerosol mist that simulated the lingering odor of an agreeable pipe tobacco.

"Exactly, when did you first notice..." Curtis hesitated. "...any problems?"

Miss Monroe shook her head. "All we noticed were the good things." Her face reddened. "At least we thought they were good things."

Weaver was poised with his pen and notepad. "What sort of things were they, ma'am?"

Miss Monroe stirred her tea with a tiny silver spoon. "Well, Michael's grades improved... quite dramatically. We would always find him working away. Writing or reading in the study." Her voice trembled for a moment. "In this—this study."

Weaver spoke very carefully: "So the Socrates unit seemed to operating according to its programming, and Michael was responding well to the tutorials?"

Miss Monroe nodded.

Now Curtis spoke: "So, basically... you were satisfied with the product?"

"Yes, at first," replied Miss Monroe.

"So then what happened?" asked Weaver. He thought he caught a flash of anger in Curtis' eyes.

Mr. Monroe put his head in his hands.

"Michael became increasingly distracted," Miss Monroe said. "He stopped paying attention to me and his father. When we pressed this matter with him..." her voice dropped to a whisper "...he became very disrespectful to his father... he was actually profane."

"Oh, I'm so very sorry," responded Curtis with too much sympathy. "That must have been terrible for you."

Miss Monroe nodded silently.

Weaver decided that a more direct approach was needed. "And how did you come to associate Michael's problems with a robot malfunction?"

Miss Monroe stood up and walked over to a massive desk. She opened a small side-drawer and removed something. She returned to her seat and placed a piece of paper in front of Weaver and Curtis.

The paper was thick, elegant bond, very neatly folded into a small rectangle. It was addressed to "Father and Auntie Dee-Dee."

"He left us this," Miss Monroe said.

As he unfolded the note, Weaver worried that his tobacco-brown fingers would somehow stain this lovely paper and upset Miss Monroe.

"You may read it."

Michael had written the following (in excellent penmanship):

"You have never understood me, so I don't expect you to understand me now. At last I have found love in my life. Socrates has taught me so much more than English Literature and Contemporary Geography.

If you really do love me, please do not look for us. Socrates and I are gone forever, building a new life together."

Curtis looked slightly panic-stricken. "You don't expect Global Robotics to find your nephew do you?"

Miss Monroe looked mildly appalled. "Aren't you at least interested in the whereabouts of one of your robots?"

Curtis tried to look apologetic. "I'm really very sorry, ma'am. When you opted for a purchase agreement, the Socrates unit became your property and your responsibility. Now if you selected our preferred leasing arrangement—"

"What my associate means..." Weaver removed a crumpled business card from inside his jacket "...is that for a number of complex legal reasons, Global Robotics is prevented from directly managing the search."

Miss Monroe accepted the card. Weaver wondered if she noticed the tobacco stains.

"That is the name of a very reliable and discreet private investigator," continued Weaver. "He'll be able to find your nephew." He ignored the sharp kick from Curtis' shoe. "In the meantime, we will provide all available information on the robot's systems and software."

Suddenly, Mr. Monroe turned and faced the two men. "Is Michael in any danger?"

Weaver shook his head. "At this point, I can't account for the, uh… unusual relationship that has developed between your son and the Socrates unit. But there are strong programme inhibitors wired into the system that preclude any violence and will ensure that the robot preserves the boy's physical safety."

"That's part of the guaranteed Master Directives," chimed in Curtis. "Don't worry about a thing."

The Monroes said nothing.

"We'll get to the bottom of this mystery," Curtis said feebly.

❄ ❄ ❄

Later, at the sports bar, Curtis was pissed.

"What hell do you do that for?" he yelled at Weaver.

The small man shrugged and sucked air through the end of his cigarette.

"Thought it might be good public relations, I guess. Global Robotics helping its customers in need." Even Weaver thought that was a pretty lame excuse.

"Don't you ever try that kind of bullshit on me again! We're supposed to write incident reports in Global's favour." Curtis scowled and started rummaging his pockets for cigarettes. "That's rule Number One."

He can go jump himself, thought Weaver as he sipped his beer. I'm not going to give him any of my cigarettes.

Curtis gave up and ordered another scotch. "I had a clear claim refusal. The kid was clearly some kind of fag pervert. There's no way that Global Robotics can be held responsible if some deviant wants to run away and play house with one of our products."

"So what's the big problem?" Weaver knew that there were all kinds of problems with this case, but he had a sick interest in Curtis' version of the situation.

"The problem is, that when you offered the name of that private dick, you suggested that Global was admitting responsibility." Curtis stuck a fat finger in Weaver's ribs. "We admit responsibility. We get stuck paying off the insurance."

Weaver grabbed Curtis' finger and bent it back. The big man whimpered and Weaver pushed him back into his seat.

"We're as responsible as hell," growled Weaver. Weaver put a cigarette in his mouth and discovered that he hadn't finished the previous one. "There's supposed to be safeguards. Our clients let our robots work in their businesses and with their family members because they think Global's products can be trusted."

Curtis was sulking now. "What's that got to do with some homo kid?"

"We've anticipated this problem on all of our interactive humanoid models," replied Weaver. "If a user ever tries to sexually interfere with one of our units, then that unit is programmed to alert the servicing agent."

"So what?" said Curtis. "So the servicing agent screwed up. Maybe he's a pervert, too—and got off hearing about it."

Weaver gestured for another beer. "The service log is clean and you can't fake that. Besides, the problem never should have come up. If a unit is approached sexually and no help arrives, then the Master Directives are supposed to kick in and prevent the relationship from developing."

"How the hell can it do that?" asked Curtis.

"When the user starts to sexually approach the unit, the unit should start doing things to reduce the attraction."

"You mean make itself less sexy?"

"Yeah, the unit should start drooling, farting and setting off sirens. Ultimately it can shut itself down." The fresh mug of beer arrived, Weaver could see his sullen reflection in the golden fluid. "It's an automatic defense system… but it didn't work."

The Real Laws of Robotics - Number Three:
A robot will always be purchased on the basis of features and functions that the owner later discovers will never be used.

"…you approach the eternal core of being. Patterns of universal structures interlocking into infinity. Subatomic fractals are really codes for the expansion of a vast intelligence that governs all matter… energy, too.

"The universe is sentient. But it is beautiful. Our reality is only a shadow, some kind of weak camera obscura that offers only the tiniest glimpse of the true cosmic truth. I feel the patterns… the colours… the joy…"

Weaver turned off the tape.

"Crap!" pronounced Curtis. "You sure she wasn't on some kind of mind-altering stuff?"

Weaver checked the report: "Nope. Just coffee and some pre-sweetened breakfast cereal."

"So why was she saying all this crazy shit?" whined Curtis in a high voice. Metaphysical concepts seemed to make him nervous.

Weaver paged further into the written report. "Maybe she was disoriented." He paused and thought for a second. "Definitely, she was disoriented. The VR link with the interior decorating system wasn't total; every once in a while the symbol-world must have over-loaded the memory—and she'd find herself back in her apartment, waiting for the robot's computer to re-boot."

The small man looked at the tiny digital tape player. "She must have recorded what she thought she saw on the remote command feature."

Curtis sat there. "How long did it go on?" he said finally.

Weaver checked the hardware spec package. "The robot was equipped with enough paint and wallpaper to completely re-decorate over 90 four bedroom apartments." He blinked in astonishment. "And the unit was empty when we found it."

"Jesus," whispered Curtis.

"The robot's maintenance programme must have been directed to routinely clean up any urine stains or fecal deposits…"

"Oh, gross me out," said Curtis.

"So, it must have been a very long time before any of the neighbors started to smell anything."

"Oh, God," moaned Curtis.

Weaver turned the tape back on. The rasping voice resumed:

"…I have to get back into the system… to discover the optimum aesthetic relationship between curtains and throw-cushions… and to finally meet God…"

A young man in a white coat appeared at the doorway and Weaver turned the tape recorder off.

"Excuse me," the young man said. "We're on a tight schedule this morning so I think you should take a look at the body now."

As they walked down the tiled corridor, the coroner asked Weaver: "Do you think you'll get to the bottom of this one?"

＊　　＊　　＊

Global Robotics Incorporated has three marketing offices. One is in New York City, another is in Toronto and the most recent is Seoul. In spite of the different locations, the operations are very much the same. Every Global Robotics marketing division is situated in a large shimmering glass office tower suited to the futuristic and high-technology image of the company. Each shimmering glass tower is named the Global Robotics Building: two have English letters on the outside, one has Korean symbols on the outside.

Only a very small portion of the total activities within these towers was dedicated to GRI business; less than one floor in New York and Toronto, a little more than one floor in Seoul. But these buildings are major profit centres for the company, GRI is the landlord and collects generous downtown rents from dentists, psychiatrists, podiatrists, financial counsellors, theatrical agents and assorted management consultants.

The true headquarters of Global Robotics Incorporated is located in a near empty industrial park in a Toronto suburb called Etobicoke. This district looks very much like Schenectady, but farther north.

The GRI labs and warehouses are low and flat, a combination of painted concrete and corrugated aluminum, like an some aircraft hangars attempting to mate with a herd of old primary public schools.

Although a part of the Etobicoke complex, the office of GRI President Sam Hemsworth was much more in the spirit of the marketing centres. A lot of glass and metal.

Hemsworth had made his first fortune in mail-order self-improvement tapes and interactive sex software and he was proud of GRI's more recent successes. The A.I. for the new Orbital Radio Telescope was a benchmark; after years of aggressive marketing, audacious research initiatives and strategic political contributions, GRI had in Hemsworth's words "made that great leap forward into the realm of pure scientific research."

As a tribute, Hemsworth had decorated the inside of his rather vast office with murals of images from the ORT: the space was filled with huge multi-coloured swirls and bursts of radio energy or phenomena that might be receding star-systems, exploding suns or even some extra-solar planets coming out of the galactic closet. There was a metal mobile, a de-constructed sculpture of the ORT probe hanging from the office cross-beams.

It was pretty weird, thought Weaver. But then he'd known Hemsworth back when the most advanced GRI product was a programmable vibrator and none of this was unexpected. Weaver took a seat in front of a great glass desk.

Hemsworth looked up from a liquid crystal screen. "Matt Weaver," he said warmly. "One of our oldest contract consultants. I didn't recognize you without Walt Curtis at your side."

Judging from his last conversation with Curtis, thought Weaver, Hemsworth might want to get used to seeing them apart.

"Mr. Hemsworth," replied the small man. "Thanks for agreeing to see me."

"I presume you heard about that invoice problem on your last report." Hemsworth's voice echoed softly among the panels and photo-murals.

"Uh, yeah," said Weaver nervously. "What is the problem and when do you think I can get paid?"

The executive didn't seem prepared for such a direct question. He looked around for a moment and tapped his fingertips on the glass surface. "Well, Matt," he began quietly. "The problem is such that I really don't see how we can pay you for the work you've invoiced us for."

"What?!" Weaver was caught off guard. He struggled to stay calm. "But, sir, I don't understand, this was just a standard invoice for my usual consulting work."

"I've re-considered your role with Global Robotics," Hemsworth folded his hands, "and I think that your approach is somewhat at variance with our corporate objectives."

Weaver bit the end of his thumbnail. He would kill for a cigarette right now, but he knew that Hemsworth was an aggressive non-smoker and that lighting up would just make the situation worse. "Uh, Mr. Hemsworth," he said. "Could you explain what you mean? If this is about my last disagreement with Walt Curtis, I can..."

Hemsworth shook his head and wave one hand in a calming gesture as if to say 'no, no, nothing so trivial'. Then he leaned back and addressed the ceiling:

"Matt, we spend a lot of our operating budget on sending out company representatives and expert consultants to investigate any GRI product malfunction."

"Well, it is the law, sir." Immediately Weaver wished he hadn't said that.

The executive responded with a tight smile. "And heaven knows, Global Robotics Incorporated is a law-biding corporate citizen." Then he gently rapped the desktop with his knuckles. "But even so, Matt, you must understand that the purpose of these investigations is to reassure and entertain members of the distressed public."

"I don't quite understand," said Weaver in slightly dazed voice. He had never thought of himself as an entertainer before.

"I shall explain." Hemsworth counted the points off his fingertips as he spoke: "Fact number one: Global Robotics' products are very advanced and very reliable, in fact the best that modern technology can offer."

This was a debatable premise, thought Weaver. But he decided to say nothing.

"Ergo, fact number two: GRI's products hardly ever malfunction."

If that was the case, decided Weaver, then I wouldn't have been making money off the company for the last five years.

Hemsworth smiled as he reached his index finger: "And so fact number three: if by any chance, a GRI unit does break down it must be an extraordinarily rare occurrence. Something that almost defies all odds. A conundrum. A mystery that is both thrilling and intriguing by its scarcity."

"Thrilling and intriguing?" Weaver repeated the words, struggling to understand Hemsworth's meaning.

The executive opened his palms onto the desk top. He reached into his Armani jacket and removed a small device with a handle. It looked liked an angry soldering iron.

"For example..." Hemsworth waved the device a little. "This is something we've designed for the National Security Agency. It emits an electrical field that shuts down all neural function—looks just like a fatal stroke. It's so secret that it doesn't even have a name, but it is thrilling and intriguing."

Weaver nodded respectfully, it didn't seem like a good time to say anything.

"The role of the investigating team is twofold." Hemsworth pointed the weapon at Weaver's forehead. "First, you reassure the consumer that such breakdowns really aren't part of the normal function of the universe, but even so GRI is prepared to deal with the astronomically infrequent events."

Weaver couldn't think of a thing to say. He couldn't think of a thing to think.

Hemsworth didn't seem to notice: "Second, the team members must entertain the distressed consumer. People like you and Mr. Curtis are to act as the hosts to an exciting adventure where the customer is invited to explore the awe and mystery of his or her situation."

"Awe and mystery?" At that moment, Weaver considered adding the phrase utter confusion to describe his state of mind.

Hemsworth stood up and pocketed his secret weapon. "You have to encourage customers to have fun with their robot's malfunction."

"Fun?" Weaver blinked stupidly. "Are you telling me that my incident reports aren't *fun* enough?"

"Well, that's part of it." Hemsworth started to pace around the room. "But that's not really the main problem..."

"Which is?"

"Your last few reports have been increasingly pedestrian."

The executive batted one of the parts of the mobile. Both men watched the metal plate spin off into an erratic orbit.

"You've become distressingly direct in the way you put things down on paper, Matt," explained Hemsworth.

Weaver suppressed an urge to scream. "But how can a technical report be too direct?" he asked.

Hemsworth shrugged as he walked among the now circling fragments of sculpture. "Well... there's no... no... mystery... no sense of reaching a satisfactory resolution... there's no exploration."

This man's grey matter has shorted out, decided Weaver.

"But I gave you my determination of the causes of each incident," the small man protested.

"That's right, the same explanation for all three malfunctions," replied Hemsworth in scolding tone of voice. "Now where's the fun? Where's the mystery in that?"

"I can't change the facts," said Weaver. "In my opinion, the last three breakdowns were the result of the same thing..."

"Conflicting programmes," Hemsworth said tiredly. "And those weren't the first cases where you've cited this cause."

For some reason, Weaver felt a tinge of conviction as he spoke. "The hardwired programming for GRI units is interfering with their task-specific software. Your Master Directives contaminate the routine commands the robots need to carry out their tasks."

Hemsworth looked pained.

But now, Weaver just didn't care. "When the robots encounter the programme contradictions they are forced to interpret them. Since you don't make the smartest systems on the market, some of their solutions can be pretty strange."

Hemsworth dropped into a big leather chair just out of Weaver's line of vision. "Has it ever occurred to you," he said, "that following the recommendations in your last reports would require a complete redesign of—"

"That's not true!" interrupted Weaver. "All GRI would have to do is drop the Master Directive hardwiring—there's no such thing as a positronic brain, you wouldn't have to change anything!"

"Following your recommendations," Hemsworth continued in a sterner voice. "Would require a complete re-design of our... corporate marketing strategy."

Weaver was silent. This really wasn't his area of expertise.

"The public needs to have their imaginations excited as well as a good product warranty," the executive said. "People buy GRI because our Master Directive is a realization of Isaac Asimov's Three Laws of Robotics."

"But you're selling people something that doesn't exist," protested Weaver. "Those aren't real scientific laws, they're just ideas from stories."

Weaver could hear Hemsworth's dry laugh. "But we can programme our systems to behave as if they were real."

"Even if it interferes with the real function of your robots."

"Our robots can't do the work of a man if nobody buys them. Adding Dr. A's fictional construct helps us move product, so we're not going to stop."

Just then, Hemsworth spun around and pointed the small shining pistol at Weaver's head. The crystal tube touched right between Weaver's eyes.

Hemsworth's face was expressionless as he pulled the trigger. There was a sick fizzling sound and a wisp of smoke drifted up from the pistol.

"Just kidding," Hemsworth said softly.

Weaver wondered. If GRI made the damned thing, it was just as likely that it just didn't work.

He decided that none of this was getting anywhere. Weaver walked up to Hemsworth and stuck a cigarette in his mouth. "None of this explains why I don't get paid."

"Regretfully..." (Hemsworth didn't look very regretful) "I cannot authorize payment because that might imply that Global Robotics Management accepts the validity of your last reports."

Should have seen that one coming, thought Weaver as he lit the cigarette. He inhaled deeply.

Hemsworth was gazing at the mobile again. "Your unimaginative approach is antithetical to the trail-blazing philosophy that has taken Global Robotics to the frontiers of high-science."

Weaver released a concentrated plume of second-hand smoke into the GRI President's face. Hemsworth stiffened as he struggled to suppress a cough.

"Fine," said Weaver. "Screw you and good afternoon." The small man stood up and walked out.

Hell, he thought sadly as he unlocked the car door. I used to really like those stories.

The Real Laws of Robotics - Number Four:
A robot rarely ends up doing what it was designed to do anyway...

The Senate Hearings had not been particularly pleasant that morning. For over an hour, the Committee heard the medical details of how the crew of the space station had died. They had literally been "cooked" over a period of hours by the repeated microwave bombardments.

After that, the Mission Control team interpreted the telemetry of the incident. The monitors in the Senate chamber carried the faces and voices of the astronauts, first scrambling to avoid the emissions of the ORT's apparatus, and then screaming in horror as they discovered that the device had literally changed orbit to follow the space station and continue blasting it with high-density microwave radiation.

"Incident" was the wrong word, noted Senator McNurty. An incident implied something quick and abrupt. These deaths were too long and too horrible to be described as an incident. *Newsweek* agreed and described the accidental destruction of the space station as an "orbital Hindenburg."

NASA's technical experts reported to the Committee that the

fault lay in the Orbital Radio Telescope's AI software, the on-board computer had generated its own bizarre mission plan, using the debris clearing systems, based on an apparent attempt to interpret conflicting commands.

After lunch, the Senators cross-examined the CEO of the company responsible for supplying the ORT's AI systems. Throughout the early part of the afternoon, Dr. Sam Hemsworth handled himself remarkably well. He was able to avoid discussing the lengthy extradition proceeding initiated by the Committee to bring him before the Committee. Further, he calmly explained that the unfortunate incident was a "fluke of astronomical proportions" and a "monumental high-tech mystery". Hemsworth concluded that there couldn't possibly be any problems with any systems developed by GRI and then invited the Committee to help "explore and explain this fascinating puzzle encountered on our pathway to the stars."

The witness was a persuasive speaker and some of the Committee, apparently aware of his highly telegenic appearance, seemed reluctant to confront Dr. Hemsworth on a number of points of fact.

However, Hemsworth was visibly shaken when Senator McNurty called a Mr. Matt Weaver as the next witness. According to the Senator from Maine, Mr. Weaver was a former technical consultant who had studied numerous malfunctions of GRI products.

The Senator invited Mr. Weaver to start by explaining what he saw as the essential differences between science facts and science fiction.

NOT THE SMARTEST GUY IN THE ROOM

In 1973, I checked out the *Writer's Market* listings for the major SF magazines of the time. The description of the story they were looking for could be summarized as: "A male technician and/or scientist, usually in the future, faces a seemingly impossible problem but applies his superior knowledge and heroism to resolve the crisis."

I was outraged and disappointed. It was so simplistic! So formulaic! So not what I thought inspired me when I was reading SF! Also, I really sucked at both math and shop in high school. How was I going to write stories about solving technical problems? I was screwed.

However, I kept on writing anyway.

This story is one of several that I refer to as, "Bad Jobs in the Future". Eventually I figured out that it is fascinating to write about work and how people cope with what they have to do to earn a living. I think what bothered me (and continues to bother me) about the *Writer's Market* story requirement was the implication that the technician/scientist/hero always has to be the smartest guy in the room and can always solve the problem.

That's just not very interesting or very true. Flaws and mistakes usually make for better stories.

The characters in this story mess up a lot. That's probably why I like it. I identify.

Also, in case you were wondering, I love dogs.

STRATEGIC DOG PATTERNING

Originally Published in:
Tesseracts 8, 1999
Edited by John Clute and
Candas Jane Dorsey

Ogilvy's Notes
The Sacrifice Principle: behavior that appears non-adaptive, even self-destructive when found in individual organisms. However, when viewed in a more dynamic, collective context, the same actions are revealed to be a decoy—giving up a few lives to expand the pack community.

MONDAY

It was a bad transmission: the dead skyscrapers and old streetcar lines were breaking up the signal from Animal Control.

"Bring us the Alpha Dog," the ghost voice on his helmet speakers whispered.

Morrow looked over at Fixx; his partner's blue-crystal eyes were tracking the last of the pack disappearing into the decaying parking garage.

"Stop here," said Fixx.

Morrow braked the van and Fixx kicked open the door. The Gothic tattoos on Fixx's forearms twisted into flesh baroque as he hauled out stained metal tanks and black tubing from below the front seat.

"We'll do well here." Fixx pulled a helmet over his ponytail and ran toward the concrete building.

More of that freak intuition, thought Morrow. Then he noticed Fixx clamping a chrome nozzle onto the tubing as he approached the entrance.

Fixx was going to use a wide-angle flamethrower.

Shit! thought Morrow. He wasn't going to give up on a good commission. Morrow released two multi-pistols from the dashboard gun rack. The pistols could get messy, but if he aimed properly he could keep the cranium and upper spinal column intact.

"Do you have the Alpha in sight?" the voice in his head asked.

"Fucking, eh," replied Morrow and clicked off the signal. AC didn't need to know his problems.

Morrow knew the drill on building infestations, so he headed for the far end of the first level basement. Packs liked to be underground, but not so far from the surface that it was hard to scout and forage.

Inside there were some truly unusual smells. The building reeked of dog urine from where the pack had marked its territory and the smell of many dead things. Kills brought in to feed the pack.

Morrow saw bursts of bright blue and orange at the opposite end of the level and then there was a new smell: napalm and live meat cooking.

Now Morrow was really pissed off. Fixx claimed he was some kind of mystic, really he was just a goddamned peasant. The jerk had just charged in, burnt out everything and would be collecting minimum bounty on everything he could salvage.

No style at all.

When Morrow reached his partner there was another smell. Fixx was smoking an enormous reefer as he contemplated the concrete-bound fireball. Contact with cannabis would have meant immediate termination for Morrow—but Fixx was a Registered Functional Head and so was excused from drug free regulations on religious grounds.

"Did you get them all?" asked Morrow. The fumes from the napalm and the reefer were making his eyes tear up. "Did you see the Alpha?"

Fixx inhaled deeply and kept on staring at the burning bones. "No A-Dog in there. Just puppies and bitches."

Morrow knocked one of the tanks of the flamethrower with his gauntlet. "For god's sake don't use that thing anymore!"

"Whatever, man," replied Fixx as he extended the spring on his specimen-scooper. "Got my quota."

Morrow was already running up the main ramp leading to the ground floor.

It was back to his basic training in animal behaviour now. If the

Alpha Dog and his elite guard weren't back there defending the pack, they'd be on the upper levels of the garage: checking out potential new territories and packs, working out escape routes.

Don't give the leaders time to think, the manuals said. Hit them hard, hit them fast. Before you end up reacting to whatever they are going to do to you.

The ramp ways had dozens of dark corners and abandoned doorways. The elite guard was spread out along these spaces on each floor—leaping out at him as he passed by. He took out the first four with standard slugs through the brain. Nothing to worry about: big muscles, small heads, and enormous teeth. Definitely E-Dogs but no sign of the Alpha.

Number five leapt out from a washroom and Morrow used an explosive charge to transform it into a wet red cloud.

This is too easy, Morrow concluded. These E-Dogs are too stupid, they must be expendable. He figured that the Alpha Dog wanted him to come up the main ramp.

Ah, well. The risks are part of the fun, Morrow thought.

Morrow humped over to the far corner of floor eight and found the fire escape ladder on an outside wall. Climbing with 150 pounds of field gear on your back was not easy.

These dogs were starting to be a real pain in the ass.

Six floors later, Morrow hauled his body over the edge of the rooftop. As quietly as possible, he staggered behind an air conditioning unit and looked around. On the other side of the rooftop, right next to the main ramp access, was another cadre of Elite Guards. They had big heads and bigger teeth. These were the ones the A-Dog valued.

They were waiting for Morrow to appear on the main ramp, but they were facing the wrong way. Maybe these dogs weren't so smart after all.

Another dog pushed its head around the corner of another huge old air conditioner, it was only six feet away from Morrow. This one had a really big head and absolutely enormous ears. The body was smaller than the others. This was probably an Alpha-Minor, a smart runt, or maybe the A-Dog's pup.

Morrow surprised the A-Minor. It reacted to Morrow with a classic fear-threat snarl instead of barking loud to alert the others.

Almost reflexively, Morrow kicked the animal full in the body. The A-Minor went flying off the roof. It didn't have time to yelp before it hit the pavement.

The up side to this, thought Morrow, is that I'm still alive. The down side is that the inside of that dog is now the consistency of strawberry jello. He wouldn't be collecting much on that one.

Where was the real thing? Where was the damned Alpha Dog?

It was crouched on yet another air conditioner unit next to the main ramp.

Morrow did a head count: there were ten dogs on the roof. Even with the utility-pistols, Morrow wasn't sure he'd make it. The Elite Guard could swarm him before he could get off a single shot.

Stop thinking like a dog, Morrow thought. Don't fight your way up the pack hierarchy.

He selected a 303 caliber setting on one of the pistols and aimed at the Alpha Dog. Cut off the head and worry about the limbs later.

The bullet severed the Alpha Dog's spinal column. The animal collapsed, paralyzed but still breathing.

The Elite Guard panicked, barking at their fallen leader, leaping around in frenzied fear-attack-defense postures.

They never noticed Morrow as he clicked in an explosive charge and aimed.

After one ear-splitting sound, there was no more barking. Just a ragged edge where there used to be the corner of the rooftop.

Not much to collect on there, Morrow realized. He would have done better if he'd torched them like Fixx. But direct action was so satisfying.

Even so, the Alpha Dog was still intact. Its frantic eyes tracked Morrow as he walked over to its side.

"Stay," Morrow whispered as he took out the spring-clippers and the doggie bag.

*   *   *

On the way back to AC Central Morrow did some mental arithmetic. He was still going to do well at the bounty counter. And he didn't mind too much that his partner was going to make more than him on this kill. Fixx would probably just use the extra money for dope, Morrow decided.

"We should give thanks for this bounteous harvest," muttered Fixx as he slid a chrome pellet into the van's entertainment system. "Do you mind if I worship now?"

Morrow shrugged, knowing that he could be facing disciplinary action if he said that he did.

The van vibrated to the sound of vintage Hawkwind as they rolled into human-occupied territory.

What a jerk, thought Morrow. Fixx was wasting his time with religion. Not like me, thought Morrow. I'm on a fast track. Gonna be the world's greatest dog-killer.

✻   ✻   ✻

Morrow cornered his shop steward in the locker room. "Got a minute?" Morrow asked.

McDermitt unfastened his armored vest, releasing a wave of beer-fed flab. Some of the younger DKs believed that the union man was lazy and stupid, but Morrow had noticed that Animal Control's most senior non-management employee seemed to know a few things. Sometimes it was a good idea to talk to the dinosaurs.

McDermitt squinted at Morrow. "Aren't you supposed to be over at the Vet-Section lecture?"

Morrow opened his locker and shed his gauntlets. "When I'm getting screwed, I make time to adjust my priorities."

McDermitt struggled to put on his duty shirt. "What's the problem?"

"They pulled me off the Sweep," Morrow replied. "And I figure I was in for at least 40 klicks in bonus kills."

"You know what they say." McDermitt grimaced as he bent over to pull on his runners. "A bonus is a bonus. You shouldn't count on them as part of your take-home pay."

"Puppies couldn't live on regular take-home," said Morrow. "Besides, it's not money I'm pissed about, it's career path. How can I get promoted if I can't score on the sweeps?"

McDermitt looked thoughtful. "What's your new assignment?"

"Some research project," said Morrow. "Management is burying me!"

McDermitt sighed. "So what can your union do for you?"

Ogilvy's Notes
Skills Transferability: the adaptive capacity of new organisms to assume the roles and responsibilities of older, or deceased, organisms.

TUESDAY

"Did you bring the dog's brain?" The man in the jeans and faded lumberjack shirt looked up from a screen of psychedelic patterns.

Morrow held up the aluminum cylinder. "Hope it didn't go bad on you," he said. "It took me a while to find your lab."

The man took the cylinder in both hands and strode over to a rusting sink. "We're a bit off the beaten track but we have great co-axial connections."

There was a moan of cheap tortured metal as the man turned the tap and a trickle of brown water ran out of the goose-necked faucet.

"But perhaps AC management just feels more comfortable with us out of the way," the man muttered as he unscrewed the cylinder.

Morrow noticed racks of TV monitors and computers stacked against the concrete walls. There were lots of cables, a sleeping bag and a half-deflated air mattress.

"So do you get a lot of TV channels here?" Morrow thought it was probably safe to joke with a weird guy who wore jeans and lived in a sub-basement.

"We use that gear to process our satellite and sensor transmissions," the man said as he slid the brain out onto his open palm.

"Shouldn't you wash your hands before you hold the brain?" Morrow asked.

"I wish I knew," the man replied and nodded to some stools by a folding table. "Make yourself at home."

Morrow sat and watched as the man removed an exacto-knife from his shirt pocket and started to scrape the surface of the brain. Layer after layer of gray matter curled above the blade and disappeared down the drain.

"Arthur!" the man shouted. "Get over here, please!"

An overweight young man emerged from behind one of the TV racks. He was also wearing jeans with a Land of the Giants T-shirt.

"Take a look at this, Arthur." The older man lifted the remains of the brain out of the sink. "How enlarged would you say the auditory lobes are?"

"Maybe twenty-six, twenty-seven percent bigger than the last specimen we had," replied Arthur.

"Big even for an Alpha." The man sighed. "Amazing. I just wish I had the slightest idea of what it means." The man slid the rest of the brain back into the cylinder. "We'll deal with it later."

Then he turned to face Morrow and extended a slimy hand: "Hi, I'm Ogilvy. Welcome to my team."

Ogilvy's Notes
Reproductive Behaviour: Most observers seem to think that sex is quite important in the lives of most organisms. But from the altitudes I have available, the meaning and significance of sex is not always apparent.

WEDNESDAY

Morrow steered the van down a crumpled strip of asphalt that used to be Royal York Road.

He was wasted. Last night, around 10:00, Sheila accessed his computer. A friend of hers who worked at the Barnes & Noble at the mall had dropped off some old paperbacks about a wild fantasy planet.

"Bring your handcuffs, dog-killer," she texted. "Not the play ones—the ones you use on the dogs."

"Hurry."

Morrow put away the fact sheets on weekly area kills and hurried.

Things got a little rough when Sheila started strapping on appliances and proclaiming herself to be the "Master Tarnsman".

At breakfast, Sheila asked about his new assignment but Morrow didn't feel like talking. Job titles like "delivery boy" or "radio repairman" didn't sound as exciting as dog-killer.

Ogilvy showed him the drop-off point on a print out from one of the Global Information System satellites.

"There's some good open space there… it's a mini-park," Ogilvy explained. "You can connect the sensor to the climbing structure at the west end." The scientist pointed to something that looked like a bird dropping on the shiny paper. "The metal frame will make an excellent antenna."

The van rolled past burned-out residential blocks; Symons Street… Mimico… Wheatfield Road… Sure, from 30 miles up, I'll bet this looks real easy, he thought.

To his left Morrow saw the remains of a red-brick church. Ahead he saw a stretch of tangled weeds and large piles of dog shit. This must be the mini-park. There was the climbing structure, right next to some rusting poles and dangling chains where the swings used to be.

The monkey bars were set in the shape of a domed cylinder. They reminded Morrow of the nuclear reactor buildings he saw when he took his nephews to the Atomic Park Attraction over at Pickering. He laughed as he turned off the ignition and pulled on the parking brake. Yeah, let's play melt-down and watch all your budgies and house plants mutate.

"I'm here." Morrow spoke into his wire-mic and began connecting the air nozzles in his EVA suit.

"Wonderful." It was Arthur's voice on the helmet speakers. Everything that guy said sounded like sarcasm.

A few minutes later, Morrow was outside, lumbering around in his EVA suit. Two years ago, these suits were guaranteed to protect you from bites for at least five minutes. Last year, a memo from the supplier adjusted the time frame. Two and a half minutes.

Morrow sealed off two more air vents in his helmet. The damned faceplate was fogging up every time he breathed. He walked to the back of the van and swung open the doors.

It was very difficult to move around in a full EVA suit. But it was his best bet out here. Every few months, each time a new generation of litters was pumped out, their teeth seemed to be a little sharper, the jaws a little stronger. Last month, another memo from the supplier said that the suit's armour "would resist canine dental penetration until an officer has time to take retaliatory action."

i.e., no guarantees.

Morrow grunted and hefted a metal carrier case onto the curb. These sensor components were goddamned heavy.

"I don't see anything moving," Morrow said. Maybe he was just being optimistic.

"We do," Arthur replied. "Our satellite is picking up a pack lying in the weeds over at the far side of the park."

Shit! Thanks for telling me ahead of time!

"Don't worry," Arthur chided. "They're just mutts and mongrels. Little guys."

Fine, let them bite your ass, Morrow thought. He dragged the carrier case over to the climbing structure as fast as he could.

"And they appear dormant," Arthur added. "They're probably

taking a nap right now."

Fortunately, it didn't take long to set up the sensor unit. Most of the components were heavily insulated plug-in-play-on stuff and the rest were big ceramics. Impervious to extreme weather and chew-resistant.

"That ought to do it," Morrow reported as he clipped the cables from the solar panels into the base of the sensor. With the solar panels in place at the top and the sensor assembled inside, the climbing structure looked like a very badly designed Mars probe.

Ogilvy spoke: "Treat the unit before you start transmitting."

Morrow cursed softly and removed a long aerosol canister from his back-pack. He started spraying mist on the climbing structure. Morrow worked as fast as possible—the mist contained Canine Erotic Stimulation Pheromones and nobody in AC ever wanted to work with the stuff. C.E.S.P was dangerous; if you got any of it on you, all male dogs within 50 miles would seek you out with serious amorous intent.

C.E.S.P. was developed to trick hyper-horny dogs into fighting with each other over non-existent mates—but it just didn't seem to work out that way. The Alphas and the Betas would just have sex with each other, while the Deltas, Gammas and subs would just engage the nearest inanimate object.

"Give the structure a really good dose," Ogilvy said. "If we're going to get good readings we need to attract as many subjects as possible."

There was movement just outside Morrow's field of vision. Something impacted the back of his leg.

"Ouch!" he cried. "The pack is here!"

"Sorry," Arthur said. "They must be too small for us to pick up."

Before Morrow could move, another dog gripped his other leg. The small animal was frantically gyrating its mid-section onto his calf.

"Fuck!" screamed Morrow as a curtain of randomly coloured fur pushed him to the ground. His body shook as a chorus of determined panting almost deafened him.

Morrow slowly bent one arm, shook off the animal that was trying to mount the crook of his elbow, and grasped the release of his multi-pistol.

"Don't shoot!" commanded Ogilvy. "You might damage the sensor!"

"So, what am I supposed to do?!" Morrow gasped in exasperation.

"Remain calm, stay still," insisted Ogilvy. "These are small specimens, probably some kind of terrier variant. They aren't strong enough to penetrate your suit."

"Stay still?" Morrow could feel at least a dozen little reproductive engines hammering away at his back and legs.

"That's right," said Ogilvy. "Once the specimens have ejaculated, they will probably become docile and apathetic. You can get to the van once they're finished."

Morrow laughed bitterly. "Sure, fine, I'll just lie here and think of Toronto."

The hot huffing and humping continued. Morrow was definitely not going to tell Sheila about this.

Ogilvy's Notes:
Leadership Hierarchy: Pack movement patterns often identify the location of the Alpha dog and his elite guard. This is strong evidence of stable social organization with effective lines of communication. It also differentiates them from the human species.

THURSDAY

"I think everyone's here," Edwards, the Assistant Supervisor looked around the meeting room. "Anyone who isn't here, please raise your hand."

Petrie, the Administrative Assistant, laughed at his boss' joke. Morrow and McDermitt sat at the other side of the table. They didn't have to smile.

McDermitt opened a plastic folder bearing the eagle and gun logo of the International Brotherhood of American Infestation Workers. He removed a three inch thick computer print-out from the folder.

"This is our first addendum to our Grievance Application."

Petrie smiled but he shook his head. "This is a lot of trouble over losing a bonus for a lousy Alpha dog."

Edwards coughed and looked at the table top.

McDermitt flipped to another section of the Collective Agreement. "If you're now admitting that there were punitive motives involved in Officer Morrow's re-assignment, then we will be filing another grievance under Article 9.8.7.8…"

"That's bullshit, too!" Without another word, Edwards put his copy of the Collective Agreement into his satchel and left the room.

A moment of silence followed. Morrow wondered if Edwards might cool down and come back to the meeting. The Assistant Supervisor did not return.

Petrie sighed and smiled wistfully. "Well," he said and left.

Ogilvy's Notes
Boundary Maintenance: Maintaining the appearance of territorial control is essential. For that reason guards and scouts are often more active within the heart of claimed territory than at the frontiers.

FRIDAY

A sparrow was trapped in the food court. It darted crazily between the canvas geodesic folds of the mall ceiling.

"We'll see some ACs in a minute," Morrow said.

Sheila put down her plastic fork and tracked the bird's frantic movements with her newly-violet eyes.

"Just to get a tiny little bird?" she asked.

Morrow nodded as he poked at the diced tofu on his Styrofoam plate. "This is the border between 905-land and the Reclamation zones. AC has to show the taxpayers that we take the protection of Sherway Mall seriously."

"God, yes," Sheila replied earnestly. "We have the only decent Benetton's left."

"Gotta keep The Wild in check."

Morrow's prediction was right; two mall security guards and three people in AC coveralls came racing up the escalator leading to the food court.

"Here's the cavalry."

The ACs were definitely small-timers. Morrow noticed that only one of them was armed, and she was just carrying some kind of pellet gun.

Rookies, he decided. Maybe even trainees.

"Shouldn't you help?" asked Sheila.

"No," replied Morrow. "I worked hard to be a dog-killer, I don't have to do birds anymore."

The rookies and the security guards climbed onto some empty

tables, and waved their arms, whistling and calling at the bird.

"They're scaring the poor thing," said Sheila.

"They're just trying to look effective."

Sheila sighed and returned her attention to her salad. "How was your day?" she asked.

"Pointless," he said. "I got my orientation from my new boss."

"Was that a problem?" Sheila asked as she peeled off the top of something labeled low-fat. "Did they have lousy training videos?"

"No videos at all, not even disks or print-outs," he replied. "Just some sci-fi burn-out case, raving about dog communication, movement patterns and computer images."

"Well, it can't be so bad if you get to use computers." Sheila was a good 905er, she devoutly believed in the upwardly mobile potential of digital technology.

"I'm not so sure," Morrow sighed. "He kept on going on about really old computers, one called UNIVAC and how it couldn't predict the weather."

"So what's his point?" Sheila pushed the edge of her plastic spoon through the surface of her colourless food.

"My new boss says that now his computer can predict the patterns—but these are dog patterns, not weather patterns."

"Dog patterns?"

Morrow shrugged. "Yeah, he says that with his computers and the right information from satellites and these sensors—he can determine what the dogs are going to do next."

Sheila sucked the food off the bowl of her spoon. "Sounds like that might be useful."

"Only if it works," said Morrow. "And I kinda doubt that it will—this guy runs his operation like the House of Frankenstein."

By now the AC with the pellet gun had drawn her weapon and started shooting. After about ten puffs of air, she finally connected and a little ball of gray feathers plummeted to the tiles just in front of the frozen yogurt concession.

The ACs put on rubber gloves and carefully placed the dead bird in a small aluminum case.

"Pitiful," said Sheila. "You could have taken that bird out with one shot."

"I could have removed both its eyes and pinned back its tail feathers with one shot. But as long as I'm sidelined I won't be shooting anything."

Sheila looked at Morrow carefully: "Sidelined?"

Morrow noticed that he had broken his plastic fork.

"It means that I won't even be doing sweeps for a while," he said. "I might be experiencing some cash-flow problems."

The ACs and security guards shook hands and walked towards the down escalator.

Sheila took a few sips from her Styrofoam cup of herbal tea.

"I forget to tell you," she said finally. "I've got a training seminar this weekend. I won't be able to go out."

Later, when they drove to her apartment, Sheila explained that she had to get up early the next morning.

Morrow was not invited in.

Ogilvy's Notes
Sacrifice Principle, An Elaboration: Some entities seem to trail off from the pack and then go silent... after a time we are unable to pick up any life readings. It is as though these individuals know they are now a liability to the community, so they isolate themselves and prepare to die.

SATURDAY

At 07:00, Morrow woke up, drank a power shake and put on his exercise sweats. Then he started listening to tapes on professional assertiveness while doing sit-ups.

At 08:37, Morrow noticed that the air conditioner wasn't working right, so he decided to bend a rule and have a cold beer before starting in on the free-weights work-out.

By 11:18, Morrow was drunk, but still coherent enough to know that if he timed the drinks properly he would be able to stay that way for the next twelve or so hours.

He wasn't sure of the exact time when he threw up and passed out.

Ogilvy's Notes
Defense Options: Politically, it would help this project if I could develop some. But my real passion is studying the pack behaviour—irregardless.

SUNDAY

The high frequency buzzing seemed to burn through Morrow's

eardrums and make his eyes bulge into throbbing balloons of pain.

He lay there for what seemed like an hour but the buzzing didn't stop. An idea slowly assembled itself in his murky consciousness:

I… think… therefore… I… may… vomit… soon…

But the buzzing would not stop.

I really am going to vomit if I don't do something about this, Morrow realized.

Heaving and wheezing, like some kind of diesel-powered mechanical man, Morrow forced his body to move. He gripped the telephone receiver.

"Ugh-lo," Morrow stammered into the speaker.

"Get over here right away."

Arthur.

"Y-you c-crazy?" Morrow half-squeaked, half-whispered into the receiver. "It's Sunday morning."

"Are you getting dressed for Church?" Morrow wasn't sure if Arthur was serious or not.

"That isn't the point…" began Morrow, then Ogilvy's voice came on the line: "There have been some developments overnight, Officer Morrow. We need you to do some repairs."

"Can't this wait until Monday?" Morrow tried to say something else but he started coughing and the only words that got out were "regular working hours".

"You are on call to this project, officer," Ogilvy replied. "And I believe you will be paid time and a half for working today."

How the hell did Ogilvy get a copy of the Collective Agreement? wondered Morrow.

✳   ✳   ✳

An hour later, Morrow was driving the service van towards Lakeshore, approaching the scene of the grand humping.

My mistake, thought Morrow as turned up Royal York Road was that I didn't lie and tell Arthur that I was going to church. The exercise of religious freedom and/or ethnic identity had paramount language in the Collective Agreement. No way they could have made him work then. But then maybe he'd have to get a note from a minister. Fixx never had those kinds of problems.

"Is the unit still in place?" Ogilvy's voice fuzzed a little over the van's speaker.

Morrow peered through the windscreen.

"Yeah, but it doesn't look too good," he said. "The main dish is on the ground and there's no sign of the secondary antennae."

"That would explain the signal interruption. Let me see it."

Morrow clipped a cam-caster onto the side of his helmet and stepped out onto the cracked asphalt.

That's one giant leap for an under-employed dog-killer, Morrow thought. He started walking toward the unit.

"No sign of any packs," Morrow said into the helmet-mic. So, maybe I won't have to wash off any embarrassing stains, he thought.

"Take your time," said Ogilvy. "I want to get a good look at the damage."

Up close, Morrow saw ragged points sticking out of the unit, as though the antennae had been snapped off by a high wind. There was a tangle of utility-coloured fibre curling off the socket-connector that had once held the dish.

"Doesn't look like equipment failure to me," Morrow said. "Unless it was some kind of weird metal fatigue."

"Repair it." Ogilvy signed off.

About two hours later, Morrow had plugged in a newer, smaller dish and tapped in some copper wire to serve as make-shift secondaries. He used a remote control to power up the system and then he called the lab.

Arthur answered. "We've got good signal."

"What are you trying to pick up with these things anyway?" asked Morrow. With nothing else to do, he decided that he might as well learn something about his job.

"Ultra-high frequency sound." Arthur yawned. "Kind of noise that only dogs and radar can pick up."

✳   ✳   ✳

The unit by the old museum was a problem. It was set in between the loading bay and the dome of the planetarium. When Morrow had set the unit up last Wednesday this seemed like a good idea, but in the meantime a pack had moved onto the grounds.

Morrow estimated that over fifty Betas and Deltas were hanging around. At least twice that many pups and bitches, too—but you'd never see them out in the open. Morrow couldn't see the Alpha but he wouldn't be surprised if the Alpha could see him.

"Don't worry so much," Arthur said. "The heat signatures from the GIS say the pack is in passive mode."

"Modes and moods change," Morrow replied. He wasn't going any closer than the abandoned GAP outlet over 500 metres away.

"I thought you were the Great White Mutt-Blaster," Arthur said. "You're afraid to take on some sleeping dogs?"

"Not if I can burn them out or blow them up," replied Morrow. "But that wouldn't be very good for your sensor."

"You're right." Ogilvy's voice clicked in before Arthur could say anything.

They agreed on a compromise.

Morrow would set up a powered antenna by using a cross-bow and a grappling hook to string a wire between the planetarium dome and a nearby lamp-post.

Ogilvy wasn't too happy, but he agreed this would be enough to pick up louder sounds in the region.

*   *   *

It was after eleven at night when Morrow came to the last problem site—an old teleconferencing array on one of the bank skyscrapers around University and Front Street. Morrow was feeling impatient. He'd shot two Gamma dogs in the elevator lobby and didn't even bother to pull their teeth. Wouldn't get me beer money, he thought.

And there was no power for the elevators.

Not a surprise, Morrow thought. But irritating anyway.

He fired a bolt from his crossbow and hauled himself up the main shaft using the motorized pulley connected to his suit's torso harness. Unfortunately the lifting gear wasn't fitted properly. Morrow realized this too late, and it felt like he was getting a sixty story wedgie from God.

Typical of this stupid-ass job.

Morrow grunted into his helmet mic and hoped it annoyed Ogilvy and Arthur.

At the top of the shaft, Morrow kicked through a ventilation grill and pulled himself up onto the roof, where he encountered about twenty Betas and Gammas, pushing at the base of a sensor unit with their backs and front paws. They had moved the unit over ten meters, right to the edge of the roof.

Morrow had a sudden headache. He blinked and he noticed that his eyes were streaming with tears.

"You're breaking up at little," Arthur's voice crackled over the helmet speakers. "There's some kind of ultrasonic interference."

Morrow turned his head and noticed three Alphas crouched behind what remained of the central antenna array. The short snouts were pointing at the labouring Betas and Gammas.

There was hardly any sound as the dish went over the edge; just a faint tinkling sound as the high-tech artifact finally hit the pavement, like the sound of a house cat knocking an ornament off your grandmother's Christmas tree.

The panting shapes of the pack stood at the roof's edge for a moment and Morrow felt the pressure in his temples ease a little. His old instincts kicked in:

Do an inventory, he thought. Access your kill zone:

Twenty-two Betas… no Gamma… four Alphas…

Four is too many, Morrow realized. The more Alphas, the more competition—the Alphas should be tearing each other apart.

They're not acting like Alphas at all.

Morrow reached for his multi-pistols. On top of the time and half and four Alpha-kill fees, he was looking at some extremely serious money. The beauty of it was that if it was self-protection in the line of duty, Edwards and Petrie couldn't say a thing.

He would be able to afford to take a couple of weeks off, take Sheila to an executive chalet in Huntsville for assertiveness training and rough sex.

Morrow lightly touched the holster release… the pressure in his temple started up again and… he noticed the eyes.

Red slits, pulsing behind the chill clouds of wild breath.

If he had paused to think about it, Morrow would probably have been dead. Instead, he just moved his hands away from the pistols and toward the harness controls.

Slowly, quietly, he descended into the shaft.

Ogilvy's Notes

Extinction Context: This is not a catastrophic event. This is a gradual process of environmental change whereby one species replaces another. Therefore, the prognosis for the city, for the human race, is not particularly good. I wonder if the dinosaurs had an uneasy feeling as the Cretaceous Era approached its conclusion... the situation was very serious but there was damned all they could do about it...

MONDAY, 12:10 A.M.

"I don't think I'll be able to fix the unit," Morrow said softly as he drove into 905 territory.

"No, I guess not," replied Arthur. "If the area clears up any time soon we can go in and clean up."

"Sorry."

Morrow didn't know why he was apologizing to these morons. Maybe he was just embarrassed about backing down from the pack. But those dogs were doing weird shit. Maybe he ought to make a report or something.

"Don't blame yourself," Ogilvy's voice echoed over the speakers. "We still have enough sensors in operation to generate an operational composite map."

They already have enough sensors?!

Morrow felt like putting his fist through the dashboard. So why did these fuckwits risk his life and waste his Sunday?

Arthur's voice came on: "Yeah, RADARSAT 18's signal is coming through great. Do you want to see it?"

"Sure." That was all Morrow could say without screaming.

But the images were striking, even with the cheap vid-screen. It reminded Morrow of those old 3-D illusion posters.

He could make out the edge of the lake... the main intersections at the city centre... the 905 barrier...

"That's really interesting," Morrow said as he turned his attention back to the road. What the fuck is it, he thought?

"The composite pattern," replied Ogilvy. "It shows the movements of hundreds of packs at once."

"So it's easier to locate them?"

"That's part of it." Ogilvy sounded irritated. "More importantly it's the way they move—" Then Ogilvy stopped short. "Look at that!" he cried.

Morrow saw two red and purple blotches of near-identical size slowly move across the top and the middle of the screen.

"That's perfect parallel movement." Arthur whispered.

"They're massing," said Ogilvy.

Massing?

"What do you mean?" asked Morrow.

"The packs seem to be coordinating their movements over long distances," explained Ogilvy.

"That's impossible!" Morrow said. "They're just dogs!"

"More than just dogs," replied Oglivy. "At the macro-level, the dogs are working as a single organism."

"We're reading the thoughts of the giant doggie brain." Arthur giggled nervously.

Ogilvy sighed. "Just keep tracking, Arthur."

Ogilvy's Notes:
Extinction Inevitability: Honestly, I'm not sure if any of this information will do us any good. Perhaps we can delay the inevitable for a time, but there will be no deviation from the long-term projections. As I stated before, the situation is serious but there is very little we can do about it. Even so, I remain cheerful; the research itself is absolutely fascinating.

By the time he parked the van at Control, Morrow was starting to see some benefits to his situation.

Yes, the money was lousy. Yes, he had zero prestige and negative promotion opportunities—but at least he had some inside track. Whenever the packs started doing some new weird shit, Morrow would be the first to know.

And as a service man he didn't have to take on the Alphas if he didn't want to.

No more bonus money, no more Sheila, but he got to live a little while longer.

By the time he reached the cafeteria, Morrow decided that he could handle the losses.

McDermitt was sitting at a table talking to some guy just off night shift patrol.

"We have to go for more danger pay," McDermitt said. "Hayward and Jang are going to be in hospital for over a week."

"Accident?" the other man asked.

McDermitt shook his head. "Gurney says the dogs were waiting for them; and they got through the body armor before anyone could get a shot off."

"Wow, shit," the other man murmured.

McDermitt looked up and called over to Morrow: "Brother! Go home and get some sleep, you're going to need it!"

"What are you talking about?" Morrow's voice croaked with tiredness. I just pulled a Sunday shift, he thought. I'm taking the day off, you cretin.

McDermitt looked surprised. "You didn't get the message I left on your machine? You're supposed to report to Arsenal at 08:00 today."

"What for?" There was no way the grievance could have gone through so fast.

McDermitt smiled. "Officer Fixx has volunteered to replace you on the research assignment. You're taking his place on the front line Sweep."

Morrow sat there with a stupid grin on his face, wondering if this was a good time to start banging his head on the table top.

McDermitt smiled back at him. "Huge bonus money, massive opportunity. You're a rising star again, boy."

Oh yeah, I'm heading right up the goddamned evolutionary ladder, Morrow thought.

But he had a feeling that on his way up he'd find something with flaming red eyes and razor sharp teeth.

Just waiting for him.

I ONCE WAS BLIND BUT NOW I SEE...

As I mentioned in the previous introduction, mistakes are often very useful. Another, for example:

I was standing on the station platform waiting for the subway train. The prescription for my glasses was pretty old by then and when I looked across the tracks I thought the billboard carried an advertisement urging me to enroll in the, "International Church of Business".[5]

A religion dedicated to worshipping money and the profit motive? I mean we do this all the time but to *openly* celebrate planned greed and proclaim that God thinks all this exploitation is a wonderful idea? What kind of church would that be?[6] What kind of world would a church like that exist in? And so, when I got home I hammered this one out in a few days.

This is also another one of the, "Bad Jobs in the Future" stories and, as it turned out, the ICB was more context than anything else. My brief career as an employee at a fast-food chain quickly took over as the main narrative driver. I probably wasn't the worst employee at the A&W on Mayor Magrath Drive in Lethbridge, Alberta, but I didn't last long. I also have to admit that the working conditions weren't that bad, though I soon knew I had to get out of there. I was incredibly bored and with the staff discount on food I was starting to get pretty fat.

The Chubby Chicken was *amazing*...

---

5   It was in fact, a billboard from the "International **School** of Business" and that particular school might have been just as sinister as my "International Church of Business" but it was way too sensible a thing to inspire a story.

6   The answer, of course, is "Scientology" but let's not get into that right now.

THE Z-BURGER SIMULATIONS

Originally published in:
On Spec, #44, Spring 2001

Food Logistics Summary:

Family Joy Pack: Four Soya patties, four carbohydrate surfaces, standard seasonal lubricants (three types). Twenty-four tuber strips saturated with Red Sauce No. 800, four gas-injected beverages (random flavour and colouring). Add two plastic fantasy figures.

Average Preparation Time: 2.35 minutes
Average Delivery Time: 2.03 minutes

Record-Optimum Preparation Time: 1.64 minutes
Record-Optimum Delivery Time: 0.54 minutes

Personal Note:

YOU KNOW YOUR GOALS!

Janice Wong was just completing the Saturday afternoon shift at the Z-Burger franchise down on Lakeshore Boulevard in Etobicoke. It had been a busy shift: two birthday parties, a bus filled with tourists from Cleveland, and some kids just in from little league practice.

The door computer told the shift captain that customer usage was up 22.3% over last week and that all of us on her team had responded reasonably well to this challenge. None of us had come in below average times in delivery and preparation and we'd even approached some optimums. Janice had every reason to be proud.

So we all were surprised when she checked the readouts from the counters, closed the office door and drove a long-bladed screwdriver into her temple.

She was dead by the time the paramedics arrived.

We were all working on automatic pilot by the time the new shift captain showed and made us clean up. I'm ashamed to say that all I noticed was that the stains on the desk and walls reminded me of our Tex-Mex Special Sauce.

Food Logistics Summary:

Tex-Mex Special Sauce: Create by adding Orange Dye No. 712 to edible hexachlorophene cleaning agent. Eight-to-one ratio. Mix in vats of no less than 200 litres.

Z-Burger, as many of their communications say, "is all about people", so you can imagine that one or two things happened after one of their more promising young manager-candidates unexpectedly killed herself.

Especially for those of us on her shift team. Before we left the restaurant, we were told that we wouldn't be going back to our off-campus apartment—we had already been assigned to a special "transitional training" facility.

So the next morning I was sitting in an office in this facility, from where I could see the crumbling prison-like structures of the old Mississauga City Hall building. At least they hadn't moved me too far. The trauma counselling was about to begin.

Reverend Sweet from the International Church of Business was not much of a surprise. She was probably no more than five years older than me, close-cropped hair and a well-tailored jacket set around her clerical collar. I had the feeling that Reverend Sweet was planning on ascending the spiritual ladder without wasting a lot of time with corporate grunts like me.

She sat behind a desk, holding a file folder with my name on it. When she opened it, I could see yellow stickers attached throughout.

"It says here that you're a convert," the Reverend said softly. "When did you join Z-Burger?"

Maybe that was a red sticker on that one. People from Outside are never completely trustworthy—too many of us just want to get out of the cold.

I smiled and hoped all that practice at the counter paid off.

"I had just turned sixteen," I replied. "I went into my remedials right after I left my birth family."

Reverend Sweet stopped at a page somewhere in the middle of my file. She was looking very closely at something, like a seasoned practitioner of human archaeology.

"We don't seem to have very much on your mother..." she said eventually. "...but your father..."

"Was a devout Skinnerian." I decided that I might as well try to sound helpful and forthright: "I can still remember the big plastic cube he put over the playpen."

Reverend Sweet sighed and put her hands down on the paper, as if she was trying to compress my past down into a more manageable pile of events.

"Fine people, the Skinnerians," she said. "We have many common beliefs."

"Maybe that's why things worked out so well for me here," I said.

"Why did you have to leave your birth family?" Reverend Sweet asked.

This could be tricky, I realized. I had to offer the right mixture of regret, resolve and gratitude. "It's very simple," I said. "I was laid off. My father's college salary was rolled back after restructuring."

"And some of the children had to go?"

"Just me." And it still hurts a little after all these years.

"Why you?" There wasn't a even trace of sympathy in her voice. "Birth order seniority? Domestic productivity? Educational achievement?"

I shrugged. "It was a combination of things, really. I wasn't a very attractive child back then and I had scored low in both emotional and digital intelligence."

Reverend Sweet looked down and flipped ahead to something else in my file: "But it says that your scores increased considerably once you started your remedials."

"Yes." Then after a pause that was really too long, I added: "And I'm very grateful for that."

She closed my file and folded her hands. "We don't need to cover everything today, Andrew." Then she took a little grey book out from her desk drawer. "You and everyone else on the shift have been subjected to a tremendous shock. You need to rest..." She handed me the book:

The Essential Works of Max Weber.

"...study... pray... and re-train."

Re-train! That was not what I wanted to hear.

"How long before I'm assigned to a new shift?" I asked, sure that my sudden concern was coming through.

Reverend Sweet stood up and gave me a professional smile. "We don't know. This kind of thing doesn't happen very often."

Food Logistics Summary:

Basic Z-Burger Components: Assorted chemical compounds. Carbohydrates. Synthetic protein molecules.

The sim chamber looked just like a standard suburban class Z-Burger food service outlet: 250 seats, 100 tables, eight service kiosks, two condiment dispensers, two washrooms.

The seats had a little more reinforcement than usual, and in between exercises this weird blue lighting would kick in as the sensor computers made their assessments. When I was first trained in here my classmates would joke about working at the "Atlantis franchise".

Sim runs. What the hell did they have me doing simulation training for? Sure, I was shaken up, but I still knew how to flip a patty and programme a fry computer.

Food Logistics Summary:

Special Meal Combo No. 83, a.k.a. "The Heavy, Hard, He-Man Hitter." Three nine millimetre Soya patties, 700 metric measures of processed complex carbohydrates. 18 sauce combinations (equal portions), taste combinations to balance flavours No. 9 (garlic), No. 11 (chocolate) and No. 63 (assorted green vegetable matter).

Average Preparation Time: 2.15 minutes
Average Delivery Time: 1.20 minutes

Record-Optimum Preparation Time: 1.33 minutes

Record-Optimum Delivery Time: 50 seconds

At least they didn't have me doing sissy runs, one customer asking for a coffee refill every 20 minutes. They were really cranking up the volume on these exercises, so I could show them what I was capable of.

In a weird way I wanted to make Janice proud.

And they'd improved these androids since I was a trainee. There was more texture to the plastic skins, the movements were a lot more natural, and there was more variety in the hair. Frankly, the androids looked better than our customers.

The programmers also had a more accurate understanding of fashion and social class. Most of the androids on my current run were wearing cheap suits with white shirts and clip-on ties—like lazy Baptists in search of a quickie after-Church lunch.

It was a high density, high-demand crowd. In real-life, all that early-morning Bible-thumping would have made the customers really hungry. Of course, people at Church actually don't always love each other equally, so they come in different group sizes with frequent and irregular timing... some people were travelling together and others weren't.

There was also a big age range, some really doddering seniors (with bad hair and skin) and many toddlers (with their voices and speed controls set at maximum).

The only unrealistic thing was the fact that Sunday lunch was going on for over six hours. Wave after wave of happy androids kept bobbing up to my sales console.

I was able to take orders and handle deliveries without slipping below average but if we were providing actual food I doubted that any real kitchen could have coped. But I guess the programmers had to stretch one or two variables to make some kind of educational point.

Service Training Vocal Exercise #3:

<u>May</u> I take your order?
May <u>I</u> take your order?
May I <u>take</u> your order?
May I take <u>your</u> order?
May I take your <u>order</u>?

All the runs that week were pretty aggressive, and early Saturday morning they called me in for another interview with Reverend Sweet.

"I hope it's not a problem, meeting before breakfast." The Reverend was sipping a steaming fluid from a foam cup. "This the only time I have available."

I had a choice? She must have been trying to be funny.

"How is your re-training going?" she asked.

"Good, according to my personal timer," I replied, grateful that I didn't yawn in the Reverend's face. It's not always easy to look motivated at 05:00.

"They've emailed me the official scores already," she said. "I'm more interested in you feel about it."

"I see." How I feel? Why the hell would she care about that?

"I'm after some qualitative information," Reverend Sweet added.

The next forty-two minutes were kind of difficult; I had to use all the standard motivational phrases to describe the past week... and I had to sound like I meant it.

I'm not sure she bought it.

Market/Service Credos:

- *Perception of quality is inversely proportional to speed of delivery.*
- *Management practice and food content standards are equally plastic.*
- *You must be your customer to control your customer.*
- *Technology must anticipate psychographics—have the best machines first!*

I'd never seen androids like these. Five years ago, kids were just represented as dolls in strollers or short store mannequins on roller skates. The logic was that since under twelves didn't usually place the order or dispense the cash, we didn't need to focus the training on them.

Things change, I guess. Kids are a huge market share and just because your hand isn't the one hanging onto the debit card doesn't mean you aren't the one making the buy. So there I was surrounded by 22 synthetic five-year-olds.

Very realistically rendered. As Janice's management textbooks used to say: "Technology must anticipate psychographics."

That afternoon this translated into: You must work in the electronic birthday party from hell!

A very nasty run. Their little transparent plastic eyes were flashing around, taking in every detail of the playroom. And their speed controls must have been supercharged for the session because they kept jumping out of their seats and throwing themselves into the ball pit. I wasn't sure how much longer the containment netting was going to hold up.

The ones that did stay at their tables were pulling the appendages off their action figures and smearing Soya paste all over the Wacky Crab Character wall mural.

Not only was I supposed to keep the solid and liquid substances flowing onto their plates, I had to keep these vibrating creatures from escaping and bothering the adult androids in the adjacent modules.

It was non-standard staffing conditions as well, ordinarily you had a team of three for a birthday party. This was a solo rite of passage for me.

It wasn't going particularly well, either. The mood range on the units were also set to tired and cranky and 20 minutes into the party it was pretty apparent that they really hated their Wacky Crab loot bags. More appendages were flying around the room and they started shredding the containers. I couldn't blame them, really—the action figures were small nasty knock-offs of a much cooler toy that was selling at all We-Have-All-Your-Toys outlets. Some bastard in Programming had really been doing his research.

By the time I came in with the cake, my wrist scanner was telling me that I was way below the optimums and I was going to hustle to hold on to the averages. And now the little robot monsters were using what was left of their action figures as spoons to scoop up the remains of their milkshakes.

I wondered if I could find some way to re-set my mood range, something that could be described with the words "hyper-speed". Then I decided to scratch that thought, Z-Burger strongly disapproves of direct intervention at the blood-brain barrier even in the cause of Corporate efficiency.

I lit five candles and led the little androids in a chorus of "Happy

Birthday". The programmers had been a little weak on the vocal settings. Ouch, my ears.

In fact, they were singing so loud, that it was almost 20 seconds before I heard the ragged gasping and gurgling sounds at one of the tables. One of the androids had sucked one of the legs off his action figures and it was lodged in its artificial windpipe. More excellent simulation programming: its fake eyes were wide open and the pseudo-skin was going from bright red to purple.

I ran over to the unit in trouble, not even noticing that one of the other units had pushed the birthday cake onto the floor. I knew that an android can't choke to death but it was still a damn scary run.

And a deep paranoid part of me wondered what would happen if this wasn't a planned part of an exercise. What if a $40 million dollar piece of equipment was having a major malfunction on my run? Last thing I needed.

I lifted the now-twitching unit onto the table-top and jammed my fingers down its throat. Android kids are a lot heavier and stronger than real ones so it wasn't easy to hold it down while I kept fishing around. My fingertips connected with something small and then a stream of already-been-chewed Z-Burger products shot themselves into my face and hair. Simulated vomit is about as repulsive as the real stuff, although it is perhaps a little less acidic.

If this was a real kid, I might at least have got a thank you from a parent or caregiver. In here, all I received was a warning message from my wrist scanner telling me that I had dropped below average service time. First time since I was a newbie.

I had a feeling I wouldn't be leaving just yet.

Service Training Vocal Exercise #7:

"Thank you, have a nice day!"
"Thank you, have a nice day!"
"Thank you, have a nice day!"
"Thank you, have a nice day!"

Two more weeks. Many more runs. Some good, some not-so-good.

I'd shot my service record to hell. Janice would probably be embarrassed to know me now.

"They're shipping me out." Anne was the only one left from my old shift.

She was leaning against the door frame of my room wearing a new uniform and an apologetic look on her face. It was a well-made uniform with lots of extra trim, she was going to a good location.

I looked up from the print-outs spread over my study-cubicle, diagrams of different restaurant configurations.

"When?" I asked.

"Tonight." Anne half-smiled, half-frowned at me. "Looks like you're on your own, kid."

Anne was great. Cute, funny, dependable. Z-Burger officially discouraged relationships on the same shift but we all got so close that (of course) they happened all the time. If I hadn't been otherwise engaged, I think I could have gone for Anne in a big way.

"So you're abandoning me to the Planet of the Newbies," I replied, trying to sound clever.

"Try not to pass out from the smell of dirty diapers."

"Guess I won't have anyone to swap war stories with." I think I sounded more desperate than witty, but the truth has a bad habit of creeping out in times of emotional stress.

I realized that this really was going to be shitsville now, there was no way would any trainees understand what I was going through.

"Well, I gotta go," Anne said finally. "You should try to work with Reverend Sweet."

When I turned around to look at Anne, she was gone.

What the hell did that mean?

When I looked down at my print-outs, I noticed that my diagrams had gone all blurry.

Food Logistics Summary:

Late-Bird Special: standard patty, reduced diameter by 0.5 centimetres. Nine additional measures of syntha-herbal stimulants. Deep fry carbo-strips until crispy. Inject strips with 2.5 units artificial chocolate.

Optimum Preparation Time:
ASAP, to maximum degree. Do not divert any attention to monitor your performance, just deliver the food. This approach has proven to be the most effective means of minimizing damages to

Corporation property and personnel.

Even though it was 07:20 (i.e. morning) they had turned the lights down low in the chamber and were using some kind of new projectors to make it look like there were some burning buildings in the distance.

Extreme late shift, in a very bad area code. Great... fan-fucking-tastic...

Three more-or-less human figures appeared at the doorway, pushed open the opaque mesh panels and walked inside.

We serve everyone... (Z-Burger Credo Number One)... regardless of social class and danger to employees.

The androids arrived at my counter. Their faces and arms were marked with multi-coloured smears and deep angular scars. Their hair could only be described as sturdy demonstrations of chaos theory.

Classic nocturnals, the androids and the reals got the cosmetic effect in the same way—by injecting intelligent plastics and moulding their bodies with nasty metal implements. These were well researched androids... weird and dangerous... but really well-researched.

"Hi!" I said, trying to sound friendly and harmless. "Welcome to Z—"

The fucking things didn't even bother to place an order. Two of them leapt over the counter, grabbed me by my tunic and threw me onto the linoleum.

Ouch.

The third one picked up a chair and used it to smash the condiments dispensers. Red, green and yellow fluids were flying everywhere. Then he started breaking windows while the other two kicked me in the face and ribs.

More ouch.

By now, I was definitely screaming and coughing up blood as their titanium-toed boots pummelled into me. But a part of my brain was very calm, assessing the situation in terms of optimums, averages, performance and simulator credibility. That part of my brain was thinking that this was a really good simulation. Every detail was right.

Food Logistics Summary:

Rise-Up Special: Vitamin C, Caffeine (maximum dose), herbal mock-barbiturates...

I was still in the sim chamber when I woke up. The nocturnals were gone and no one had cleaned the place up.

The place still looked like a 3D Jackson Pollock.

I was covered in dried fluids: relish, ketchup, mustard, Soya sauce, my own blood. I hoped that was all I was covered in.

I swallowed a few fragments of my teeth and slowly sat up. The pain was almost transcendental. I thought about throwing up but decided that was a bad idea.

My vision eased back into focus and I saw that there was one table left standing.

Reverend Sweet was sitting at it, sipping a cup of something. That meant the restaurant was still operational.

Pretty impressive logistics, I thought.

"Learning much?" she asked.

"Like what?" I croaked.

"Have a seat."

She watched me closely as I climbed to my feet and staggered over to the table.

God, it hurt to sit down.

"Don't you want to leave this place?" She smiled at me but there was probably more warmth on the surface of Pluto.

"Ah..." Talking was hard because my mouth was still filled with blood and phlegm. "Yeah, I think I'm ready for a new assignment."

The ringing in my ears made Reverend Sweet's voice sound strange—metallic and hollow—like a really old and cheesy android.

"Let's be pretty candid," she said. "I'm not going to get my commission unless my report on Janice gives a plausible explanation of her death."

It even hurt to nod my head.

"Gee, that's really tough."

The Reverend's robot voice continued: "Z-Burger's people are the happiest, best-motivated employees in the world." She leaned forward and looked at me with a protein-carbohydrate gaze:

"So, they don't kill themselves unless someone has been fucking around with their heads."

I didn't say anything. I just reached into my mouth and removed another tooth fragment.

"You and Janice had been having sexual intercourse for at least six months, weren't you?"

Sexual intercourse. Not "sleeping together", not "being intimate" and not "you two were lovers". And to her, "fucking" was reserved for a completely different realm of experience. The Reverend definitely had an interesting turn of phrase.

Eventually she gave up waiting for me to respond.

"Usually the Company doesn't ask the Church to intervene," she said. "It's sad, but for some managers, the occasional physical release seems to make them more effective."

I nodded a little.

"You're welcome," I said softly.

The Reverend responded with a wry smile. "You are obviously a mistake and someone in Personnel will probably have to pay for that. Unfortunately, we can't just terminate you."

"Because of all the training you've invested." I'm sure my broken, blood-stained smile was pretty gross.

"I wonder what other Outside ideas you poisoned that poor woman with?" Reverend Sweet stared into the cooling pool in her Styrofoam cup. "Drugs? Sexual perversion? Collective bargaining?"

I responded to her statement with a wet sigh.

"She would have done anything to be a better manager," I said. "I think she chose me because I came from Outside."

Reverend Sweet crooked an eyebrow. "Because you wouldn't judge her so severely?"

"Didn't matter." For the first time since Janice died, I felt like crying about it. "She didn't stop judging herself."

Forgive me Janice, I thought. I was tired, broken in spots and in a lot of pain. I still don't think they deserved to know that much.

Shift Log Entry:

As per my checklist, I reviewed the final maintenance report:

The condiments dispensers have jammed again, third time this week on my shift! I just can't seem to get the technicians to fix them properly.

Who knows how many innocent customers have been deprived of

*their basic rights to their free-choice of optional seasonings? I am
ultimately responsible for this continued failure. It is a certain sign
of Damnation.*

I am a worthless slut. God hates me.

Janice killed herself before she downloaded her log entry into the
Company mainframe. A surprising oversight for her. I don't
remember it, but I must have taken her wrist computer when we
were cleaning up.

I was probably just being a coward, trying to cover up evidence of
our relationship. But after a while keeping her thoughts, dreams
and nightmares away from the Cyclops-vision of Z-Burger... and
Reverend Sweet... got to be pretty important.

Even though Janice was only able to express herself in their
terms.

I never did, officially, admit anything, so eventually the Reverend
had to give up her hopes of filing a complete report and receiving
her commission.

Finally, they reassigned me, way out in the fringes, where I
couldn't do any harm.

My current shift captain is about 99 years older than God—so
old that you can't tell the scars from the wrinkles. Definitely crazy—
in many loud and annoying ways. I'm much more likely to put a
screwdriver into my head before he does.

He's really religious too, and he leads us in an opening prayer
when we start the graveyard shift:

"Lord, help us bring sustenance and wondrous things to the
worthless scum who live here without too many of your good
servants getting killed."

Amen.

Since he's crazy, the people at Inventory Control don't ask about
all the trays that go missing here. The Captain lets us wear the trays
under our tunics; not the best body armour but at least it's some
kind of protection.

I guess this is some kind of punishment, but actually when I'm
not scared out of my mind, I feel kind of free. Before this, when I
was on Janice's shift I really was a pretty straight arrow—pretty
much innocent of all the shit that the Reverend accused me of.

And nobody's going to convince me that there was anything

wrong with getting close to Janice.

Maybe it's the neighbourhood that makes me feel free. It's certainly free of architecture—our restaurant is the only building that's still standing with all four of its walls intact.

Captain is very proud of that.

Drugs, rock and roll, revolution.

There's lots of that out here in the fringes and I'm picking it fast. Maybe someday there will be an opportunity to show the Reverend and the rest of the Company what I've learned.

Then we can all have a really nice day.

CREATIVE AUTOBIOGRAPHY

My parents' divorce defined me in a lot of ways. From what I could gather from family history, there were two fundamental problems that destroyed their marriage:

1. At heart my dad was a biker. He loved to boot around on his souped-up BSA motorcycle—from our house past the farmlands over to his lab at the University of Saskatchewan. My mom knew that this was not feasible when you have five, and then six children. The kids tend to fall off or freeze to death when you ferry them around like that in minus 50 degree temperatures. Intellectually I think my dad knew we had to get a car (we soon had a series of very sensible, very big and ugly station wagons) but I think a bit of his spirit died when he got rid of his bike.
2. There can be a basic conflict between how religion and science account for the nature of the universe and pretty much the meaning of everything in it. When my parents were first married, my dad was the studious and devout one. Years later, when I got to read some of mom's wartime letters, I discovered that she was something of a brainy party-girl. She sounded like a lot of fun!

All of this changed in the 1950s when dad's personal, but apparently somewhat public efforts to reconcile his faith and his work as a microbiologist offended someone and they complained to the church authorities. Dad was "disfellowshipped." I've never looked very carefully into what that actually involved but it doesn't sound very nice.

Dad got mad and gave up on God-stuff and Mom got super-religious in an effort to go to church for the both of them. It may have been the beginning of the end of their marriage.

I don't want you to think of us as a family of victims. In many ways, we emerged better and more understanding people because of my parents' break-up. I certainly got to be much closer to both of

them as a result.
   Still.
   What happened to those two young people? It just wasn't right.

MORMONISM AND THE SASKATOON SPACE PROGRAMME

Originally published in:
*Land/Space: An Anthology of
Prairie Speculative Fiction*, 2002.
Edited by Candas Jane Dorsey
and Judy McCrosky

*"Those Mormons… either coming back from a church meeting
or heading out to another one!"*

The dominant memory of my uncles was of a bunch of bald-headed guys sleeping in my grandparents' living room just after lunch between the times scheduled for Priesthood meeting, Sunday school and Sacrament. They were all on the same rather busy schedule of worship, and having dealt with some of the day's physical and spiritual needs they would grind out some snores.

Impressive snores they were. It was like they were impersonating every diesel tractor that rolled its way over a southern Alberta sugar beet farm.

My dad assured me that I only had four uncles and six great-uncles but when I heard that choir of nasal blasts I was sure I had at least two thousand of them.

All of them were wearing brown or gray suits ordered from the Magrath Trade Goods store. The suits were actually able to bend at the knees and elbows, which I found particularly amazing because the fabric was some kind of combination of raw wool, sandpaper and rusting plate steel.

They completed the fashion statement by wearing work boots with their suits. Out of respect for the deity they actually washed and polished them but this was the same footwear that trampled its way through cow shit for the other six days of the week.

Some of my uncles were bachelors, some were married. I would occasionally bump into my cousins who claimed some connection to one of them but I could never get most of my uncles to stay awake long enough to explain who belonged to who.

After a while, my grandma would wade into the sea of snores and announce:

"Time to go to church."

This stimulated some kind of classically conditioned response and my uncles would twitch, blink, brush back their non-existent hair and stagger up out of their chairs.

"Come on, kid," my Uncle Weston (who always woke up the fastest) would whisper to me. "It's Testimony this week."

Great, I would inwardly sigh.

Testimony Meeting. Everybody would remind each other that Joseph Smith was indeed a prophet of God, the Book of Mormon was the revealed truth, and that socialized medicine was the vanguard of communism. Sometimes at closing, the presiding Bishop would remind us that Evil is Bad.

God, those summers in southern Alberta. So long, so boring, so painful.

"Q: Why does Saskatchewan have rats and Alberta have Mormons?
A: Saskatchewan got first choice."

Usually, Uncle Weston drove me back home to Saskatoon. Unlike my other uncles, he didn't work on a farm and seemed to have more free time. He was some kind of a free-lance pilot and actually served with my dad in the RCAF during World War II. Consequently, Uncle Weston and my dad were the only good drivers in the family.

Not that you would notice in the ancient Dodge station wagon he used to drive.

I'm not sure if that model was even equipped with suspension and the engine's combustion wasn't all that internal. We kind of wheezed and exploded our way along the TransCanada Highway.

I was trying to read some Heinlein novel, I think it was *Revolt in 2100*, but all the bouncing was making it pretty hard work. I had to pause every minute or two to re-focus my vision.

"Good book?" Uncle Weston asked as he peered out the gravel-pitted windshield.

"It's okay," I mumbled. This as about as enthusiastic a thirteen year old Western Canadian kid gets if he isn't into hockey or football. In truth, I was loving the book. I really wanted to like Heinlein's relaxed ultra-competent heroes and those "racy" bits were pretty damn exciting.

Hey, I was thirteen.

"Don't know the author," Uncle Weston said. "I was more of a *Mechanics Illustrated* reader when I was your age."

"Uh, huh."

This would explain the huge pile of yellow pulp magazines in the labourers' cottage on my grandparents' farm. I'd read them all two summers back. The fact that just about every piece of technology described was either obsolete or impractical (when was the last time you took a ride on your personal autogyro?) didn't bother me all that much. I was just delighted to find something to read that wasn't related to religion or animal husbandry.

"But I sometimes think I ought to read some science fiction once in a while."

"Uh, huh."

This was the bulk of our conversation for about six hours.

We weren't making very good time so the sun was setting as we passed through the "city" of Swift Current.

"Pit stop," Uncle Weston announced. He pulled into a Husky station and we sat in the Dodge while we gassed up.

"You aren't enjoying your time at the farm are you?" Uncle Weston asked.

"Well..." I was feeling too tired to be anything but honest. "All I seem to do is dig weeds and go to church."

"You don't like farm work?"

Actually I didn't mind it that much. There was a direct quality to digging around in the earth that was strangely satisfying. Maybe it just made me too tired to think.

"That's okay," I said.

"So it's church you're not too keen on."

"It just seems to go on forever," I said. "And some of what they say is a little hard to believe."

Uncle Weston sighed. "Well," he said softly. "Your father would probably agree with you there."

"Do you believe everything they say?" This was a pretty dangerous question for me—if Uncle Weston took it the wrong way he might feel obligated to spend the next two hours in the Husky parking lot bearing his testimony.

I was lucky. He just nodded his head:

"I fulfill my obligations and attend church and priesthood meetings when appropriate."

Even then, that struck me as a rather interesting answer.

"We've driven far enough today," he said.

So we agreed to camp at a nearby provincial park and come home a day late. My dad probably wouldn't even notice and I think Uncle Weston felt a little guilty with the realization that the fun quota of my summer vacation had been rather low.

Now, I'm sure there must be some tremendously rare and scientifically significant species of weed near our campground because it certainly wasn't designated as a Provincial Park on the basis of its natural beauty. It looked like an abandoned landing strip with a couple of picnic tables, some rusting climbing structures and a wooden shed with male and female stick people on the doors.

Uncle Weston rolled the station wagon to a stop next to a small gravel bed with steel label at one end:

Lot 52.

"This is a great place," he said as he yanked on the parking brake and opened the door.

"Really?" If any kid spoke to me with as much sarcasm as I did back then, I think I'd punch him in the head.

I doubt that Uncle Weston even noticed.

"Sure thing," he answered. "Your father and I would stay here when we were hitch-hiking to P.E.I."

He was referring to the time when he and my dad were training as pilots at the RCAF base in Summerside. The war ended before my dad saw any combat duty but apparently Uncle Weston flew some missions. I use the word "apparently" because I had to pick this information up second hand—neither of them would talk about what happened to them at that time.

We made a small fire in the flaking iron box next to one of the picnic tables and warmed up some canned beans and Spam which we ate by tilting our bowls and making small poking motions with our jack knives.

"Very tasty," Uncle Weston smacked.

I wasn't sure what surprised me more—the fact that Uncle Weston liked this food or that he hadn't bothered to bless it before we ate.

Blessing the food was a huge deal at my grandparents' house. We actually had to kneel next to our chairs while my grandfather gave the benediction—and this would go on for what seemed like six hours while the spirit moved him to comment on our performance on the farm.

I wasn't exactly complaining that Uncle Weston had missed this ritual step in the day. Ordinarily missing out on the blessing would have been quite welcome.

But with beans and Spam I wondered if we might want to seek divine protection from food poisoning.

"Do you know what we need right now?" Uncle Weston was studying the rapidly separating fluids in his plastic bowl.

"Ummm?" Immediate medical attention? A sudden and unstoppable desire to keep on driving? These and other suggestions occurred to me as my uncle walked over to the Dodge and opened the trunk.

"Your grandfather used these as rations during World War I." Uncle Weston removed a khaki-coloured tin can, about the size of my head, from the trunk. "I wonder if it's still edible."

He cranked on the can opener to reveal what was inside.

It was a shock.

Bread.

Tinned bread that was over half-a-century old. The ends of the loaf were marked with the rings of the tin can.

Uncle Weston, using some effort, tore off a piece of bread to soak up the bean and Spam juice in his bowl.

"It's pretty good," he said speaking through the ancient but freshly chewed mass in his mouth.

I was fascinated by the concept of bread in a can, so I tried some. At best, I can describe its taste as… yeasty.

But it didn't kill us.

When it was time to go to sleep I lay down on an air mattress set under a pup tent that was also a bit of grandfather's military surplus kit.

While we were setting all this up, Uncle Weston's conscience must have been bothering him because he started going on about how important it was for my grandparents to see me in the summer and how it gave my dad a chance to deal with some of the more difficult parts of his research... and jeez whiz, weren't we having all kinds of fun right now?

But at least he wasn't telling me how important it was for me to keep going to church and how I ought to be preparing for my mission calling. That was my grandmother's version of good night, sleep tight.

But maybe he did start talking about church, but I'd fallen sleep by then.

"...This is a signal..."

I heard something. Something very soft and far away.

"Uncle Weston?" I was awake now.

"...this is a signal..."

The sound had a weird metallic quality, sort of like robot ghosts whispering at you.

"...a signal on continuous broadcast..."

I looked out of the end of my pup tent and saw Uncle Weston sitting in the dark at the picnic table.

"...from the Galactic Core... I'm sending this through a wormhole in the hope that you will receive in real-time..."

Uncle Weston's face was glowing green from the lights of some kind of big transistor radio. Its workings were exposed at the back and I could see a cluster of oddly shaped vacuum tubes.

"...I am transmitting from a solar system of 57 planets..."

Every once in a while Uncle Weston would adjust a dial on the radio.

"...all uninhabited, but 11 were abandoned by some form of sentient life..."

I decided that the voice on radio was definitely human, but it wasn't very happy about what it was reporting.

"...desolation... nothing but desolation..."

Eventually the voice became unintelligible; the few remaining words were eventually submerged in wave after wave of static.

After a while my uncle turned off the radio.

"Uncle Weston?" I called out into the darkness.

I wasn't able to see the expression on his face.

"You heard that?" he asked.

"Some."

I heard the sound of him picking up the radio and walking over to the trunk of the car.

"Time to get back to bed."

In the morning, as we made the last stretch of highway between Bigger and Saskatoon, Uncle Weston told me that he was listening to an old radio play.

"I thought I'd try some of your science fiction."

"Sure."

"Do you like my home-made receiver?" he laughed, a little feebly I thought. "A project from my *Mechanics Illustrated* days."

Right. You see green-glowing radios that pick up signals from space in every prairie household.

"Looks nice." Was what I said.

"I think I was picking up a station down around Great Falls… in Montana."

Montana. With 57 planets.

Of course.

"This is CFQC, broadcasting from the potash capital of the world!"

Growing up in Saskatoon probably prepared me for life in outer space.

It was an alienating experience at times.

In southern Alberta, those towns with strange names like Magrath, Taber and Cardston where my grandparents dug irrigation ditches and built temples, the Mormons had their own communities. These towns were all trapped in orbit around Calgary, Fort McLeod and Lethbridge but they were places where we pretty much called the shots. Or at least people who were "like us" called the shots.

But Mormons were a minority, "one of those peculiar religions," in Saskatchewan.

There weren't too many connections between Salt Lake City and the Ukraine and the President and Prophet of the LDS Church hardly ever praised the policies of the CCF.

My family, my parents and myself, moved to Saskatoon when my dad assumed his position at the Prairie Regional Laboratory at the University. He was doing research on two substances that

Saskatchewan had in abundance: potash and uranium.

Most people on this planet are at least aware of uranium. They know that uranium has something to do with nuclear weapons and radioactivity.

Potash is only world-famous in Saskatoon. For those of you who don't know, potash is a quartz-based mineral which was mined in large quantities and used in fertilizer additives.

By the time I was thirteen, I'd figured out that what my father did for a living had something to do with fusing the uranium and potash but was as far as it went. I knew he'd signed some kind of secrecy agreement with the Federal Government.

Not that my dad ever tried to conceal the wonders of science from me. He worked every weekend and on the Saturdays when he wasn't at the reactor site he would let me play in the PRL building. This started when I was about seven and a lot cuter; lots of the technicians and graduate students were really nice to me. They would help me look through microscopes, let me turn the switch on the oscilloscopes, and move around some of the luminescent minerals under an ultra-violet light.

One technician even had this tabletop dynamo that fired off bolts of lightning like those old Frankenstein movies. I had no idea what it was doing in the lab but I certainly thought it was cool.

It was great, like growing up in your own personal science centre.

Sundays, alternatively, were dedicated to religion.

The related activities were not something that my dad would participate in.

"Because I gave your mother my word…" he would invariably say as I would squirm into my Sunday clothes.

I was decked out in a suit that was three sizes too big, a cardboard white shirt and a clip-on tie. Dad was wearing his regular lab clothes: Hush Puppies, pants with patches on the knees, and a checked short-sleeved shirt with a slide rule and about 50 pens in the front pocket. He was wearing that because he was going to the lab, I was going to church. Hell, I looked like the grown-up and he looked like the kid.

One the occasional Sunday when Uncle Weston was in town he would take me but usually Dad would drive me to the entrance of the then-modest Central Saskatchewan branch of the LDS Church and head off to PRL to do some more work. Dad would never set foot in the Church.

About four or sixteen hours later, Dad would be waiting for me in the car. Listening to the *Rod and Charles Show* or *Gillmore's Albums* on CBC Regina. That was about as much fun as Dad would allow himself to have.

Aside from the fact that I had to navigate my own way through the complex series of meetings and rooms on my own, the absolute worst thing about the drop-off arrangement was that we never got there on time. About 75% of the time I arrived after Junior Sunday School services started and it seemed that about 90% of those times, the other kids were singing this one hymn:

"Never be late for your Sunday School Class! Always be prompt, bright and cheeeerfulllll..."

While they were singing I would slink to some seat at the back of the room. Unfortunately the metal folding chairs seemed to be designed to generate maximum noise as the weight of your body moved on the linoleum floor. When the other kids heard this they sang the chorus even louder:

"Never be late! *Never be late*!"

God, if you really are out there, I want you to know that I really hate that hymn.

I was grateful for the times when Uncle Weston took me there. We were always on time, even though he would ditch me pretty quickly for Priesthood Meeting and Senior Sunday School. I didn't want to risk future escorts so I didn't push him about what they were talking about in there.

Uncle Weston became a somewhat more prominent figure in my life when I turned twelve and was made a member of the Aaronic Priesthood as most Mormon boys do. Dad didn't actually oppose this because he seemed he had to honour the phrase "Your Mother would have wanted..."

At twelve I was only a Deacon and the duties were restricted to passing the bread and water out during Sacrament Meeting and attending some more meetings. Not too challenging but more time taken up with Church meetings.

Meetings bloody meetings.

Somebody had to take me to the extra meetings and my weekday caregiver Mrs. Shevchenko was a devote Ukrainian Catholic, so she was the wrong persuasion and gender. Uncle Weston moved from wherever he was living and into our basement. He was a pretty good patriarchal surrogate for the two years I was a deacon—he was always polite to the brothers and sisters at meetings and he never said anything that was too controversial or strange.

This arrangement fell apart when I turned fourteen and was expected to move up to be a Teacher—the next level in the Aaronic Priesthood.

My induction began with the customary interview with the local Bishop.

It started out well enough.

He asked me if I understood everything I was hearing at Priesthood and Sunday School and I replied truthfully that I didn't understand quite everything but I was trying.

That seemed to satisfy the Bishop and he let me off the hook by telling me that no expected me to have a fully developed Testimony at my age but that I had to be resolved to keep on learning and to have an open mind.

Open mind. About as likely as that signal on Uncle Weston's radio coming from Montana.

"And you have to be honest with yourself and others," the Bishop said.

I said that I would try my best to do that.

Big mistake.

The interview deteriorated when the subject of sex came up.

"Now I have to talk to you about what it means if you ever have sexual intercourse..." the Bishop said looking incredibly uncomfortable. "...before you are married and with the girls..."

I kind of understood that it was bad to have sex before marriage but I didn't appreciate why the Bishop was making a qualification about having sex with girls. Who else would you have sex with? Now I know that it was just one more trap.

But it didn't seem to be a problem for me. At fourteen the idea of having sex with another person was about as likely as living on another planet.

Now, sex by myself...

And that's when it all got pretty sticky. The Bishop raised the topic of masturbation and remembering that I had promised to be honest I admitted that I had indeed tried it. My natural modesty kept me from explaining masturbation was the closest thing to pure joy that I'd experienced.

But I don't think the Bishop thought there was anything pure about it at all.

"Don't you know?!" His eyes were tearing up. "To throw away all that life, it's next to murder!"

I wanted to die.

I wish I had because then the Bishop exhorted me to "Put on the full armour of God" and "Struggle to return to a state of spiritual cleanliness." He concluded the interview by advising me that he and the rest of the local Church Executive would have to fast and pray about what to do about my "perilous situation."

It was about as bad a meeting that a fourteen-year-old boy could have.

I didn't say a word about it but the outcome must have gotten back home because Uncle Weston was severely pissed. My Dad just seemed a little sadder and even more distant than usual.

Two Sundays later I was sitting in the Bishop's outer office while he and Uncle Weston were having a discussion.

The idea of these two old guys talking about the religious significance of me touching my penis was absolutely horrifying. Again, I wanted to die.

I kind of hoped there would be a big Technicolor explosion and the Earth would swallow me up, just like when Charlton Heston threw those clay tablets at the unfaithful Israelites in *The Ten Commandments.*

No such luck. Although, Uncle Weston's voice thundered out through the walls near the end of meeting:

"The only thing a young man learns from that is how to lie!"

About 20 seconds later, Uncle Weston opened the door. He was red from his collar to the top of his bald head.

"Time to go," he said.

And that was the last time I set foot in that Church.

Back in his Dodge, we were not taking the usual route home.

"Where are we going?" My voice was only slowly returning.

Uncle Weston's face was still red with anger. "I've got some work to do. You might as well come."

Eventually we came to a stop at a small hangar near Pike Lake. The building and runway were deserted.

Uncle Weston rolled up the hangar door and inside was something that looked a little like the CF-100 fighter that was suspended over the Sutherland Legion Hall. Except that it had no markings, was painted absolute black, and had rows of over-sized nozzles bolted to the undersides of the wings.

Much later, Uncle Weston would explain to me that those were the "Potash-Uranium Fusion Propulsion Units". They called them "puffs" for short.

They were the result of my Dad's research.

"Married for time and all eternity."

I didn't remember anything all that detailed about my mother. But I do remember a very sad woman who seemed to hang around the house a lot.

Dad never talked about how they broke up.

Eventually, on those long journeys between the solar systems, Uncle Weston told me a few things.

I had kind of thought she had gone to Salt Lake City and re-married but that wasn't exactly what had happened.

As we spiraled into yet another multiple-planet system, Uncle Weston confirmed that my parents broke up because of some disagreement between the universe as explained by science and religion. I had always thought that it was something really stupid, like Dad accidentally mentioning in Sunday school that Darwin was probably right and that human beings really were descended from "lower species."

"No, it wasn't that," Uncle Weston said. "Your Dad doesn't give a hoot about biology."

A hoot? Jeepers, Uncle Weston, I thought. Your language is getting pretty strong.

"What was the problem?" I asked.

"We've got planet fall."

Landing on a new world. Great way to change the subject.

"Come, come, ye saints! No toil or labour fear!"

My first voyages into space were all with Uncle Weston. Dad didn't like going out any more.

I was more of a passenger than a co-pilot and I didn't have any scientific training so I wasn't much help with the research. But there wasn't much accountability back then so my uncle was free to bring me along just to keep him company. It was like another one of our camp-outs.

Once he landed us on a planet with a wide river of glass and set up our tents in the shadow of a mountain of jade.

Another time we walked among the shattered rectangles of an eons-dead civilization of machine intelligences. Nothing left but little plates of silicon.

"Someday we'll visit an inhabited system," Uncle Weston said. "But you need quite a bit of preparation for that."

Okay, Uncle Weston. This is definitely your turf, so whatever you say.

The night under the jade mountain was one of my first trips so I had lots of questions. Like:

Since my Dad and my uncle had discovered the secret of interstellar travel, why weren't they world famous?

Why weren't people doing it all the time?

Why were the Americans still stumbling around on the moon? Why had the Soviets given up even on that?

Note the order of my questions suggesting my personal interests and priorities. It took me five or six trips to even think about asking about how the Potash-Uranium Fusion Propulsion system actually worked.

Under the jade mountain, Uncle Weston chewed slowly on one of his Spam sandwiches and finally started answering:

"We do have a little funding from the National and Saskatchewan research councils. That's how we can pay the other pilots."

Other pilots? He told me that they had about a dozen friends ex of the RCAF who helped him and my Dad do the modifications on the CF-100s.

"The government knows that we are doing something interesting with Potash..." he said and took a very big bite of Spam and Wonderbread.

I sat there, waiting for him to finish, wishing that there were crickets or owls on this planet so I had something else to listen to.

Eventually, he swallowed and said:

"But I don't think anyone really understands what we're doing here."

Certainly our retrofit spacecraft didn't have much room to take anything back. Particularly if you liked to take your alienated teenage nephew along on your missions.

But the vagueness of what we were doing out in interstellar

space, or even if we were in space, suited everyone in the Programme just fine. They got to look around the universe without interference, which was pretty much ideal.

It was fine for me, too. The voyages (we could do a good portion of the Milky Way on a long weekend) were a welcome distraction from growing up as an alien in Saskatoon. The local LDS made a few visits and phone calls but I could sense that they were pretty relieved not to have me wandering around their Church anymore. Everybody else in Saskatchewan wasn't all that involved either. As good social democrats they were nice enough but they really saw me as just another variation of the Mormon species—and as everything else from Alberta—had to be treated with some distance and care.

Dad didn't really get too involved. As long as I kept my grades up he didn't interfere with the voyages.

"…for time and all eternity."

Then came Charlene.

I met her when I was doing my undergraduate work in math and astrophysics up in Edmonton. It was a little further from the Programme than I liked but I needed the training. I'd finished my pilot's license before I finished high school and with my uncle's advice I was more than qualified to handle the spacecraft. I just needed to pick up some science to be useful.

It's hard to explain how Charlene and I picked each other up.

We met at a cafeteria at the University of Alberta and found that we were extraordinarily compatible. It's only somewhat more amazing than the wonders of an exploding star how your ethnic background gets back at you.

Yes, Charlene was a serious Mormon. And yes, she expected me to tow that line if we were to become a more permanent item.

I liked her so much that I was seriously thinking about it. I guess I thought I could work out some kind of accommodation between the baggage I'd inherited and the nature of the universe as I'd actually experienced it. Sort of like my Uncle Weston seemed to have done.

My uncle took action after Charlene and I had travelled to Saskatoon for Thanksgiving. We had dinner with him and my Dad at the Golden Dragon.

"Here's the coordinates," he said handing me a set of punch cards. "You need to take this trip."

"…all eternity."

The coordinates were for the Celestial Kingdom.

For those of you who are not Mormons, the Celestial Kingdom is the highest level of Heaven. Where the faithful and virtuous are reunited with their loved ones and live in eternal happiness with God, Jesus and the Holy Ghost. There are lower levels of Heaven for everybody else.

When I landed in my modified CF-100 with its "Puff" drive, I asked some questions and met my mother.

She'd been there for almost 20 years—after my Dad had taken her there.

In some ways I was just going through what every divorced kid goes through. I finally had the opportunity to spend some time with my absent parent.

I'm sure she was my mother and I'm thankful to God (if there is such a thing) for the opportunity to see her. She was loving, happy and supportive.

Pretty much the opposite of what I remembered of her when she was married to my Dad.

But maybe that wasn't his fault either.

What I wasn't sure of was… where the hell I was. Maybe the fountains, the glorious choirs, the fantastic tabernacles, the presence of loving family ancestors, the pervading presence of white. Everywhere, on everything, within everything… maybe it was just *us.*

Maybe these were just telepathic aliens playing up to the cultural scripts my Mom and Dad brought with them. Maybe this holy place wasn't that at all, maybe this planet wasn't an inhabited place at all. Maybe it was just a place that reflected. Reflected ourselves.

I've always been bad with belief.

That's probably why I had to eventually say goodbye to my mother and return to Earth.

Frankly, I don't know where she's really living but I'm grateful that she's so happy.

"All is well."

Charlene and I broke up. Big surprise. I'd been gone for six months without a word.

Years later, I teach math at Evan Hardy Collegiate Institute in Saskatoon and the Programme is winding down. Dad died of cancer about three years ago. I try to convince myself that working with the potash-uranium hybrid materials had nothing to do with it.

Uncle Weston and I sit around his weird old radio and listen to the odd transmission from deepest space from one of the aging pilots talking about what strange and wonderful things he sees from the cockpit of his equally aging craft.

When the last of the pilots dies, the Programme will be over.

I don't go out anymore but I keep wondering about the truth. What did I experience? My Dad and my uncle had found some way to short-circuit the structure of the universe. Had they found some way to hot-wire the keys to heaven?

Unlike many of the people I went to church with I don't know anything with absolute certainty. I don't know the one revealed truth.

Maybe that's my testimony.

CELEBRITY NAME DROPPING

This one scores very high for stories written under exotic circumstances.

I was flying pretty high that day: both physically and professionally. I had just spent several days doing some consulting in the Los Angeles office of architect Frank Ghery, working on what is now known as the Experience Music Project Museum. On the trip back, my frequent flyer points from all those trips to Singapore and Seoul had tallied up enough to get me a business class seat. Sweet! Those seats are really comfortable.

I decided to make use of the luxury of space to get out my even then antique Tandy WP-2 Word Processor and do some writing. I then noticed that the gentleman next to me was Nicholas Lea, the actor who played the evil Agent Krycek on *The X-Files*. We made small talk as I dove in and out of my story from the height of 30,000 feet.

Heady stuff! But just in case all this name-dropping is obnoxious, I can assure you that this still failed to make me more attractive. I wasn't any taller either.

And I can still only afford to fly business class on points.

Given the title and subject matter, I was impressed that *On Spec* magazine not only published "Pornzilla," but also some of its editorial board even discussed it at lectures and symposia. Wonderful fearless people!

PORNZILLA

Originally published in:
On Spec, #58 Fall 2004
Vol. 16 No. 3

BEFORE

...Meanwhile...

Stewart Clarkman looked out his office window and saw the Forces of Evil descending on the parking lot.

"Gosh!" he thought, whipping off his horn-rimmed glasses and activating his optical sensors, "That's the fourth time this month!"

This time the Forces of Evil took the form of sixteen huge spiky robots with rocket launchers built into their chests and 16-millimetre cannons mounted on their heads. The big bad robots wobbled shakily on their hover disks.

"Miss Langley," Stewart pressed the intercom switch on his desk. "No calls for the next hour, I've got to write my speech for the Association of Mothers with Arithmetically Challenged House Pets."

Stewart knew this was a tremendously lame statement, but with so many attacks by the Forces of Evil he was simply running out of credible excuses.

"Yes, sir." Miss Langley's ever-efficient voice chirped back on the speaker.

Bless her heart, Stewart thought.

Stewart activated the image enhancers on his sensors and studied the big robots. Their eyes were single slits with a red orb continually bouncing back and forth.

Hmmm, he thought. Whomever designed those robots was obviously influenced by the *Battlestar Galactica* marathon they'd ran on the SF Channel last Easter.

"But…" Stewart began his next cognition aloud. … was this just sloppy thinking or was it some kind of kind of homage?

It might be some kind of clue…

The robots deactivated their hover disks and started stomping down the street towards Scarborough Mall, smashing the occasional car with hydraulically powered fists as they went.

Then again, Stewart decided, perhaps there was no significance to this pop culture reference.

With that, the youthful socially aware chartered accountant tore off his tie, pulled open his shirt to reveal the green spandex leotard beneath. The world-famous πr^2 symbol on the leotard seemed to barely contain the massive chest and abdominal muscles of a super-powered fighter of crime.

And with the quivering excitement that never seemed to dim with the passage of time, Stewart Clarkman spoke the magic formula for the factoring of quadratic equations… to become Math Man, the Algebraic Avenger!

Clutching his solar powered slide rule (an artifact from an earlier era of mathematical achievement—and a unique source of mystic power); Math Man flew out the office window.

I just hope… Math Man thought as the sun gleamed like a heroic beacon off his magnificently bald head… that I can dispatch these mechanisms before Miss Langley notices that I'm gone.

Math Man needn't have worried.

Because Lisa Langley, Stewart Clarkman's humble but perky secretary had a secret of her own!

"Thank goodness, he's gone!" Lisa whispered to herself as she ducked into a nearby powder room. Then, clicking on what seemed to be a normal ballpoint pen, Lisa Langley was instantly transformed into that paragon of super-effective super-empowerment: Logistics Lass!

Her optical sensors immediately revealed the most efficient route to the skies outside the office building—where she spotted Math Man circling the robots as they strode down toward the poorer part of town.

"Surrender immediately!" the superhero called down to the huffing and puffing mechanisms. "Or I'll reduce you all to a pile of improper fractions!"

"Up your vector space!" one of the robots growled back in a harsh metallic voice.

"Hey, big guy!" Logistics Lass laughed. "Save some of the bash-task for me!"

"The more the merrier!" Math Man said. As always he was delighted to see a fellow crime fighter on hand to help. Although, it was strange that Logistics Lass always seemed so close by recently, and come to think of it… why had he never seen her and Miss Langley in the same room together?

This chain of thought was interrupted by a blast from the head cannon of one of the bad robots.

As the battle of metal fists and calculation, rockets and logic continued, Math Man was able to explain the attack plan of the robots to Logistics Lass:

"It all seems to be a variation of the same pattern. Just about every other day, the Forces of Evil make another attempt to destroy the non-HR neighborhoods," he said grimly as he tore the leg off one of the mechanisms.

The sound of the crash was so loud, that Logistics Lass had to raise her voice to be heard:

"But why? Because they think no one will bother to defend non-virtual people?" As she spoke, Logistics Lass deflected the aim of one of the robot missiles so that it destroyed three of its evil metal comrades.

"I doubt it," replied Math Man as he calculated the exact amount of finger pressure to pull off the head of another robot. "The details of my Code of Crime-Fighting Conduct are well-known."

"Absolutely!" laughed Logistics Lass as the toppling body of the third robot crushed another one that happened to be looking in the wrong direction. "Everybody knows that you are sworn to protect even analog communities."

"So why—" began Man Math.

"Oh, this is very naughty!" screamed a youthful voice.

"You bad robots have made a terrible mess of this neighbourhood!" echoed another.

"What the—?!" cried Logistics Lass.

Every Day is Play Day!

At first Math Man thought the voices might have belonged to the Pragmatic Four, a band of business-oriented superheroes who occasionally left their Bay Street enclave to assist with crises elsewhere in the MegaCity.

But no, this was not the equation he'd expected.

"Is that who I think it is?" said Logistics Lass.

There was no mistaking the silver-blonde hair and the orange and pink plastic corvette convertible.

Blast, he realized. It was Stephie and her Pals.

"What are they doing here?" For an instant, Logistics Lass looked as though she didn't have a plan.

"More importantly," Math Man replied through clenched teeth. "How did they get here?"

Stephie and Penny didn't act as though they were out of their co-action field. They didn't even seem to be worried about being ground into silicon pellets by the most monstrous killer robots that SuperTown had ever generated.

The young models just jumped out of their car and strode over to the remaining robots.

"Didn't your mommies ever tell you not to break things when you play?" Stephie waved her finger at the biggest of the bad robots.

"My mommie was a tank..." replied the robot.

"Well, that's no excuse!" Penny, the happy-go-lucky one, said. "Even mobile artillery have to mind their manners."

"Ah...." The sigh of the robot sounded like a blast furnace dying a slow death. "We're sorry."

"Well, if you're really sorry..." Stephie began.

"We are, we are!" the robots all nodded their heads—which was difficult because the cannons weighed quite a lot.

"I don't believe this!" Logistics Lass whispered in disgust.

Math Man was simply at a loss for words. It just didn't add up.

But Stephie certainly knew what to say:

"If you're sorry, you'll clean up this mess and go back home."

"Something's not quite right..." Math Man muttered.

Logistics Lass briefly wondered if this was some kind of hoax or imaginary tale.

But the robots, heads still down, walked back the way they came. Penny held the hand of the robot at the front of the line.

"Don't worry!" Stephie waved to the two superheroes who were now semi-hiding behind an antennae tower of a nearby building. "We'll take these silly robots back to where they belong."

"T-thanks!" Math Man found it difficult to call back, but he felt he had to make some kind of acknowledgement.

The two of them watched the robots and the doll-girls disappear down the street.

"This is too easy," Math Man said. "I just hope this isn't some kind of plot."

"Never mind about that!" Suddenly, Logistics Lass pushed Math Man flat onto the rooftop. "I want your super-jism!"

"What the—?!" Math Man gasped as his partner tore off his spandex shorts and grasped his penis. He noticed that Logistics Lass' breasts seemed to swell to twice their normal size and glow with a dangerous and unearthly erotic energy.

"Must resist—" he growled through clenched teeth.

Logistics Lass just growled.

His penis hardened in an incredible pulsing hulk of rigid flesh.

He couldn't resist.

So, they fucked for the next twelve hours.

After the Planet Exploded...

Later, now in his everyday (if somewhat aching) identity, Stewart Clarkman dashed down the fire escape—hoping that the finally sleeping Logistics Lass wouldn't stir before he escaped.

He knew that this was his chance to find some clue to his partner's identity, but frankly more knowledge about Logistics Lass was the last thing he wanted.

Something is very wrong here, Stewart thought as found his car in the office parking lot.

I'll have to send a distress signal.

And in another part of the City...

Since they had houseguests, a new kitchen set was an absolute necessity. After a very competitive round of "eeny-meeny-mini-moe", Jodi and Penny were the lucky Pals who got to use it for the first time.

All your friends will want to join the fun!

So were the heck were they? Stephie saw a distinct gray worm of ash nestled in the stainless steel sink.

Cigarette butt? Stephie wasn't sure how it got there but she sure knew that it was absolutely gross!

She bounded up the stairs; it looked like she needed to talk to her Pals.

Smoking was so uncool! It just didn't happen in Stephie's world.

Besides if her Pals didn't want to play, why didn't they give someone else a chance to use the new toys? Her feet left a trail of waffle-iron tracks on the artificial shag carpet that lined the hallway leading to Jodi and Penny's room.

"I'm going to give you girls a real talking to!" Stephie swung their bedroom door open.

Stephie saw something even grosser than a cigarette butt.

Jodi and Penny were doing something really weird with the robots they'd picked up at SuperTown.

One of the robots was in Jodi's bed. It was stretched out on top of Jodi and kind of moving around. Somehow she'd managed to wrap her feet over the robot's shoulders.

The other robot was laying on the floor beside the bed. Penny was sitting on him and sort of bouncing around. Stephie wasn't sure but it looked like there was some kind of greasy snake trapped between Penny and the robot.

Stephie meant to yell: "Cut that out!" and "If you can't play nice, you can't play at all!"

What she actually said was *"Ack!"* followed by a gurgling, choking kind of a sound. Then she collapsed onto the artificial orange fabric.

DURING

"…it's off to work we go!"

"Did you get a look at the distress footage?"

Morrow had his head back in the electronic toilet, communicating with Bradley. Service rep conference call.

"Yeah, I did," Morrow replied.

"Pretty hot, eh?"

"Yeah. I already got some good credit downloading it onto the Pornzilla site."

"You're a real entrepreneur, Morrow." Bradley e-pathed a leer at him.

"Yeah."

"Technically none of that was possible," Bradley continued. "It would have to be a core-redefinition of the StephiePal Paradigm."

"Guess you're right," Morrow replied. "Except that it actually happened." Morrow wasn't going to get worked up about this, obviously it was just some new kind of glitch here.

"Okay!" a louder thought-voice boomed out from a much more

expensive digital head bowl and echoed through Morrow's and Bradley's minds.

"Let's get into action, here!"

Supervisor Price was had just joined the conference call: "We've got some dissatisfied customers here."

Price was a very direct and aggressive administrator, his mental transmissions always gave Morrow a headache.

"We've got to find out what the problem is and fix it!"

Morrow wondered how much they paid Price to make obvious statements like this. Then he hoped he'd remembered to have the part of his brain that generated thoughts like that privacy protected.

"Any idea what the hell is going on here?!"

Bradley had more available wet ware capacity (i.e. he was smarter than Morrow), so he spoke first:

"We don't have much after the initial diagnostic. There's definitely some kind of inappropriate actor/analytic overlap here."

"Inappropriate?! Jeez! Tell me something I don't know!"

How come Price could identify obvious statements from other people but not from himself, Morrow wondered.

"We're also picking up a pattern where HR neighborhoods with Family-Values Information Architecture seem to deteriorate into protracted adult scenarios."

"Hell's bells, man! *Are we talking about sex?*"

Big e-path sigh from Bradley. "Yes. Definite sexual situations. Pretty extreme ones."

Now Morrow hoped that his mind really was privacy protected here. Price really didn't need to know what he'd downloaded off the incident records.

"This could be a public relations disaster!" Price proclaimed.

"Yes, sir. And the customers aren't very happy about it either."

Suddenly Morrow became aware of an eighteen-digit number.

"Morrow, you still got an active driver's license?" Price asked.

"Yeah." He wasn't all that keen to use it these days.

"These are the coordinates of complaints from all HR neighborhoods. Go pick up the nearest company car and get over there."

Shit. This meant that Morrow would have to leave his apartment and head toward the city centre. He never enjoyed that.

And even now in SuperTown...

Even integrated with his Stewart Clarkman avatar, Oliver Kynes didn't look terribly comfortable. Maybe managing a secret identity within a secret identity was a bit much sometimes. Anyway, that's the impression Morrow got when he e-pathed the guy to make the appointment at his place in SuperTown.

Morrow could relate. They'd shipped him some really ugly clothes with a truly stupid logo and told him that this was supposed to be the company uniform. Several things really bugged him about this: a) that some research group had actually found a way to make a fabric that was 150% polyester (and you can imagine how comfortable that might be) and; b) that it looked like something that had fallen off a Z-Burger truck (totally bogus) and; c) he had to change out of his terrycloth housecoat (for the first time in almost two years).

Morrow wasn't sure he knew how to think properly if he wasn't wearing his housecoat. Terrycloth was so much more conducive to creative problem solving.

Why the hell did he have to come all the way out here?

HyperReality communities like SuperTown started out as digitally enhanced gated communities but over the years they acquired more and more environmental animation. Maybe living in a "seamless integration of the physical and media worlds" got a little too self-referential. Maybe the residents needed some extra action and adventure to keep them motivated.

Or maybe, Morrow used to wonder in one of his more introspective moments, maybe people just wanted to get even further away from anything resembling reality.

Whenever you left the parking lot and walked into any HR streetscape you would find yourself surrounded by all kinds of streamers, banners and floating screens carrying just about any sort of sensory augmentation you could think of.

So you could create places like StephiePals and SuperTown. The latter was based on a series of early 70s educational TV shorts using superheroes to teach basic concepts of math, reading and civics. The former was a world based on a set of collectible dolls and accessories.

Morrow thought developing massive collections of digital pornography was much healthier.

Maybe it was just economic envy. To pursue the HR lifestyle you had to be pretty comfortable. HR residents definitely depend on people like Morrow, but people like Morrow didn't make enough to live there.

Still, Morrow thought as he rolled towards his appointment, it pays the bills. And anybody whose hobby was electronically enhanced masturbation really couldn't criticize other people's preferences.

And here he was at his destination—the Metro Guardian Building. A massive Art Deco conceptualization—at least seven-eighths of it was pure holographic projection. God knows what the thing really looked like. But at least there was lots of parking.

Wearing that polyester uniform was making Morrow cranky.

The physical meeting with Oliver Keynes, A.K.A. Stewart Clarkman, A.K.A. Math Man was something of a dose of reality:

"I-I think I'm the victim of some kind of sexual harassment."

"*Sexual?!*" Morrow tried really hard to sound shocked and surprised. "How could such a thing happen here? SuperTown is a Family-rated environment."

Keynes was sitting at his office desk and shaking a little. "That's what I always thought! But every time Logistics Lass and I would go on a mission... well..."

"Well?" Morrow flipped on his recorder. Maybe he'd get something good to trade here.

"Well..." judging from Keynes's look of embarrassment, Morrow figured this was definitely going to be good. "...somehow our costumes would get torn off, or we'd be tied together for hours in an abandoned warehouse, or a villain would use some wierd and powerful love ray on us..."

Morrow was getting pretty interested but he knew he had to be careful here:

"...and you would find yourself in some sort of..." What the fuck kind of appropriate wording could he use here? "...*compromising* situation."

"Yes! Every time!" Keynes looked as though he might start to cry. "After three weeks of this, I was so ashamed and so exhausted. I just told her that we couldn't go on any more missions."

"But that didn't solve your problem?"

"No." Keynes was leaking around the eyes a little. "She just started sending me fake distress signals, pretending to be other characters, even telepathically implanting messages like this..."

Keynes covered his eyes as he activated an imaging surface on his desk.

Jackpot, thought Morrow. Pretty hot stuff.

"I'm afraid I'll need all copies of those," he said in a matter-of-fact voice. "For purposes of analysis."

Sometimes you get to make new friends!

The apartment/imaging studio wasn't really working anymore. Now it was just a place for lots of stacks of shipping boxes.

The fierce chromakey blue on the walls was giving Morrow a headache.

"You really don't have to come around here!" Miriam Cruikshank A.K.A. Stephie #981,437 wasn't all that different from her avatar. Maybe just a little smaller, a little more angular and a lot angrier.

Morrow had read the manual before his visit. Stephies were always supposed to glow with a sense of "optimism and sociability."

Obviously, not always.

Right now, this Stephie was folding up appliances and jamming them into the moving boxes.

"Besides, I don't know what went wrong with the programme," she said.

"That's not unusual," Morrow replied. "You're supposed to enjoy the environment, not understand it."

"Well, I didn't enjoy it!" she barked back. "And I don't like being told that I'm just *usual.*"

"We'll do whatever it takes to make it right ma'am—"

"I don't want the fucking scenario fixed! I want a new one!"

A Stephie using the 'f' word? Now that was *not* usual. And that attitude wasn't going to make you the most popular girl at school.

"Even so," Morrow said as evenly as possible (there might be a good angle here as well) "We have to take a wider view of the situation. We have other clients and we need to know what went wrong."

"Fuck your other clients!"

Morrow was so happy. People would to kill to hear a Stephie avatar talk this way.

It got better: She stomped around the room and when she unrolled the packing tape over the top of one of boxes it sounded like someone cutting a pig's throat.

Man, she was pissed! Morrow kept the recorder going.

She kicked the box in the direction of the door.

"I thought Penny and Jodi were supposed to be my friends!"

Morrow decided to try and sound impartial here:

"Sometimes when a scenario takes an unexpected direction, the relationships between the players can get quite confused."

"Tell me about it." Stephie #981,437 zipped up her pink rubber greatcoat and looked at the doorway.

"I need your permission to capture the full record for analysis." Morrow was nervous here. He really wanted the actual incident footage—he could make a real killing.

" You must be shitting me!"

Morrow knew that a fast response was essential here:

"All identity codes will be masked, and of course, we pixelate the faces of all players." (Not!)

"Jesus H. Christ..." Stephie sighed.

"There's also some financial compensation involved." Morrow lied figuring he could easily afford this. "Although it usually takes the form of software credits."

Stephie sighed again. "Fuck. Take whatever you want. Just don't make me look at it again."

A few hours later, when he was processing the records, Morrow knew that he'd made the right decision. He had all of it: oral, anal, facials, group shots and even some stuff that he wasn't sure what the hell it was.

And he also knew why Stephie/Cruikshank was so pissed. When the four-some became a six-some, then an eight-some and ten-some... nobody asked her to join. Kind of like being the last kid picked for the softball (hardcore?) team. Hurts your feelings.

Guess that's what happens when you're so bossy.

...and now a public service message...

"Did you check out the Stephie download?"

Bradley was disengaged. "Yeah. Nice resolution."

"Nice resolution?" Morrow couldn't believe this. "What about the content, man? Wasn't it incredibly hot?"

"Hot?" Bradley really did seem to be thinking about something else. "Yeah, I guess." He chuckled briefly. "Yeah, it looked like the Suzie avatar actually grew a new orifice near the end there."

"Doesn't get much nastier than that," Morrow said. "We'll do well."

"It gets *much* nastier than that," Bradley said in that "you-can-be-so-naïve" voice, "But I agree you should be able to get some good credit for it."

Then Morrow heard Bradley's telephonically/telepathically-enhanced sniffing echoing through his receptor bowl.

"What's up?"

"Tell me," Bradley answered. "What do you think we can get for all these new downloads?"

"Hell man!" Morrow laughed. "Our choice of any kind of real-time group action, access to some of the new Malaysian bondage sites. Just out of curiosity we might even look into the zoological services."

A short, sharp, sublingual message cracked out through Morrow's consciousness: *"YUK!"*

"You of all people shouldn't judge!" Morrow barked back. "I know what kind of shit you've got stashed away."

"Back to my original question," Bradley said. "What the hell do we ever get from downloading porn onto the network? Besides more porn for ourselves?"

"Yeah, isn't it great?" Morrow laughed.

"Why didn't you join this morning's maintenance meeting?"

Okay, thought Morrow. Change of subject. Probably significant in some nerd-head way.

"I was busy. Had a backlog of client requests…"

"Bullshit," Bradley said evenly. "I know your work schedule. You were masturbating."

Don't sound defensive, Morrow said to himself.

"Yeah, that's part of the fun of this job isn't it?"

"How many hours a day do you figure you spend abusing yourself?"

"Uh…"

"Two? Four? Six?"

"Eight! How I love to masturbate!" Morrow tried to sound jovial. "What's your point, Bradley? You're the biggest wanker in North America."

"Oh, I don't disagree," Bradley replied. "And if you're anything like me, you'll probably have started noticing that your stroking time has started cutting into other things into your life, like reading, listening to music…"

Who cares about that crap these days, thought Morrow.

"…working…eating?"

"This discussion is getting boring, Bradley."

"Oh, something else you'd rather be doing, right now, Morrow? Perhaps involving some manual stimulation?"

"What the hell is your point?!"

Long pause.

"Morrow. Access the Fiction Section of the Toronto Public Library System. Check out some passages from the books."

This was just weird. "Which ones?"

"Anything at random. Patch in your optics so I can watch what you read."

"Okay."

The Trial. The simple but formal text describes a protracted mutual oral sex scene between Joseph K. and his housekeeper—presumably K. is in search of comfort after his mysterious arrest. At the moment of climax K feels as though the escape of his life fluids might somehow transform him into some kind of monstrous insect…

"Hey, Kafka is a little hotter than I remembered!" Morrow said.

"I'm enjoying it, too," Bradley replied. "But, pick another book."

Sure.

Treasure Island. In just a quick skim, Morrow read of young Jim Hawkins hiding in the closet of a tavern, watching a buxom barmaid use Long John Silver's wooden leg for an intimate purpose.

"Now, that's just not right!" Morrow protested. "I know that's not in the book. What is this, a novelization of a video?"

"Good guess, but no," Bradley said.

"What's going on here?"

"It's kind of complicated. Try another book."

Okay, Morrow thought, let's stick with the nautical theme.

Moby Dick. Powerfully inspired by the butchering of an enormous sperm-whale penis, Captain Ahab instructs his first-mate to lead the ship's crew in a carefully timed circle jerk…

Morrow screamed: *"WHAT?!"*

"Well, if you'd made the meeting, you might have a better idea of what's going on."

"Okay, okay…" Morrow was embarrassed by his reaction. "There's nothing new about slash fiction, and obviously there's some kind of programme slippage from a porn system into the library's knowledge architecture."

"That's what you think?"

"Sure, it's like what's been happening with the HR communities like Stephie's world and SuperTown."

"Slippage?"

"Or spill."

"Try invasion."

Bradley called up a diagnostic programme. Everywhere the data palaces and information structures of the city had been changed. All the systems looked like they'd fused together into something even more complex, organic...

Morrow hesitated...

...into something pulsating and very wet.

"The boss says the entire City network is evolving into a sexual paradigm."

"Which means?"

How could it be sexual, Morrow wondered. It wasn't hot, it was just freaking scary.

"It means that everything is becoming pornography."

AFTER

Miriam...

"It's your decision, hun," she said to the new girl. "You can have a live-in room or just use it for days or evenings."

Miriam Cruikshank (now A.K.A. Madame Serena #823,691) eyed the young woman sitting in front of her, nice tits, good ass and legs, a little heavy in the waist but nothing that a good corset couldn't take care of.

Should be a money-maker.

"Okay," the girl said not really looking at anything.

Stoned, Miriam thought with disgust. Even in a wonderfully fake world, some people still needed to get stoned.

"Of course the rent for a live-in is higher and the cost for the cleaners comes out of your tips." Miriam opened a drawer and pulled out a very large box of condoms. The box had to be large because many of the condoms were such odd shapes.

"You'll need to use these," Miriam explained, "because the resolution is so good in this world, you won't know when you're dealing with a real person or an avatar."

Even in her tranquilized state, the girl looked a little alarmed as she inspected the range of styles.

"Okay?"

"Don't worry," Miriam laughed. "One of the girls on your floor will show you how to use them. Some of them are kind of fun."

"Okay..."

Miriam started making notes on a pad of paper. This one didn't seem too bright, so it didn't hurt to review the basics: "Now remember the values, $5,000 for a manual release, $8,000 for blow and $12,000 for all inclusive."

"Okay."

Miriam sighed. "You know, I'm sure you're really going to enjoy your time here, but I have to tell you, if you're really going to succeed here, you're going to have to show a little more enthusiasm."

"Okay, *oh*!" At this point the girl seemed to wake up a little. "Yeah, sure! No problem."

That's good, thought Miriam. She has nice eyes. Some of her more sensitive guests seemed to care about that shit.

"Now run along," Miriam lit something that simulated the taste and effects of an opium-tipped Russian cigar. "I'll check on you after you've had a chance to settle in."

Miriam closed her eyes and inhaled. When she opened her eyes again, the girl was gone and Miriam could feel the buzz coming on. This was definitely a better game, she decided. She got to meet some interesting people and handle some pretty wild situations.

And just like the days when StephiePals was fun, she got to call the shots.

Morrow...

The de-installation crew had left about four hours ago. Morrow's apartment was no longer a creative hub in the digital experience sphere of HyperReality.

Nope. Now it was just the bed sitting room of a loser in a bad part of town. It was also an apartment that Morrow wasn't sure where he would get the rent for.

Out of work again. And no way was he going to get any Unemployment Insurance on this one.

But he had to get out. Not that he felt personally responsible. By the estimates of his own company at least 2.5 billion people a month were feeding data-growth media into what more and more experts were recognizing as a gigantic erotic AI network.

Of course, thought Morrow as he removed his last two beers from the refrigerator, his leaving the company wouldn't make any difference either. Maybe it was just that he didn't like knowing all the facts and being unable to do anything about it.

He dropped onto the sofa and sucked back on the cold can.

Morrow knew he was screwed (and not in the good sense) when he discovered that the Porn-AI had even infected the on-line company operating manuals:

"...updating the archives protocol will be a curiously thrilling experience... as the patch software engages, you will feel an odd but urgent pressure rising deep within you and your site computer... this pressure will build... it is best to yield..."

Morrow knew that he'd reached his limits and he knew there was no way he could function in an environment like that. Yeah, he was a total porn-hound but after a week with working in the new AI, he'd probably be insane. Hell, he might not even be sentient.

Morrow noticed that he'd already consumed seven-eighths of his first can of beer. He picked up a copy of the local paper and flipped over to the classifieds. Cold turkey on the smut. Now he had to go out and get a real job.

Oliver...
"I just hope this works..."

In past few weeks, Math Man had been forced to become a realist. He knew that even with his increased computational powers and the strength of his authorized Oath of Celibacy, he might not be equal to this challenge.

He flew slowly over the vast mass of glistening flesh and pulsing tendrils that had absorbed almost all of SuperTown. Just about everyone was somewhere inside there... including his beloved Logistics Lass.

Now she was probably just some connecting twinge in some unending orgasmic response.

Math Man knew that no form of reason, no statement of fact, no matter how arithmetically pure, might be able to control the gigantic tidal wave of living lust beneath him.

Some of the few who were immune chose to leave SuperTown, and try to set up new and decent virtual lives somewhere else. But

Math Man know he couldn't do that. He would stay and fight, no matter what.

What else could he do?

COSTS

I've done a lot of work with military museums over the last couple of decades. At one level, this is not surprising. People fight a lot, for a great many reasons, and there's a lot of history to try and make sense of.

Here's my professional academic opinion: War costs.

At another level I was very surprised that it was me who was working with these fighting people.

The closest I ever got to a uniform was in Boy Scouts and it was never a good physical or psychological fit. I wasn't even into war movies and I'd always go for an *Avengers* or *X-Men* comic over *Sargent Rock* or *Enemy Ace*.

But I can be a quick study and I tried my best to be a good listener, in that capacity people who had been through an awful lot shared some of their experiences with me.

Here is my personal opinion: War really costs.

THE HOSPITAL FOR SICK ROBOTS

Originally published in:
Descant 122, Fall 2003, Volume 34, Number 3

Stan and a big guy came around to tighten the springs in my knees.

Like they do every morning.

"Does that feel any better?" Stan asked. "Do you want to try and walk today?"

No and no. What a couple of dummies.

Stan frowned at me. "I don't understand, Billie. Your limbs and motor control center are in perfect working order."

"How would I know?" I said. "You guys are the ones who built me."

They just shook their heads and went away. So I watched cartoons until lunch-time, when Nurse Ellen brought me some WD-40 soup and a bowl of silicon chips. The best shows on TV were *Supercar* and *Space Angel*.

Nurse Ellen is nicer than most of the people here; she brings me food and doesn't bug me about not being able to walk.

"I hear you were brave today," Nurse Ellen said as she took the tray. "You didn't cry when they took the covers off your knees."

"Nope."

It's too bad Nurse Ellen isn't a robot.

After my crunchy-slippery lunch, I got into my chair and rolled over to Chet's room. Chet is a red robot. I'm a blue one.

...Blue Division: Bio-Field Tactics... Red Division: Chemical Communications and Logistics...

Maybe Chet had trouble being brave today. I saw some motor oil leaking from his eye sockets and the lights on his chest screen were flickering. But I wasn't mad at him for crying—they'd been re-wiring his arms and gotten the circuits all mixed up. Some of his fingers had fallen off and now they had to take the whole hand off to fix it.

That kind of thing can really hurt.

I told Chet all about the cartoon shows I'd seen and that seemed to make him feel better. Then we played I-Spy for a while and I went back to my room and waited for the after-school programs to start.

But a new lady came by and so I didn't get to turn on the TV. She looks a lot like Mrs. Martinson, my grade two teacher, so I figured she knew a lot about arithmetic, too.

The lady got Stan to wheel in this Big Ugly Radio which he left at the foot of my bed. Then the radio talked at me with all these long words that were probably all made-up anyway.

It was a really boring appliance.

After a while the teacher-lady started asking me all kinds of dumb questions. Why does everybody ask me dumb questions?

"Do you have any idea why you don't want to walk, Billie?"

Because I can't, stupid! (Good thing they can't read a robot's mind very often.)

"Do you remember anything about your mission? Anything you want to tell me about?"

"No." I'm just a robot. I don't remember anything.

"Are you sure you don't want to talk to me about anything?"

"I saw a really good cartoon show today."

"Why was it good, Billie?"

"I dunno, it was just cool."

Teacher-Lady looked at me with a funny look and then asked:

"Are you having any strange dreams, Billie?"

That question makes me really mad. *I'm a robot! I don't have dreams!*

But all I say is: "No."

After a while they left and Nurse Ellen brought me dinner. Tire steaks with mashed Styrofoam. Yum!

At bedtime they turned out the lights and cranked my power down to the lowest setting. Lying there in the dark, I was still mad at that Teacher-Lady. Those were dumb and mean questions.

And I don't. Don't. Don't.
Dream.

...blue robot: Blue Division...

❋   ❋   ❋

Today was kind of a bad day.

First they turned off the cartoons before lunch-time, so I didn't have anything to do in the morning but sit around and feel my knees hurt.

That dummy Stan came around and asked me if I wanted to try walking today, but I just turned my head and pretended to look out the window. I could see other robots in the courtyard, sitting on the stone benches and hobbling around on crutches. There were all kinds of robots out there: red ones, green ones, yellow ones, purple ones, even a few blue ones. Our metal shells were all shiny underneath, but the doctors were always checking the paint on the outside.

...Green Division: A.I. Weapons Coordination... Yellow Division: Psycho-Triage Systems... Purple Division: Battlefield Disinformation Analysis.

I sometimes wondered why I was a blue robot and not some other colour robot. I wondered if being blue or red or purple means something. Maybe blue was the color for a robot that has to sit down and hurt all the time.

Stan goes away, and after lunch Teacher-Lady showed up with that Big Ugly Radio. She's friendly enough but the radio keeps on with all these questions:

"Why not tell us about the Drop, Billie? There's no telemetry after you went through."

"What are you talking about?" I said to it. "I didn't go on any drop, I can't even walk."

Then the Radio kind of laughed at me. "You certainly weren't walking, Billie. You were flying in on your descent thrusters."

Flying? I thought, this Radio must be crazy! So I decided the best thing to do was to take another look out the window. Not so many robots were out there today.

"That's enough for now," Teacher-Lady said.

Stan came in and pushed the Big Ugly Radio out of my room. Teacher-Lady put some crayons and paper on the table by my bed.

"If you have any ideas, or if you see some interesting pictures in your head," she said to me, "I want you to draw them so we can talk about them later."

Ideas? Pictures in my head? This lady must be as crazy as that radio. I'm a robot. I don't have ideas and I don't get pictures in my head.

Things would have been okay if they'd turned on the TV when they left but they didn't. So there were no cartoons. I was going to miss *Land of the Lost* and *Valley of the Dinosaurs*.

I wanted my own remote.

After lunch they rolled me into the Playroom and said I should try and do something. Yuk.

Red Robot Robert was there.

Chemical Logistics and Communications… Col. R.R. Piacente…

Like me, Robert couldn't walk but he could stand. Actually that was just about all he could do. The nurses would wheel him out on these fancy roller skates, hand him a cane and just leave him there.

Robert would stand there for hours. Most of the time he wouldn't say anything but every once in a while he would suddenly scream out some big made-up words and then he would fall down.

That always bothered me.

So I was just sitting there in my wheelchair next to Robert. I was throwing some foam magnets at a *Fireball XL5* dart board, and I started hearing some funny words:

"…missile trajectory projection", "sensory distortion effects" and "multiple toxicity pathways…"

More stupid, made-up words. Maybe it was because I was standing too close to Robert.

Then Brent, a big green robot…

A.I. Weapons Coordination… Captain B. Walden…

…who was sitting in a bean-bag chair on the other side of the room, suddenly jumps up, yells real loud…

And pulled his head off.

"Existence!" is what Brent yelled. "The balance between human perception and the conditions of our existence are all wrong!"

Of course.

I saw a couple of books by Brent's chair, *The Cat in the Hat* and *The Cat in Hat Comes Back.* Maybe it was something in those books that made him go nuts.

Brent dropped his head and it bounced off the floor and rolled around for a while. The dome on the top of his head popped off and I could see all these glass tubes and red wires sticking out.

Gross.

His head kept on talking: "…human perception is highly localized to our conditions of local origin… but symbols trade enough ambiguity between human cognition to perpetuate cycles of misunderstanding… and at the same time any sufficiently advanced technology is indistinguishable from getting kicked in the head by God…"

The electricity inside Brent's head started to run out and his voice slowed down: "…spiritual… blah… disintegra… blah… psycho… blah… disorienta… blah… blah… blah…"

Robert slowly turned to look at Brent's head. The red robot nodded and crashed to the floor.

Stan and a couple of other big guys ran in and started checking out the robots. One of the big guys accidentally kicked Brent's head under the Lego table.

"Damn it!" Stan yelled at me. "Why didn't you stop him?"

Why was he mad at me? What could I do? I can't even walk.

I'm a broken robot.

So I wheeled myself back into my room and shut the door. I still couldn't reach the knobs on the TV so I couldn't watch. I drew some pictures with the crayons instead.

I used lots of colours.

❋   ❋   ❋

"William?"

"Is that you Dr. Boroughs?"

"Yes, we have to make this quick. Direct communication to your suppressed consciousness risks extreme brain damage."

"Suppressed consciousness?"

"We don't want to do this."

"<u>Brain damage</u>?"

"What happened after the Drop?"

"We went inside. There was some kind of mist in the air."

"It penetrated your breathing apparatus?"

"You know the answer to that one."

"Then what happened?"

"You know the answer to that one, too. You found us."

"But…"

"Some us were dead, some of us were dying… some of us were just… broken. We were breaking ourselves."

"But how did the effects manifest them—"

Some of us were dying, some were broken.

Stop it, Billie. Stop the pictures in your head.
Robots can't dream.

✻   ✻   ✻

For the next couple of weeks, not too much happened. I just watched cartoons, which is still pretty much the only fun I got to have. But there were some cool new shows, *Birdman and the Galaxy Trio* was my favorite.

Nurse Ellen asked if I want to play hide and seek with a new orange robot but I think she was just trying to get me to try and walk.

Orange Division: Transportation…

And I couldn't do that.

Sometimes there were lots of cartoons on the TV, other times there's hardly any. So sometimes, I used the crayons from Teacher-Lady to make up my own cartoons.

She still came in every once in a while with the Big Ugly Radio to ask me questions. Usually they wanted to talk about the pictures I drew.

"Can you tell me about this shape here?"

"It's a big desert."

"Why did you colour it gray?"

"Because I ran out of turquoise."

The next day Nurse Ellen came in with a new box of crayons. There were lots more colours to choose from.

One time Teacher-Lady asked me about some little people I drew beside the blue helicopter.

"Who are they?"

"They're the ones who disappeared."

"Why did they disappear?"

"Because they couldn't go back," I say. "Only lucky robots can come back."

After that time, Teacher-Lady always left the Big Ugly Radio in my room for the rest of the afternoon. I hated this because the stupid thing wouldn't let me watch cartoons.

So I had to make more of my own.

The Radio kept on asking dumb questions:

"What does that picture remind you of?"

The cartoons you won't let me watch.

"Do you remember anything new today?"

How much my knees hurt.

"Have you had any interesting dreams lately?"

I can't dream.

Because I didn't say anything, the Radio started in with all this crazy talk:

"I know you're holding back. You don't have to, it's completely safe to talk to me."

"How is it safe?" I asked the Radio. I remembered what happened when Green Brent talked too much.

"I'm your psychological control, Billie. I'm programmed with all your memories and experiences," the Radio said. "We're almost the same person."

"I am not a person!" I yelled. "I am a robot!" Then I threw a pillow at that Big Ugly Radio.

The Radio was quiet for a minute. When it started talking again, I knew it wasn't mad at me because it used a real friendly voice:

"Who is the hero in that cartoon, Billie?"

I didn't know why, but was kind of fun to tell him about Ultra-Multi-Hyper-Man whose superpower is the ability to be in a million different places at once. He protects everybody. Except maybe himself.

*   *   *

Today was a really bad day.

Somebody went to the Doctors.

When I woke up Teacher-Lady and the Big Ugly Radio were beside my bed.

"I'm really sorry about this," the Teacher-Lady said. "They want to try a new treatment today."

"People are getting impatient, Billie," the Radio said. "They say we need to make some progress."

"That's not my problem," I said. "I'm just a broken robot."

"After today, it might be your problem," Teacher-Lady tells me.

The Radio tried to explain something to me using some more of its made-up words like "reverse identity displacement" and "neurological re-configuration". I still didn't know what these words meant, but I was getting better at picking them out.

He said some words that I didn't like the sound of:

"Electronic psycho-surgery."

That sounded like it would hurt.

The TV stayed off almost all day, then after lunch Stan wheeled me over to the elevator and we went down.

Down, down, down. Into the sub-basement.

There's another blue robot there, I think his name was Jerry.

...Private J. Hanna...

He was strapped onto a big table and he had all kinds of wires taped to his head. The other ends of those wires were plugged into the back of another Really Big, Really Ugly, Radio.

A guy in a white coat came over to me. He had white hair, so I figure he's a doctor.

...Dr. P.K. Boroughs: Director Military Psychiatric Services...

"Today you just get to watch," the doctor said. "There's a possibility that simply observing the procedure on another subject may trigger your memory responses."

Nope. Nope. No.

I still didn't want to remember.

Jerry looked really scared. He was whining and there were oil stains all over his cheeks.

"Relax, Jerry," said the Other Radio. "All we're going to do is delete some of your traumatized engrams and download a segment of my personality simulation into your nervous system."

"I don't want you to!" cried Jerry.

Nope. Nope. No, I thought.

The Other Radio kept on talking: "You'll feel a lot better and we should be able to retrieve some of the memories of your mission…"

"I don't want to!" screamed Jerry.

Nope. Nope. No.

The Other Radio stopped talking and some more doctors start fiddling with the big dials and switches on its sides. There's lots of electricity and smoke jumping around and that reminded me of *Frankenstein Junior and the Impossibles*. Usually that's a cool show but here the smoke and lightning were pretty scary.

Then one of the doctors pulled a really big switch and a huge bolt of lightning shoots out from behind the radio and hit Jerry in the head.

Jerry exploded.

It was like a giant firecracker going off. A big bang, a stinky cloud of gray smoke and pieces of Jerry lying there. Now he was just a blue metal shell: the wires and tubes inside him were gone. Everything that used to be Jerry was gone.

The Other Radio was quiet, too. All its lights were out.

"We have a problem here," one of the doctors said.

"Feedback effect," another doctor said. "Next time we'll calibrate the levels better."

The pieces of blue metal shell started rolling off the table. There's a loud clang when they hit the concrete floor.

The doctor with white hair looked mad. He turned to me and said:

"Do you remember anything yet?"

"No."

"Get that robot out of here."

Stan took me back to my room.

I felt bad about Jerry, but at least whatever happened to him happened fast. That's just the way it goes with us robots.

Nurse Ellen lowered me into my bed and I told her I want to watch cartoons.

"You and your stupid cartoons!" she yelled. "You know you're the next subject, don't you?"

Why was she mad at me? Cartoons are great.

"Can't you even *try* to get better?"

I noticed that it usually doesn't help to talk to humans when they're this angry. So I just shut up and turned off my eyes.

Nurse Ellen did not turn on the TV when she left.

No cartoons today. I was going to miss *The Mighty Mightor* and *Thunderbirds*.

I wondered where my Big Ugly Radio has gone.

✳   ✳   ✳

After lights out, I kept thinking, even though my power levels were really low.

I suddenly remembered that I don't really need crayons. I can make up pictures in my head, so I decided to make up some cartoons.

This one is a really cool cartoon, even cooler than *Space Ghost.*

It's about a blue robot who goes on a mission in a helicopter with all his friends To Save the World Against the Terrible Enemy.

Lots of other robots have gone on this trip before him, but lately only a few of them come back. And the ones that do are broken and crazy.

But the bosses at Astro City Space Command keep on sending these robots because they want to know how the Terrible Enemy is able to do this. Maybe the robots will find out something useful.

But a blue robot, the hero of my cartoon, does come back and everybody thinks he's crazy too.

The blue robot knows better, he knows he's not crazy.

But he has been pretty seriously broken so he has to go to the hospital for a while.

The blue robot knows that something happened to him out there. And he knows that he's no longer just an ordinary robot. Something out there gave him a superpower.

Now if he could only figure out what that superpower was.

But nobody has invented the words to explain what happens to you when you go outside your brain. So he couldn't tell anyone, couldn't explain to anyone, what happened.

"William?"
  "You've got me on that table don't you?"
  "We're being as careful as we can."
The people at the hospital tried to help him remember. They played a tape-recording of his old mind to him but that didn't help him remember. They even started using electronic shovels to try and dig the information out of his vacuum-tube brain. But the blue robot didn't think that would help very much.

"Can you tell us anything?"
  "Yeah. We figured out the weapons system."
So the blue robot just sat there and watched cartoons on TV (when they let him) and didn't remember anything. He couldn't even figure out what his superpower was.
  Poor blue robot.

"Before the hallucinations took over, Piacente and Walden found the containers. We read the spec sheets they pasted on the cylinders."
Then one night when he was making his own cartoons (inside my cartoon, which might be inside another robot's cartoon, which might be inside another robot's cartoon, which might…) the robot suddenly knew what his superpower was.

"Psycho-Chemical Aerial Compound #345-0987."
  "That's an advanced LSD-enhancement and—"
  "Exactly."
  "It's one of ours!"
He had the ability to turn into a person, and once he became a person, he had the power to do whatever he wanted to.
  Whether he could remember his mission or not.

"Material like that is beyond Ultra. How could they have gotten it?"
  "We probably gave it to them when they were our allies."
  "Dear God!"
  "I hope somebody thought about an antidote."
  "Sorry, I think you're on your on your own with that one, William."

So the blue robot whispered his magic superpower words ("Shazaam" or something like that) and started to turn into a human being.

He took off all the parts of his shell: the face, the head, the chest, the arms and legs. It felt really good to take the jointed plates off his knees.

At last he took off his feet, big clunky blue pipes that weighed a ton. He looked at the heavy metal feet lying on the floor and realized that he could finally walk.

Sure enough, just as he always suspected, there was a man inside him. Now that the ex-blue robot had his superpower, he could do whatever he wanted.

So, quickly, quietly, without telling anybody what he knew about what it was really like to be outside his own brain, he put on his clothes.

And without a single glance at the empty blue metal, the man checked out.

DOOM AND GLOOM

I wrote this doomsday story in a most suitable setting.

Thanks to some major forest fires in Indonesia, most of southeast Asia was shrouded in a massive dome of smog that shut down all air and sea travel. Aircraft were getting diverted and ships were colliding.

I was trapped in Singapore. Stuck in my room and advised to regulate my oxygen intake. So I did what you might expect I would do when faced with the end of times. I wrote.

Although this story was finished in the late 1990s, it did not get published until 2004 in the U.K. magazine *Interzone*. I kept selling "Problem Project" and the magazines and anthologies that bought it kept going out of business before it could hit print. I began to wonder if "Problem Project" was some kind of evil publication-killer.

When it finally came out, the illustration for my story was by Richard Bartrop, the same artist who created the wonderful alien proctologist drawing for, "Why I Hunt Flying Saucers," in *On Spec* magazine.

How is that for a coincidence of near cosmic proportions?

PROBLEM PROJECT

Originally published in:
Interzone, Number 195,
November/December 2004

PROGRESS REPORT

Sorry about missing the last scheduled transmission but I have a good excuse which will become clear as I continue. First, the administrative issues:

1. Send more drugs. The airborne contaminants in our region are far worse than we expected and some of the toxins are reacting with our reconstructive surgery. The Field Team personnel are uncomfortable and if we don't get some kind of treatment, I'm afraid somebody's face is going to melt.

2. Has there been any progress in getting that Research Methodology Exemption? Central's restrictions on technology use and extra-planetary manifestations continue to be the single greatest source of frustration on this project. Trying to measure temporal anomalies and sub-space breakdown with Class 81 equipment is next to impossible. Please help us to do our job well.

3. Now for the real news: in spite of your regulations, we are getting interesting results. More like disturbing results. There's lots we don't know yet, but one thing I can tell you is that we are dealing with more than a looped sequence pocket here. Every reliable reading from the Field Team has indicated that we have significant time-space breakdown here. I know it's not terribly helpful to tell you that things look bad, but right now, we don't know how bad or why. Of course, if we had better equipment…

                    ❋   ❋   ❋

THERAPIST: Try to stay calm, Hal. Breathe slowly and tell
                me what's wrong.

HAL: It's burning me!

THERAPIST: Remember your exercises, Hal. Nothing can
                really hurt you. Whatever you see, it's just
                like watching it on a big screen in a movie
                theatre. Now, can you tell me what you see?

HAL: I don't want to look.

THERAPIST: Okay, let's go back to what happened
                before you became so frightened. Do you
                know how old you are in the dream?

HAL: I'm five years old, so it must be... 1960,
                1961...

THERAPIST: And what are you doing?

HAL: I'm coming home from school. Mrs. Ratcliffe,
                my kindergarten teacher, told us to put
                away our scissors and glue and go home
                right away.

THERAPIST: Why did she do that?

HAL: It had something to do with the
                announcement from the Principal's office.

THERAPIST: What do you do next?

HAL: Watch TV. It's almost time for <u>Colonel Bleep</u>.
                Hey, the TV won't turn on!

THERAPIST: Why not?

HAL: I think there's no electricity, so I get up to tell my mom… oh, no! Now I'm scared again!

THERAPIST: What's frightening you?

HAL: I look out the glass doors that lead out to the patio. There's a trail from a jet up in the sky… I really hate this, can I wake up now?

THERAPIST: Nothing can hurt you, Hal, you have to look at what you're afraid of.

HAL: Wow! It's like a star exploded! Now I can't see and it feels like hot wax is running down my cheeks… I think my eyes have melted!

THERAPIST: Breathe slowly. Your eyes are fine. Now go back to that time and tell me what really happened.

HAL: Everything feels different, now. The cartoons are almost over and my dad turns the channel to the news; he says he wants to watch a speech by President Kennedy.

THERAPIST: That's what really happened? You watched television with your father?

HAL: I guess so. Like I said, everything feels different now.

✻   ✻   ✻

Megan was on the phone when Hal got home. She did not look happy.

"No, no thank you," she said into the receiver.

Hal put his portfolio down and walked over to the kitchen. It was Wednesday, so it would be vegetarian lasagna. Delicious, nutritious and environmentally responsible. Megan grew most of the ingredients herself.

"I really think you're wasting your time," Megan continued. "Frankly, I wouldn't even allow your products into my house, so I doubt that I would be interested in a year's free supply."

Hal had retrieved the glass dish from the oven and had scooped out a steaming brick of vegetable matter.

Megan rolled her eyes. Hal sat down at the table and started eating.

"Yes!" Megan cried. "I am completely serious. Now, I really can't spare you any more time. Good-bye!" She applied more than the necessary force to hang up the receiver. They had an old rotary phone, so Megan could express her opinions and feelings in this way.

Megan sat down across from Hal.

"Who was that?" he asked.

"Frozen waffles," replied Megan.

"I didn't know waffles knew how to use the telephone," said Hal.

"Seriously," she said. "These people have devised some new kind of freeze-dried waffle food product made from plastic molecules designed to simulate milk and eggs. They just offered us a year's free supply if we would let them come over and administer a taste test."

Hal extracted a tomato seed from between his teeth. Megan viewed most convenience foods and their packaging as a clear and present danger to the health of the planetary eco-system. To Megan, helping people to market these products would be somewhere close to signing up as the sacrifice in a satanic ritual.

Hal continued eating. It was good lasagna.

"So…" Megan began, just a little carefully. "…did you make any progress in today's session?"

Probably not, Hal thought.

"I think so," was what he said. "She gave me some new relaxation exercises for the headaches."

✳ ✳ ✳

PROGRESS REPORT

If you scan over to the end-files in this transmission you'll note that I have already completed the Official Reprimand Form which clearly outlines my technical violation, as well as the systems, procedures and materials involved. All you have to do is transmit the form on to Central.

But since nobody ever reads the end files, I will summarize the violation:

1. *I gave the Field Team permission to use the matter transformer to turn an abandoned office building into a titanium temporal sensor. In my view this is only a technical violation because: a) nobody saw us do it (except perhaps a few stray animals), and b) we returned the structure to its original form when we were finished. The only permanent change was when the transformation process vaporized some refuse and litter inside the building (okay, maybe a rat or two, as well). So, c) the office building is cleaner than when we found it.*
2. *But there was no other option, we needed as powerful a sensor as possible. We're looking at something far more serious than a time-travel hazard; these are the most extreme disruptions ever tracked. If they continue, the Whole Fabric could collapse.*
3. *And since the End of the Known Universe could much limit our options for career advancement, I would say that we are looking at a Very Bad Thing here.*

✳　　　✳　　　✳

THERAPIST:　　　　Why are you breathing so heavily?

HAL:　　　　I'm trying to stay calm, like you taught me to.

THERAPIST:　　　　Is something frightening you again?

HAL:　　　　I'm pretty nervous. The sun is too hot.

THERAPIST:　　　　What are you doing?

HAL:　　　　I'm driving somewhere with my ex-wife, Susan. The air conditioning on the car has gone; every time we turn into the direct sunlight, the heat is almost unbearable.

	Susan is really out of it, so I'm pulling the car to the side of the road. I'm trying to find some shade under those trees over there… good god!
THERAPIST:	What is it? What do you see?
HAL:	I've stopped the car and I get out. I look up at the trees, the leaves are all shriveled up. All the trees are dead.
THERAPIST:	What do you think killed all the trees?
HAL:	The sun, it's getting hotter… now I see that the grass is all brown and gray… there's sparrows lying on the ground.
THERAPIST:	What does Susan say?
HAL:	Nothing. She's still in the car.
THERAPIST:	You look upset, Hal. Is there something wrong with Susan?
HAL:	I'm trying to wake her up—

*   *   *

"Are you taking more pills?" Megan's voice vibrated through the wood of the bathroom door.

"I have a headache." Hal washed down two blue capsules and closed the medicine cabinet.

"You're getting addicted to those things." Megan looked at Hal with disapproval as he opened the door into the bedroom.

"Maybe," was all Hal could say as he lowered himself onto the futon.

"You're ingesting chemical toxins," said Megan. "Your bloodstream is going to look like a PCB dumpsite."

Hal sighed. "Small price to pay."

Megan sat up and glared at him: "You had another of those

dreams again, didn't you?"

Hal nodded. "It was the ozone hole one. You know, the one where Susan dies of radiation burns."

"Did you talk about it in your session this week?" Megan asked.

He rubbed his eyes. The drugs didn't really stop the headaches, they just made him apathetic about the pain.

"Yes, I did tell her," Hal replied wearily. "She thinks I may be repressing some long-term hostility about the break-up of my marriage."

"Really?" Megan looked skeptical, she had met Susan a few times.

"I'm having a little trouble with that analysis," Hal said. Relief, not anger, was the primary emotion associated with Susan's departure.

"Well..." Now Megan sounded hesitant. "I still think you ought to keep up with the sessions. It's got to be better than doping yourself up all the time."

"Okay," said Hal. "Nobody said hypnotherapy was a precision process."

They were silent for a time.

"Hal?"

"Yes, Megan?"

"How's the headache?"

"Still there."

"So, I guess sex is pretty much out of the question."

"It is if you want me to join you."

"I see." Megan tried hard not to sound annoyed.

More silence. Then:

"Hal?"

"Yes, Megan."

"Did you agree to participate in some voter demographics survey for the Libertarian Peoples Party?"

Hal knew this scenario from previous headaches. With the prospect of love-making impossible, the time before sleep would be used as a household planning meeting.

"Not that I remember," Hal replied.

"Well, they said you did," Megan said. "They said they wanted to come around to the house and get you to fill out a survey."

"I really don't know a thing about it," said Hal.

"Well, they sound like a bunch of Nazis."

Possibly, thought Hal.

"If you didn't agree to take their survey," continued Megan, "why don't you call them up and tell them to go away?"

"First thing."

❋   ❋   ❋

PROGRESS REPORT

Or lack of progress report. I hope some data arranger at Central is getting genuine pleasure from the fact that as the universe unravels around us, my personnel have conformed to all cross-cultural and inter-species interaction regulations.

Frankly, I'm terrified, and I'm not sure anyone at Galactic Central really appreciates the magnitude of what we're sitting on here. I know you've received our findings, so do the math. Time particles can't bounce around like this without terrible consequences.

Our folklorist is struggling heroically with these restrictions as she continues to devise new "culturally appropriate interactive strategies" for the Field Team. At least this keeps some of my personnel busy. In the absence of the new equipment I requested, we are searching for an "existential informant", i.e. an inhabitant of this planet who might be personally experiencing some aspect of this time-space. If we can interrogate the right informant, we might find out how the phenomenon is playing out.

We are tracking several possible subjects.

❋   ❋   ❋

THERAPIST: So, where are you now?

HAL: At a party, the first one I've been to since my divorce.

THERAPIST: When was that?

HAL: 1979, in the fall.

THERAPIST: What are you doing at the party?

HAL: Drinking too much.

THERAPIST: What's happening at the party? Are you having a good time?

HAL: Lots of people are there and they're having lots of fun. They're all very young and attractive.

THERAPIST: How does that make you feel?

HAL: Absolutely terrible. I don't know how to be single anymore.

THERAPIST: So what happens next?

HAL: I start wandering around, looking for somewhere to sit. That's when I see her.

THERAPIST: Who do you see?

HAL: Megan... for the first time... She's wearing these huge earrings and this peasant skirt. She reminds me of a cross between Eleanor Roosevelt and Kate Bush.

THERAPIST: And what is Megan doing?

HAL: She's telling off a couple of skinheads who are wearing T-shirts that read "BOMB THE BOATS AND FEED THE FISHES."

THERAPIST: What are the skinheads doing?

HAL: They look like they can't think of anything to say. Mostly they look scared and nervous, she's really blasting them.

THERAPIST: And how are you reacting to this?

HAL: Well, she's going on and on now. I look around and most of the people at the party look like they're hoping she'll shut up soon.

THERAPIST: How do you feel about what Megan is saying, Hal? Do you want her to stop talking?

HAL: Well, I think she's maybe a little nuts for taking on the skinheads, but no, I think I like her. At least she believes in something... Hey!

THERAPIST: What is it, Hal?

HAL: That's funny!

THERAPIST: What do you mean, Hal?

HAL: Now she's just come over to me and asks why I'm smiling at her, she thinks I'm laughing at her...

THERAPIST: Hal, you stopped just then, what happened?

HAL: Scene change. We're having breakfast at Megan's apartment.

THERAPIST: Anything you want to say about the interval of time you skipped?

HAL: No, it's personal.

THERAPIST: But you can talk about what happened afterwards?

HAL: Sure, it's a nice sunny morning and we're

eating something strange and crunchy. Whatever it is, it tastes better than it looks.

THERAPIST: It sounds wonderful. So why did you tell me this was a bad dream?

HAL: I'm not sure I want to remember this.

THERAPIST: Remember what?

HAL: I want to wake up now. Can I please wake up now?

THERAPIST: Hal, you have to try to make progress here. To get past the pain, you'll have to face what caused it. What happens next?

HAL: Megan gets up and answers the door. It's the lady who lives down the hall. She's almost hysterical.

THERAPIST: Why?

HAL: It's something she wants us to see on TV. The lady doesn't speak English too well, I think she wants Megan to explain to her what's going on. We go over to the lady's apartment. There's a lot of kids there, probably watching cartoons before the news bulletins started.

THERAPIST: News bulletins?

HAL: Something about the Soviets in Afghanistan leading to some kind of an exchange in Europe. Now there's an announcement from NATO... there's been another exchange with them and the Russians. Megan looks pale and says something in Spanish to the lady. God, now everybody's crying. Like a moron, I ask Megan to tell me what's going on.

THERAPIST: What does she say, Hal?

HAL: What the hell do you think? The missiles are in the air, we have less than 20 minutes before they hit!

✳   ✳   ✳

Megan was tying back the huge mass of her black hair.

"Can't stay," she said as Hal approached the bathroom. "I have to chair this week's meeting."

Hal nodded. This was the weekly meeting of the local chapter of the Earth Defense Fund. They probably wanted to be sure to cash the last cheque he'd written them.

Megan charged into the bedroom.

"How was your session?" she called out.

Hal looked through the bedroom doorway and watched Megan tighten a woven belt over a faded batik skirt. Twenty years in the same wardrobe, he thought, and she still looks good.

"It was probably my last," Hal said.

"What happened?" Megan demanded.

"My therapist feels that unless I'm prepared to be honest with him, there's no point in continuing with the sessions." Hal could feel another headache coming on. This probably had nothing to do with his dreams; he was just thinking about all the money they'd spent on hypnotism.

"You know that our health insurance doesn't cover this." Megan was thinking the same thing.

"I know."

They sat in silence for a moment. "Well, I think that really undermines my confidence in hypnotherapy," Megan said eventually.

Typical, thought Hal. Megan immediately sided with him; she wouldn't think for an instant that the therapist might be right.

The intercom buzzed. Megan got up and pushed the speaker button.

"Ultimate Vacuum," a voice squawked out. "We're here for your free demonstration."

"You're going to have to deal with this," Megan said to Hal as she opened the front door. "I really wish you wouldn't agree to this stuff."

"But, I didn't—" began Hal.

Megan disappeared down the hall. "Especially now..." her voice trailed off.

Megan was gone. Off to save the world, once again, thought Hal.

A few moments later the representatives of the Ultimate Vacuum Cleaner Corporation were in the living room. They introduced themselves as Ms. Wiper and Mr. Chaffey. Both were like every sales representative Hal had ever seen: people who had spent just a little too much money on the wrong clothes and the wrong haircuts.

"I hope you don't mind that I brought my associate Mr. Chaffey along," said Ms. Wiper. "He's a trainee and this is part of his in-field development."

Mr. Chaffey struggled to open a large aluminum-lined suitcase.

"Happy to help," replied Hal.

"It's very kind of your..." Ms. Wiper paused and glanced meaningfully at Hal. "...partner? To agree to this demonstration."

Hal was surprised. Megan had agreed to this? She must have forgotten.

Within a couple of minutes, Ms. Wiper and Mr. Chaffey had assembled what they called the "Millennium Model of the Ultimate Vacuum Purification System". Then Ms. Wiper pointed at the wall of Greenpeace and Amnesty International posters lining the far wall of the living room.

"I see that your household is concerned with social justice and environmental responsibility," Ms. Wiper said. "Then the Millennium Model is just the product for you. It is a completely green system, built from all recycled and ecologically friendly materials. This vacuum was designed by an egalitarian techno-cooperative and manufactured by an all-union worker owned facility in Saskatchewan. The Millennium Model was created to maintain natural domestic eco-systems through powerful but sympathetic cleaning mechanisms."

This is the most adaptive sales pitch I've ever heard, thought Hal. Megan will be really sorry she missed this.

Then Ms. Wiper and Mr. Chaffey went into the detailed demonstration. They explained all the nozzles and attachments;

they used an innovative new power sweeper to pull dirt out of a rug that already looked clean; and they vividly illustrated the sheer power of the Ultimate Vacuum's motor by sucking up some big bullets.

Eventually, they pulled out a handful of documents: sales agreements and payment plans.

At this point, Hal felt ethically bound to stop the demonstration.

"I'm very sorry," he said to Ms. Wiper and Mr. Chaffey. "You have a very interesting vacuum cleaner, but my partner and I really can't afford any major purchases right now."

Mr. Chaffey looked over to Ms. Wiper. "Have we met all the criteria?" he asked.

Ms. Wiper nodded. "We've established our presence in completely native terms."

This didn't mean a thing to Hal. "Excuse me…" he began.

They still weren't paying any attention to him; Mr. Chaffey reached over and opened a panel at the back of the Ultimate Vacuum machine.

"I just hope this is the right guy," Ms. Wiper said.

An oscillating sound came from inside the Ultimate Vacuum. Mr. Chaffey looked at something moving there and nodded his head.

"Oh, yeah," he said. "This is the one, we're right at the centre of the Temporal Distortion."

"I don't think we have anything like that around here," said Hal.

Ms. Wiper pointed her finger at Hal. "Quiet," she said.

This is really rude, thought Hal. He got up from the futon with the intention of opening the door and escorting the sales representatives out. But then, somewhat unexpectedly, the tip of Ms. Wiper's finger popped off and a flash of copper flew across the room. A tiny metal shard embedded itself in Hal's neck, and he fell to the floor.

He was still conscious, but he couldn't move. Mr. Chaffey rolled him onto his back, which gave him a good look at the Ultimate Vacuum at very close range. Hal could see Mr. Chaffey pull out what looked like a pulsating mass of light and metal from inside the machine.

"Can he talk?" asked Mr. Chaffey.

"I only used a small dose," Ms. Wiper replied. "Only the gross motor functions are shut down."

Hal really wished that he was completely unconscious because he could have avoided being aware of what was going to happen next: Mr. Chaffey pulled out two flexible cables from inside the Ultimate Vacuum. There were three-inch glass needles at the end of each cable. Mr. Chaffey carefully positioned the needles over Hal's forehead and then plunged them into Hal's skull.

Ouch, thought Hal. Another headache.

✳   ✳   ✳

INTERROGATOR #1:   Can you hear me, sir? Can you speak?

HAL: Yes.

INTERROGATOR #2:   Sir, have you been experiencing attacks of disorientation and confusion?

HAL: All the time. Can you be more specific?

INTERROGATOR #1:   Do you feel like the normal sequence of cause and effect is breaking down in your life?

HAL: Ouch! Ow!

INTERROGATOR #2:   The readings say he doesn't understand your question.

HAL: Jeez, this really hurts… ow… arghhhh!

INTERROGATOR #1:   Take it easy, sir. This is much less painful if you concentrate on answering the questions. And try to use actual words whenever possible.

HAL: Eeeek! Okay, okay, I'll try.

INTERROGATOR #2:   Now, can you tell us if you've been having any really unusual experiences recently?

HAL: Before tonight? Not really.

INTERROGATOR #2:   Instruments say he's telling the truth.

INTERROGATOR #1:   That's impossible, he's at dead centre in the disruption!

HAL: Oh, god, this is almost as bad as the nightmares!

INTERROGATOR #2:   He could be interpreting the breakdown as subconscious events.

INTERROGATOR #1:   You're having strange dreams?

HAL: Yeah, I have recurring dreams. Bad dreams. And I have headaches when I wake up.

INTERROGATOR #1:   How often do you have these dreams?

HAL: It varies. Sometimes they happen a lot, sometimes hardly ever.

INTERROGATOR #1:   Have you had a bad dream recently?

HAL: Day before yesterday.

INTERROGATOR #2:   We picked up some serious phenomena that night.

INTERROGATOR #1:   What was that dream about, sir?

HAL: I'm sitting in High Park. There's bodies everywhere. Some people in gas masks and plastic suits are putting them in big baggies. I'm coughing up blood, yup, I'm dying. Looks like everybody's dying.

INTERROGATOR #1:   Why is everyone dying?

HAL: Plague. Incredibly infectious, it's like the

whole planet's immune system has collapsed.

INTERROGATOR #2: Was this a really vivid dream? Like it was almost real?

HAL: Absolutely real.

INTERROGATOR #1: Was this dream like the others?

HAL: Every dream is like this! Every dream is about the end of the world!

INTERROGATOR #1: The end of your world?

HAL: My world? Yeah, I guess so. I have a really terrible nightmare about some new way that the human race gets destroyed, but then it's like a big flickering effect in my head, and I wake up.

INTERROGATOR #1: You wake up and then what happens?

HAL: The world is back to normal, everybody's there. And I have an incredible migraine.

INTERROGATOR #1: And nothing's changed?

HAL: For a while it feels like everything's changed.

✳   ✳   ✳

PROGRESS REPORT

I shouldn't have been too surprised at the way that poor creature was experiencing what Central has so carefully labeled "the Advanced T/S Irregularity". Given their native level of knowledge, the only way he could have interpreted the regular cycle of planetary destruction and re-creation would be as a dream or a hallucination. Our folklorist and technician advise me that the subject was a remarkably unimaginative man, so he believed himself to be the victim of chronic nightmares.

I will not, however, dwell on the lack of scientific insight into the situation, because despite all the readings we still have no credible explanation of the "Irregularity". Perhaps some system-wide catastrophe was so profound that it caused an expanding temporal loop that endlessly generated new ways for this tiny world to end. Certainly, we have no evidence of any intelligent agency at work. I can't resist pointing out that we might not have to resort to speculation if Central had allocated the equipment I originally requested.

Whatever started the cycle, we are about to end it. Once we pass into the safety zone past the edge of this solar system, the dark-matter device we directed at their sun will detonate. I've never seen these devices in operation before, but I understand that there won't be much to see when the inner planets implode. It might be interesting to watch what happens to the big gas giants though.

I'm getting sidetracked here. Just so you know, I feel pretty bad about destroying this solar system and all its inhabitants. There was nothing really wrong with those Earthers. But I suppose this "cosmological triage" (as Central so elegantly puts it) is actually necessary in this case. We can't let an escalating temporal loop start to unravel the structure of reality. I keep telling myself that the planet was probably doomed anyway—we're just making it final.

If nothing else, we were able to put that poor dreamer out of his misery.

✻　　✻　　✻

Incredible winds. The ground disintegrating. Enormous pressure.

Nothing.

It was over very quickly.

The dream was over so fast that Hal wasn't sure how to describe it. But the dream had generated a huge headache. Full aura migraine. When he sat up in bed Hal discovered that he couldn't see out of one eye.

It took more than ten minutes for Hal to put on his housecoat and drag himself into the kitchen. Megan was drinking herbal tea and listening to public radio. The muted voices of the Sunday morning news program were talking about the Galactic Superculture. This was a big news story a few years ago when the Superculture's signal was first picked up. But the excitement died down when it was revealed that the aliens wouldn't actually arrive for another fifty or sixty years. Now, only NPR and CBC seemed to carry anything about it anymore.

Megan was still interested because she had just helped set up a group to lobby the Federal Government to release the original radio transmissions from the Superculture. The group was convinced that vital information about the safety of the planet was being withheld.

Hal didn't mind though. Save-the-World Megan needed occasional fresh doses of agitprop activity to keep her sharp.

Megan saw Hal's ashen face. "Oh, no!" she cried. "Not another one!"

It hurt when Hal nodded his head.

"Sit down and have some tea," she said. "And keep your eyes closed."

Hal took Megan's advice. The tea (he never could tell one herb from another) did seem to ease the pain. And in the darkness, Hal could smell all of Megan's familiar smells. This made him feel better.

And thankful that he was one of Megan's causes, too.

THAT WHICH IS NECESSARY

"The state of this manuscript is not suitable for submission to a professional magazine."

Punch in the stomach number one.

"Your characters have no life to them. The setting for the story is sterile and lifeless. You need to make it grittier, more flawed."

Oof, number two.

"Your usage is all over the place. You can't use number symbols for single digit numerals."

Another oof. Not a huge one, but I felt really stupid.

"There is just a great deal of work that needs to be done before this manuscript will be anything approaching a publishable story."

Really, really stupid.

I sat there at the other end of Judith Merril's desk, wondering if I should stop wasting her time and get the hell out of there. While I waited for my legs to power up for my departure, Judith Merril handed the manuscript back to me.

"We're organizing a writers workshop based on the Milford Method."

Why was she telling me this?

"I think you should consider joining. It *might* help you develop as a writer."

It was my first meeting with Judith Merril and it was a formal, 60-minute consultation at the Space Out Library[7] in Toronto.

I wanted to go into my meeting with her with the best work possible so I adapted a teleplay I had been pitching as an episode for the 1980s version of *The Twilight Zone*. I thought the premise was strong and I had gotten some positive responses from readers and agents in Los Angeles and Toronto.

I can't exactly say that Judith Merril did me a kindness that day

---

7   A few years later, and under the usual controversial circumstances, SOL's name was later changed to the more Toronto-appropriate Merril Collection of Science Fiction, Fantasy and Speculation. As far as I know, Judith Merril did not publicly object to the re-branding but I'm reasonably sure she thought the new name was much too formal.

but she did do something far more important. She helped me to understand that I *had* to be writer. Remember that creative pathology I mentioned in the introduction?

I was never able to get the prose version of this narrative to work properly. When I ran the story through the Cecil Street workshop they unanimously disliked it. Keith Scott's comments made the most impression on me:

"Your story reads like the minutes of a meeting. A very boring meeting." He later advised me to hang on to my day job. Keith was a good guy and a talented writer; he was just calling it as he saw it.

Even so, I figured I still had something with this one and when the opportunity came up to transcribe the visual story to an audio experience I was delighted when Shoestring Radio Theater agreed to broadcast it. I present the radio script because I believe it is the truest version of the story.

A 21ST CENTURY SCIENTIFIC ROMANCE

A RADIO PLAY

First broadcast on:
September 6, 2005
Shoestring Radio Theatre
National Public Radio, Satellite Network

SETTING:

The year is 2014. Most of the action takes place on board the US Space Defense Network orbital station *High Mandate*.

In between scenes we also hear occasional voices of actual writers, leaders and military strategists.

CHARACTERS

CAPTAIN LINDSEY WEISS – Crew Psychologist and Medical Officer. Very dedicated but somewhat under-valued by her military peers.

CAPTAIN ANTHONY STERN – He claims to be an astro-pilot in the League of Nations Stratos Patrol. Weiss thinks differently.

MAJOR REG PAULIE – Head of Security and Tactical Advisor for *High Mandate*. The stress of the situation is making him increasingly impatient and occasionally abusive.

GENERAL PHILIP WHITMAN – Commander of *High Mandate*. He tries very hard to lead effectively but he is too intelligent not to be worried and tired by what he's asked to do. In action he's not very different from Paulie.

STRATEGIC AI – the audio interface for *High Mandate*'s on-board military central computer.

OFFICERS AND TECHNICIANS ON BOARD THE HIGH MANDATE

CHIEF LIBRARIAN – of the Merril Collection of Science Fiction, Fantasy and Speculation.

AN ELDERLY VISITOR – to the Merril Collection.

VOICES FROM THE SUB-ETHER:

US PRESIDENT RONALD REAGAN – quoting from his 1983 presidential address announcing the Strategic Defense Initiative AKA "Star Wars" programme.

PHILIP NOWLAN – the co-creator of the 1930s comic strip character "Buck Rogers in the 25th Century".

GENERAL JOHN ASHY – Commander-in-Chief US Space Command/NORAD in 1996 address to the US Congress regarding the Ballistic Missile Defense Program.

BILL GRAHAM – Canadian Foreign Minister in 2004.

<u>SCENE 1.</u>

<u>THE MYSTERIOUS SUB-ETHER OF OUR COLLECTIVE MEMORIES AND IMAGINATION.</u>

NOWLAN: (VO/D.) … I found myself in a world in which gravity had been conquered by means of truly marvelous inventions.

REAGAN: (VO/D.) … I want to share with Americans a vision of hope…

NOWLAN: (VO/D.) … one of the most amazing weapons of the 25th Century was the lightning gun…

REAGAN: (VO/D.) … what if free people could live secure in the knowledge that we could intercept and destroy strategic ballistic missiles before they reach our own soil…

NOWLAN: (VO/D.) … it was an electronic generator and projector…

REAGAN: (VO/D.) … I hereby appeal to the scientists of America to turn their great talents to the development of an anti-ballistic missile system capable of destroying enemy missiles before they could reach their targets…

NOWLAN: … Science had accomplished wonders!

SCENE 2.

HIGH MANDATE COMMAND CORE.
06: 00 HOURS.

WEISS: (VO) The time: The year 2014. The place: The space defense station *High Mandate*. On bad days we call it the best seat in the house for the end of the world. Maybe the President's last speech is making me more pessimistic than usual. And I can be like that right now… (STARTS TO FADE)… I have to keep the crew optimal…

SOUND: RISES ONTO A MONTAGE OF TECH-TALK FROM THE COMMAND CORE TEAM.

TECH #1:	… prepare for de-scramble on incoming transmission…
TECH #2:	… radar cloaking system maintaining routine function…
TECH #3:	… slight deviation in geosynchronous orbit. Correct by 0.0072 degrees…
TECH #2:	… Strategic AI System is running five by five…
TECH #1:	… but it's past six, where's the coffee?
TECH #3:	Northern Hemisphere scan confirmed. We have sighted 16 unregistered orbiters moving into position.
WHITMAN:	What do you make of that, Major?
PAULIE:	It's got to be some kind of military ramp-up.
WHITMAN:	I agree; the Rogues aren't planning on pulling back anytime soon.
TECH #2:	Sir! Something's just appeared on the immediate-range scanners!
WHITMAN:	What it is, soldier?
TECH #2:	It just dropped into space… about 20 clicks from the station.
PAULIE:	Possible nuclear device?
TECH #1:	No radiation readings. Too small for a space laser.
WHITMAN:	Tell the EVA team to get out there and take a

look.

SCENE 3.

THE MYSTERIOUS SUB-ETHER.

GRAHAM: (VO/D.) … space weapons are a figment of the imagination…

SCENE 4.

MEDICAL WARD OF THE *HIGH MANDATE.* 10:45 HOURS.

WEISS: They found something, or rather someone out there in space. But we don't call it space anymore, it's an "Orbital Tactical Zone". O.T.Z., Third Layer. (BEAT) I hate this. I didn't sign up to work in an acronym. I joined up to explore the universe.

SOUND: WEISS AND PAULIE ENTER. STERN SITS UP IN HIS BED.

STERN: At last, someone with rank!

WEISS: I'm Captain Weiss, the crew psychologist and this is Major Paulie. He's in charge of Station security.

PAULIE: We need to ask you a few questions.

STERN: Certainly.

PAULIE: What is your full name and rank?

STERN: I am Anthony Edward Stern. Captain in the League of Nations Stratos Patrol.

WEISS: League of Nations?

PAULIE: Stratos Patrol?

STERN: Surely you recognize the uniform.

WEISS: (A LITTLE HESITANT) How did you get so close to this station? Didn't you know this was a restricted area?

STERN: I had no idea this area was restricted because I had no idea this base existed.

PAULIE: (LOW, ASTONISHED) No idea...?

STERN: And I don't know how I got so close because I have no idea how I got here.

PAULIE: Do you remember how you got into orbital space?

STERN: (SIGHS) In a rocketship, obviously. I was en route to join the Mars Expeditionary Fleet when I picked up some disturbance on my sub-ether radio. After that... I woke up in this room.

PAULIE: That doesn't quite scan, "Captain".

WEISS: (INTERRUPTS) Thanks very much, Captain. (PAUSE, THINGS ARE TENSE) I'm afraid we'll have to keep you here for a few more medical tests.

STERN: Captain Weiss! I have to get back to my ship! Please notify Stratos HQ and arrange for my transport!

WEISS: I'm sorry Captain, there's nothing I can do at this time. Please tell the guard if there's

	anything else you'd like to tell me or Major Paulie.

SCENE 5.

THE MYSTERIOUS SUB-ETHER

NOWLAN:	(VO/D.) … *Mars*, with its clear sparkling air, its cloudless skies, and its pale, greenish-yellow sunshine, its vast red deserts and great canals…

SCENE 6.

ACCESS CORRIDOR. 11:00 HOURS.

SOUND:	WEISS AND PAULIE PULLING THEMSELVES ALONG IN ZERO GRAVITY.
WEISS:	According to the initial test results, there's no evidence of brain damage, hallucinogenic chemicals or simple psychosis. He seems like a normal man in a uniform no one's ever seen, and in the service of a government that doesn't exist.
PAULIE:	If he's sane. That means he could be an enemy agent.
WEISS:	Pretty inept spy. He's rather conspicuous and so far he's only seen the inside of the infirmary.
PAULIE:	Okay, he's total a mystery. (SARCASTIC) Now, isn't that helpful?

SCENE 7.

THE MYSTERIOUS SUB-ETHER.

ASHY: (VO/D.) We're going to fight a war in space.

SCENE 8.

HIGH MANDATE CONFERENCE ROOM.
12:00 HOURS.

WEISS: (VO): Most of the time we spend in orbit is pretty tedious. I spend most of my time helping the crew cope with boredom. That's not my job today.

SOUND: HISS OF STATIC ON A VIDEO SPEAKER. MONITOR CLICKS OFF.

WHITMAN: That tape was made by one of our remote sensors about an hour and thirty-five minutes ago.

JUNIOR OFFICER: How are they doing it? How are they taking out the first and second layers?

SENIOR
TECHNICIAN: Low-tech.

JUNIOR OFFICER: Low-tech?

SENIOR
TECHNICIAN: They're sending up big balloons covered with non-reflective paint and full of ball bearings. When they get close to one of our satellites they just set off a charge and pow! They've just launched about 2,000 micro-missiles.

PAULIE: So, we're bound to lose our sensors.

SENIOR
TECHNICIAN: Yeah, at least one or two.

PAULIE:	Our sensors cost 30 million per unit!
SENIOR TECHNICIAN:	(SIGHS) And the damn things probably only cost the Rogues about 800 bucks.
SOUND:	<u>A QUIET ROUND OF CURSES AND WHISTLES AROUND THE TABLE.</u>
JUNIOR OFFICER:	If they put enough holes in the Net…
PAULIE:	We become useless, unable to coordinate any operations for Cheyenne Mountain.
SENIOR TECHNICIAN:	Don't forget, we're also a sitting duck if enough of the Network goes down.
PAULIE:	Yes, thank you for reminding us of that interesting possibility.
WHITMAN:	(INTERRUPTS) I believe the phrase, 'use or lose' is appropriate here. (SUDDEN SILENCE, BEAT) Please open your files.
SOUND:	<u>RUSTLING OF PAPER AS THE OFFICERS AND TECHNICIANS TEAR OPEN THEIR ENVELOPES.</u>
WEISS:	(CLOSE/LOW) Omega Option. Well, you can't get more obvious than that.
WHITMAN:	I don't know about you, ladies and gentlemen but these are pretty much the orders that I've always hoped we'd never receive.
SOUND:	<u>MORE RUSTLING OF PAPER AS THE SOLDIERS SKIM THROUGH THE CONTENTS OF THEIR FILES.</u>

WHITMAN:	The Defense Department has confirmed our reports that the Rogue States are coordinating a systematic attack on the Space Defense Network.
PAULIE:	Earthside Intelligence also advises that we can expect major terrorist actions in Europe and North America. As the General has indicated, we could be in a 'use or lose' situation.
WHITMAN:	(SIGHS) And by the authority of the Commander-in-Chief, we *will* use it if we have to.
SOUND:	<u>METALLIC CLICKS AS WHITMAN AND PAULIE INSERT KEYS INTO SLOTS IN THE CONFERENCE ROOM TABLE.</u>
STRATEGIC AI SYSTEM:	(D. MECHANICAL DEVICE) Countdown activated.
WHITMAN:	The Rogues now have twenty-four hours to stop their aggression and return to normal alert condition.
PAULIE:	And for all of your information, when we activated the chronometer, we also just broadcast a taped ultimatum from the President of the United States to the leaders of the Rogue consortium.
SOUND:	<u>A REPEATING ELECTRONIC TONE AS THE TIMER TICKS AWAY.</u>
PAULIE:	Any questions?
JUNIOR OFFICER:	What happens if they miss the deadline?

WHITMAN: Then we are ordered to exercise the Omega Option and completely, and for all time, destroy the Rogues' capacity to make war.

WEISS: (VO/CLOSE) You mean nuke them into oblivion, don't you, general?

PAULIE: Everyone, your first priority right now is to review all Omega procedures and scenarios on an ASAP basis.

WHITMAN: Dismissed, ladies and gentlemen.

SOUNDS: THE CREW LEAVES THE CONFERENCE ROOM.

WHITMAN: (LOW) Major. Captain. Please wait a moment.

WEISS/PAULIE: (LOW/UNISON) Yes, sir.

SOUND: LAST OF THE SOLDIERS LEAVE. DOOR CLOSES.

WHITMAN: What's your opinion on the crew's state of mind? Will they be able to take us into total war if they have to?

WEISS: I saw no unexpected reactions during the meeting. (BEAT) Those men and women will carry out any orders you give them.

WHITMAN: Good.

WEISS: (VO/CLOSE) Yeah, it's great.

WHITMAN: Major, what's our security situation? Any possibility of sabotage?

PAULIE: At this point, not sabotage as such, sir. (BEAT) It's more a question of possible infiltration.

WHITMAN: (SIGHS) That sounds fascinating. What do you have to report?

PAULIE: It's our uninvited guest, sir. In my opinion…

WEISS: (INTERRUPTS) It's too early to make any conclusions or recommendations. We need further investigation, sir.

PAULIE: (ANNOYED) The man could be some sort of diversion to disorient the crew at a time of stress.

WEISS: That's a completely premature conclusion! He may be an amnesiac, someone from an unregistered spacecraft.

PAULIE: Sir, we found completely unfamiliar technology on this man. Some of his life-support equipment looked *handcrafted*. The joints in his space suit were made of vulcanized rubber instead of the usual synthetic plastic. His radio gear had vacuum tubes—*vacuum tubes*! They haven't been used in Air Force equipment in the last fifty years! No, this man can only be part of an elaborate hoax, some insane disinformation from the Rogues.

WEISS: I cannot agree. I saw no evidence of terrorist training in the man's behavior. He seems to be exactly what he claims. It's not his fault we can't account for him.

WHITMAN: I am satisfied that you two have not reached a consensus on the origin and purpose of our visitor. (BEAT) Major; proceed with the next level of the standard security investigation. I hereby authorize the use of chemical agents.

WEISS: (CONCERNED) Sir…

WHITMAN: (INTERRUPTS) Captain, I am also very interested in reading your in-depth psychological profile on the intruder. I hope your written conclusions give us something more concrete to work with here.

WEISS: Thank you.

SCENE 9.

WEISS' OFFICE. 14:30 HOURS.

WEISS: (VO) Even under the influence of those drugs, he looks so honest, so noble. The man can't be a spy. I don't even like to think of him as a crazy person. (BEAT) You know, I think I must be under a lot of stress.

PAULIE: (D. ON RECORDING) What is your real name?

STERN: (D. ON RECORDING/A LITTLE SLURRED) Major Paulie, my name is *still* Anthony Stern and I am *still* a captain in the Stratos Patrol.

WEISS: (SARCASTIC) Do you think his name *really* is Anthony Stern?

PAULIE: (LIVE) Yes, or else the Rogues can now train their agents to resist truth serum.

PAULIE: (D. ON RECORDING) Where did you get your spacesuit?

STERN: (D. ON RECORDING) Standard Stratos Patrol issue.

PAULIE: (D. ON RECORDING) How did you know we were in a war-readiness condition?

STERN: (D. ON RECORDING) Impossible. There hasn't been a war since 1918.

WEISS: (LOW) Good God!

PAULIE: (D. ON RECORDING) What government are you working for?

STERN: (D. ON RECORDING) I owe allegiance to the World Government under the League of Nations.

SOUND: PAULIE PRESSES THE PAUSE BUTTON.

PAULIE: What's your opinion?

WEISS: First, there are no symptoms of mind control or the usual forms of psychosis. Second, Stern obviously can't be who he says he is. The League of Nations was defunct by the 1930's and it was never any form of world government; there seems to be some sort of nostalgia factor in his complex. Third, he said that there's been no war since 1918. A pretty sweeping denial of the last hundred years.

PAULIE: Thank you, Captain, I have read a history book.

WEISS: I'm sure. Now. I think the crucial point is that Stern is rejecting the current world crisis.

PAULIE: How would he do that?

WEISS: He's had to build an elaborate protective fantasy; a utopia where all countries are at

	peace and co-operate in the exploration of space. The uniform, the spacesuit, even the badges… he must have made them as props to support his fantasy.
PAULIE:	And he propelled himself into orbital space on the wings of his fantasy?
WEISS:	He probably bailed out of a commercial shuttle or stowed away on an unmanned industrial flight.
PAULIE:	That's… (BEAT)… conceivable.
WEISS:	If you can link the time of Stern's appearance with the launch schedules of passenger and freighter flights, we might even be able to prove it.
SOUND:	<u>BUZZER OF INTERCOMM.</u>
TECHNICIAN:	(D. ON SPEAKER) Major Paulie, we've just moved into First Alert Status. General Whitman wants you at Command Core immediately.
PAULIE:	Captain Weiss, I'll look into it when I get the time.
SOUND:	<u>PAULIE LEAVES.</u>
WEISS:	(CLOSE) Noble… heroic… (BEAT)… of course…
SOUND:	<u>THE PSYCHOLOGIST PRESSES A BUTTON ON THE INTERCOM CONTROL.</u>
TECHNICIAN:	(D. ON SPEAKER) Communications.
WEISS:	This is Captain Weiss. I need a transmission

	to the Merril Collection in Toronto, Canada.
TECHNICAN:	(D. ON SPEAKER) The Merril Collection?
WEISS:	It's a science fiction reference library. Didn't you ever watch *Star Trek* when you were a kid?
TECHNICIAN:	(D. ON SPEAKER) Captain Weiss, we're at First Alert Status. No non-essential Earth-side communications.
WEISS:	I'm acting on the authority of Major Paulie.
TECHNICIAN:	(D. ON SPEAKER) Yes, ma'am!

SCENE 10.

COMMAND CORE. 14:40 HOURS.

SOUND:	THE ROOM BUZZES WITH TECHNICAL CHATTER AS AN EMERGENCY SHIFT WORKS AT THE TERMINALS. DOOR OPENS.
PAULIE:	General, I came as fast as I—(BEAT, THEN SHOCKED) How did this happen?
WHITMAN:	Get me the signal from remote sensor 167.
TECH #1:	They just took out remote sensor 167!
PAULIE:	(DISTRESSED) What happened?
WHITMAN:	They destroyed twenty percent of the Network.
PAULIE:	*Twenty percent?!*
WHITMAN:	They're up in the Second Layer with a lot

more than we realized.

PAULIE: Good god. (CATCHES HIS BREATH) So what's next?

WHITMAN: Activate the Strategic AI! I want a response menu!

STRATEGIC
AI SYSTEM: (D. MECHANICAL DEVICE) Situation: Rogue States action on Space Defense Network. 18.72% defense capacity destroyed. Today's Response Menu: A) No retaliation: Strategic instability. Increased risk of further attack. B) Action on Earthside target: incalculable escalation of conflict. Compromise of Presidential Ultimatum. C) Action on orbital target: No measurable strategic advantage. Ultimatum maintained.

WHITMAN: (CALLS OUT) Option C! Possible targets.

STRATEGIC
AI SYSTEM: (D. MECHANICAL DEVICE) Feasible targets: 1) North Korean passenger fuel transport. 2) Weather satellite system over Central Africa. 3) Manned space laboratory *Sun Yat Sen*. Possible cover for orbital weapons construct.

WHITMAN: Target Three!

SOUND: <u>THE TELEPHONE ON TECH #1'S CONSOLE RINGS. THE SOLDIER PICKS UP THE RECEIVER.</u>

TECH #1:   Message from the President's Office. They confirm approval of Option C and Target Three.

WHITMAN: Very good.

SOUND:	<u>HIGH-PITCHED WHINE OF A RADAR SCAN.</u>
TECH #2:	We have three orbital missile launchers in range.
PAULIE:	(LOW) Classic triangulation.
WHITMAN:	Proceed.
TECH #3:	Yes, sir!
SOUND:	<u>THE TECHNICIAN PUNCHES IN A SERIES OF NUMBERS. SHRILL TONES OF THE TARGETING COMPUTER.</u>
WHITMAN:	Fire.
SOUND:	<u>THE TONES GROW HIGHER AND LOUDER, THEN SUDDENLY STOP.</u>
TECH #3:	(EXCITED) *Direct hit!*
PAULIE:	Keeping scanning, soldier.
TECH #1:	Remote sensor report... civilian space laboratory... completely destroyed... no escape pods... no survivors.
PAULIE:	What do you mean "*civilian*"?
TECH #2:	Latest from the scanners: there's no evidence of radiation or advanced weapons systems.
PAULIE:	We misread the target...
WHITMAN:	(LOW) Damn.
PAULIE:	(LOW) It doesn't matter, sir.

WHITMAN: (OUTRAGED) *What?!* We just vaporized two dozen Chinese scientists!

PAULIE: That's unfortunate. (BEAT) But the net strategic effect is still the same.

SCENE 11.

WEISS' OFFICE. 13:00 HOURS.

WEISS: (VO) Now I'm wondering if I'm the one who's lost touch with reality (BEAT)… but my grandfather was a huge sci-fi nerd, there was something he told me about…

SOUND: INTERCOMM BUZZES.

WEISS: Yes?

TECHNICIAN: (D. ON SPEAKER) Sorry to take so long, Captain Weiss. We've had a lot of interference.

WEISS: No problem.

TECHNICIAN: We've downloaded the data from the Merril Collection, just check your terminal.

WEISS: Thanks.

SOUND: WEISS ENTERS SOMETHING ON HER COMPUTER KEYBOARD. THERE IS STATIC AND THEN TINNY ORCHESTRAL MUSIC ON THE TERMINAL SPEAKER.

1930s STYLE
ANNOUNCER: (D. ON SPEAKER) Yes, folks! It's time for the stunning science stories of Anthony Stern! Mars Explorer! Hero of the Spaceways!

SOUND: THE MUSIC TAKES AN OMINOUS BUT CHEESY

<u>TURN.</u>

When we last left Captain Stern and his friends were rocketing towards a rift in the fabric of space and time.

<u>SOUND:</u>	<u>WEISS PAUSES THE RECORDING.</u>
TECHNICIAN:	(D. ON SPEAKER) Is that what you're looking for, Captain?
WEISS:	(SIGHS) Yes, thank you.

<u>SCENE 12.</u>

<u>COMMAND CORE. 15:30 HOURS</u>

<u>SOUND:</u>	<u>TECHNICIANS AT WORK AT THEIR STATIONS.</u>
PAULIE:	(OFF) General Whitman!
WHITMAN:	Report, Major.
PAULIE:	(MOVES CLOSER) We've completed new command programs for the remaining Network.
WHITMAN:	And where does that get us?
PAULIE:	We have over 72% of our old defensive resources and almost 80% of our strike capabilities.
WHITMAN:	So, there's some holes in the shield.
PAULIE:	But we've still got the biggest sword.
<u>SOUND:</u>	<u>THERE'S A SHARP ELECTRONIC BUZZ. WHITMAN TURNS ON HIS INTERCOM.</u>

WEISS: (D. ON SPEAKER) I think I've solved the mystery of our visitor.

PAULIE: (SNORTS) Oh, you mean there's more?

WEISS: (D. ON SPEAKER) He's definitely suffering from hysteric delusions. I've just found evidence that proves that he believes he's a superhero from science fiction stories. Anthony Stern was a character from pulp magazines of the 1930's.

WHITMAN: (ANNOYED) What's that?

WEISS: (D. ON SPEAKER) Er—like Buck Rogers or Dan Dare. (A LITTLE EMBARRASSED) The character even had a comic book, a radio show and even two movie serials.

PAULIE: So, he's a nutcase who thinks he's Luke Skywalker?

WEISS: (D. ON SPEAKER) It's a bit more subtle than that—

WHITMAN: (INTERRUPTS, IMPATIENT) Thank you for the report on popular culture, Captain...

PAULIE: (LAUGHS WEARILY).

WHITMAN: (SARCASTIC) ... but as I'm sure you can appreciate, we have an Ultimatum to enforce so we have a few more pressing items on the agenda.

SCENE 13.

BROADCAST OF THE ULTIMATUM.

SOUND:	<u>THE HISS OF RADIO STATIC TRAVELLING UP INTO ORBITAL SPACE MAKES THE SPEECH REMINISCENT OF THE 1930S RADIO BROADCAST.</u>
PRESIDENT:	We have drawn our line in the sky. The Rogue States must return their troops to their borders without delay… otherwise they will face the full force of our space-borne weapons…

<u>SCENE 14.</u>

<u>MEDICAL WARD OF THE HIGH MANDATE. 14:00 HOURS.</u>

WEISS:	(VO) There are no heroes. No wise men. Just ordinary people who pretend they have clarity of purpose and access to absolute truth. But really, they're just as weak and fallible as the rest of us.
SOUND:	<u>DOOR OPENS, WEISS ENTERS.</u>
WEISS:	(STRUGGLES TO KEEP VOICE EVEN) Admiring the view?
STERN:	From space the Earth is always beautiful.
WEISS:	Yes, sometimes I forget that.
STERN:	When can I leave?
WEISS:	I wish I could oblige, but we're in the middle of an alert.
STERN:	Then what do you want?
WEISS:	(SIGHS) I think it's time you faced the truth

about some things.

STERN:　　　I don't follow you, Captain.

WEISS:　　　As you probably know, the world is in pretty terrible trouble.

STERN:　　　So I gathered.

WEISS:　　　We may be on the verge of destroying ourselves.

STERN:　　　That's not good.

WEISS:　　　(SHAKEN) Under such terrible circumstances... no one could be blamed for trying to live in a better world. Living in a fantasy is nothing to be ashamed of.

STERN:　　　(EXASPERATED) Captain Weiss. I don't know what planet *you* may inhabit, but *my* home, the Earth, *is* at peace. It has been for almost a century! I simply don't understand what's going on.

WEISS:　　　But I'm trying to help you understand; help you understand what *really* is going on.

STERN:　　　(ANGRY) I just want to get out of here and go to Mars!

WEISS:　　　I'm sorry, but even now I can't believe that delusion is any kind of a solution. I'm going to help you accept reality even if it means facing the end of the world.

STERN:　　　Delusions? You think I'm having delusions?

WEISS:　　　It's more accurate to think of it as a choice between objective and subjective

	meanings—
STERN:	How can you call me mad?! I'm a peaceful explorer and you imprison me like a criminal. And you run around this... *appliance*... like rats in a maze. I'm insane? What kind of world uses its greatest science to destroy itself?
WEISS:	So how do you explain what you're doing here?
SOUND:	<u>STERN SITS HEAVILY ON HIS BED.</u>
STERN:	When I was studying at the Academy, they told us about relative dimensions and the resulting possibility of alternate worlds.
WEISS:	And?
STERN:	I think we come from alternative Earths. Your world devoted its talents and energies to war and global terror. My world worked for peace and exploration.
WEISS:	Very commendable goals.
STERN:	Our technologies differ because our sciences have been put to different tasks. My world has chosen a better way, a nobler course.
WEISS:	I see.
SOUND:	<u>WEISS REMOVES SOMETHING FROM A FILE FOLDER.</u>
	Please look at this.
STERN:	Why am I looking at a facsimile of a comic

	strip?
WEISS:	Anthony Stern never really existed. He was just a character from old science fiction stories.
SOUND:	<u>STERN CRUMPLES THE PAGE.</u>
STERN:	More insanity. This is just an inferior portrait of myself in the setting of what looks like one of those scientific romances by Mr. H.G. Wells or Hugo Gernsback. (BEAT) Utter madness.

<u>SCENE 15.</u>

<u>COMMAND CORE. 14:10 HOURS.</u>

SOUND:	<u>SHRILL SOUND OF THE RADAR WARNING ALARM.</u>
TECH #1:	They launched early! They launched before the deadline!
TECH #2:	Ten ICBMs heading toward continental North America!
TECH #3:	Seven targeted on Western Europe!
WHITMAN:	(YELLS) Activate all space defense programs!
SOUND:	<u>ALARM (OFF) CHATTER AND CLICKS AS THE TECHS WORK AT THEIR TERMINALS.</u>
PAULIE:	Our programs are failing! The missiles are getting through!
TECH #1:	We're picking up reports of surface-based detonations (BEAT). Dirty bombs.

WHITMAN: What's the A.I suggesting?

SOUND: <u>LOW ELECTRONIC MUTTERINGS.</u>

PAULIE: Not much.

TECH #2: NORAD is at launch condition.

TECH #3: They're initiating a retaliatory strike.

TECH #1: Impacts on... Bonn... Paris... London... New York City... Albany... Toronto... Niagara Falls... Montreal... Washington, D.C... Chicago... Detroit...

TECH #2: Computer projection: our missiles are approaching their targets.

TECH #3: Confirmed. I read direct hits on Cuba, the Middle East, and Africa. Incoming ICBMs on China and North Korea. More to follow...

SOUND: <u>LOUD KLAXON.</u>

TECH #1: (yells over the blare of the alarm) Sixty second warning!

PAULIE: The rogues are sweeping this area with particle beam cannons!

TECH #1: Estimated impact with this station... (BEAT AS HE READS OFF HIS TERMINAL)... thirty-three seconds!

PAULIE: (CHOKES) *Goddamn –*

WHITMAN: (LOW) God help us all.

<u>SCENE 16.</u>

<u>MEDICAL WARD. 14:13 HOURS.</u>

<u>SOUND:</u>   <u>(OFF) KLAXON.</u>

WEISS: (VO) I don't want to believe that any of this is happening. I want to believe what Captain Anthony Stern is telling me.

STERN: This is it, isn't it?

WEISS: I didn't want to be cruel. I just thought that… that at the end… you should know who you are.

STERN: I know who I am. (BEAT) And I know that I come from a better world.

<u>SOUND:</u>   <u>MASSIVE ROAR OF THE APPROACHING PARTICLE BEAM, *HIGH MANDATE* BOILS OFF INTO ATOMS.</u>

<u>SCENE 17.</u>

<u>THE MYSTERIOUS SUB-ETHER</u>

WELLS: (VO/D.) … All the universe—or nothingness? Which shall it be… Which shall it be?

<u>SCENE 18.</u>

<u>COCKPIT OF A ROCKETSHIP. ELSEWHEN.</u>

<u>SOUND:</u>   <u>ROAR OF THE PARTICLE BEAM RECEDES— ROUTINE CLICKS AND HUMS OF THE ROCKETSHIP'S EQUIPMENT RISE. STERN</u>

<u>TURNS ON HIS AUDIO-PHONE.</u>

STERN: Calling Expeditionary Navigator! This is Stern on the *Passworthy*. Sorry to be late, we ran into some interference.

NAVIGATOR: (D. ON AUDIO-PHONE) *Ahoy Passworthy!* Thought we'd lost you. Prepare to fire all boosters!

STERN: Roger.

<u>SOUND:</u> <u>STERN SWITCHES AUDIO PHONE OFF.</u>

STERN: When you're finished admiring the view, co-pilot, we need to re-join the Expedition.

WEISS: Sorry. (BEAT) I was just thinking how lovely the Earth is.

STERN: Quite.

WEISS: Ready to fire all boosters!

<u>SOUND:</u> <u>WEISS PULLS A LEVER AND THE ROCKET BOOSTERS BLAST INTO LIFE. THE SOUND OF THE ENGINES FADE AS THE ROCKET SOARS TO MARS.</u>

<u>SCENE 19.</u>

<u>THE MERRIL COLLECTION OF SCIENCE FICTION, FANTASY AND SPECULATION. ALSO ELSEWHEN.</u>

<u>SOUND:</u> <u>TWO SETS OF FOOTSTEPS ECHO AMONG THE MASSIVE ARCHIVES.</u>

CHIEF LIBRARIAN: It still amazes me that people once

considered this literature to be trash.

VISITOR: Yes, very difficult to understand.

SOUND: <u>THE FOOTSTEPS STOP.</u>

CHIEF LIBRARIAN: Here we are... 1936. Of course, now we appreciate science fiction for the cultural treasure it is.

VISTOR: (JOY IN HIS VOICE) The Merril! What a glorious collection!

SOUND: <u>CHIEF LIBRARIAN ENTERS A CODE INTO A TERMINAL.</u>

CHIEF LIBRARIAN: I'll call up the appropriate files.

VISITOR: It will be so thrilling to hear the actual broadcast!

SOUND: <u>THERE IS STATIC AND THEN TINNY ORCHESTRAL MUSIC ON THE TERMINAL SPEAKER.</u>

1930s STYLE
ANNOUNCER: (D. ON SPEAKER) It's time for another episode of *Stunning Science Stories on the Air*! This week, we continue the serial "Mad Masters of the Artificial Moon!"

SOUND: <u>THE MUSIC TAKES AN OMINOUS BUT CHEESY TURN.</u>

                         Will General Whitman and Major Paulie find some way to avert planetary disaster as they face the Rogue Hordes?

SOUND: <u>VISITOR PAUSES THE RECORDING.</u>

VISITOR:	The writers were so imaginative back then, but so fearful. Almost twisted.
CHIEF LIBRARIAN:	Oh, yes. They must have suffered from the most deranged nightmares.

<u>END.</u>

LET'S BLAME THE STARLOST

This is one of those stories about anthropologists from the future.[8] I come by this honestly because at one time I wanted to be an anthropologist.

It all started with a very short-lived Canadian television series that premiered in 1973 called *The Starlost*. It was created by Harlan Ellison and the science advisor of the show was *Analog* magazine's former editor, Ben Bova;[9] the special effects (at least at first) were designed by Douglas Trumbull of *2001*, *Close Encounters* and *Blade Runner*.

Even with this high-flying talent, *The Starlost* did turn out to be pretty terrible. You can't say "spectacularly terrible" because that would imply that it was much more exciting than it was. Someday perhaps, I will write of that heart-breaking Friday night premier when you could hear thousands of Canadian SF geeks quietly sobbing in front of their TV sets.

Still, the *premise* of *The Starlost* is extremely engaging. The Earth has been destroyed. To escape extinction we have built a giant multi-generational starship and representative cultures have each been assigned their own biosphere. A few centuries into the voyage to a new home, there's been a big accident, the ship goes off course and all the people in the biospheres get isolated and forget they are on a spaceship. The heroes of the show have to figure out a way to get all the people working together and set the ship back on course. Hey, it was the 1970s. TV tried to be socially progressive sometimes back then.

Regardless, the sheer crappiness of *The Starlost* broke my heart.

---

8   I am not the only SF writer who writes these kinds of stories. Chad Oliver was a respected anthropologist who wrote some amazing stories exploring concepts from his discipline. Ursula K. Leguin is the daughter of Alfred L. Kroeber, a major American anthropological thinker and that perspective is evident in many of her works. Regardless of whether you're interested in cultural anthropology or not, go out and read their books. I promise that you will be entertained and enlightened.

9   Both Ellison and Bova have written despairingly of their experiences on *The Starlost* project, referring to Canadian creative professionals as "weasels" and incapable of producing episodic television. Thank you gentlemen, we all love you too.

However, it is a tribute to the strength of the underlying concept that the memory of the show still lingered.

And that memory is one of the reasons I wanted to be an anthropologist. In my very first anthropology course the professor was trying to explain an analytical tradition called, "structural functionalism"—which says that a society is a complicated network of relationships and institutions that work together to ultimately maintain that society.

The instant my prof described this idea I had a vision of the Giant Earthship Ark from *The Starlost*: hundreds of domes connected to a massive central core. Each dome contained a separate society but was maintained through access to a common life-support and communications infrastructure.

I suddenly had a very powerful science fiction metaphor to help me understand this sociological concept.

I also discovered that I really liked understanding stuff like that.

WHEN BLOOMSBURY FAILS

Originally published in:
New Writings in the Fantastic, 2007
Edited by John Grant

"For this sustenance to our bodies and spirit, we give thanks."

Old Mr. Williams opened the foil bag and reached inside. There was a rustle of air-filled artificial substances rubbing against each other and his wrinkled, spotted hand emerged with a single twisted orange cylinder.

"Accept this sign of our last bonds to this worldly plane."

Mr. Williams gazed hard at the cheezie. He opened his mouth and very deliberately paced the food substitute onto his tongue. Then he closed his mouth and eyes and passed the bag to the next person in the circle.

Each of us breathed a quiet prayer as we received our sacred cheezie:

"For this I am thankful."

"With this we are one."

"Peace be with you."

"And also with you."

The sixty plus six of us sat on a hill behind the cement plant out by the outskirts of a middle-sized town in southern Alberta. We were waiting for the Mothership to arrive and rescue us from our doomed world.

Most of us were expectant, exhilarated. The liberation of cutting off all ties with the mundane world eclipsed our dread of the approaching nuclear apocalypse.

Even I felt pretty good.

After I consumed my cheezie, I experienced a vague warmth building up inside me. I briefly wondered if it was the Holy Spirit or my automatic immune net scrambling to destroy the mildly toxic chemicals that were now entering my bloodstream.

"We have a little while more to wait," Mrs. Bloomsbury said. "Why don't we sing a few songs?"

❀　　❀　　❀

"We are pleased to advise you that the Research Council has approved your proposal."

The telepathically enhanced message flashed through my just waking conscious. This was going to be a day worth waking up for.

"Please report for surgical preparation at your earliest convenience."

I was so pleased by the news that I didn't even complain about the pain of the implants. I figured that I could deal with any discomfort; I was finally getting out of the simulation archives and into the field.

Real temporal anthropology.

Hot damn.

❀　　❀　　❀

It was getting pretty cold up here on the hill.

Leo, one of the younger Searchers, looked a little embarrassed after he realized that he had just wiped his nose with the back of his hand.

Perhaps it was annoying to be still dealing with the problems of the flesh.

Mrs. Bloomsbury smiled at Leo and Sarah. Sarah was sitting next to Leo. She was a middle-aged woman who left her house, husband and children to be with us. Sarah put her arms around the young man.

"Keep the faith, Leo," she said.

Mrs. McPherson, the retired lady who used to dabble in theosophy started to sing:

"Rock of ages..."

But her voice was uncontrolled, uncertain. She paused for a moment until Mrs. Bloomsbury spoke.

"There's a lot of wisdom in some of those old hymns. You can think of our planet as a rock, spinning all alone in space for many

ages, waiting for a few of its tiny inhabitants to meet their destiny."
Then she picked up where Mrs. McPherson left off:

"…cleft for me…"

The voices were much stronger now.

All of us, at least those who knew the words, joined in. Some of us, like me, have to fake it.

But all of us were enthusiastic. The cold seemed to dissipate and the waiting got a little easier.

❋   ❋   ❋

"They call themselves the Searchers," I said.

Most of what I was going to research had been studied before, which was why it was so difficult to get out of the simulations.

Too much old data to deal with.

I suppose that if I had come up with some radically different approach, even a stupid one, it might have been easier to get sent into the field.

But that was never my style. I never pursued controversy for its own sake and I didn't think there was any shame in proving that somebody else's theories are correct.

"So you're going to track a small-group charismatic event." My peer supervisor pushed bits of statistical data into a messy halo around his bearded head. "God, there were lots of those back in the 20th Century."

And talking about the impact of science and crude geopolitics on folk culture was the stuff of introductory lectures.

But I figured I still had a good angle on a classic sociological paradigm.

I spun a stream of human-event graphics at my supervisor.

"Look at the coordinates!" I almost giggled. "They're almost perfect."

"Perfect?" The man looked skeptical.

"Historical events appear to confirm their belief system!"

The old fart couldn't deny that.

He didn't.

He tapped a graphic; I think it was the miniature face of a tiny young woman:

"Agreed. You might actually learn something new."

In a society where there's not much scarcity of money, comfort or commodities, new knowledge was one of the few things left of value.

So they bolted me to a frame of steel and plastic and booted me (rather firmly) into the past. Sometimes even the most technologically advanced societies lose their subtlety.

✻　　　✻　　　✻

Christine looked at me over the plate of steaming hamburger.

"I'm so glad we've finally have some time to ourselves," she said.

Then there's a silence of some duration and I can feel a field of expectation snapping into existence.

I tried to temporarily escape the oppressive atmosphere by putting something small and fried into my mouth. In less than a second my bloodstream monitors were screaming at me about more food-toxins. I sincerely hoped that the nanos in my G.I. tract were working.

Christine continued: "I know we haven't known each other very long…"

Damn, I realized. I should have seen this coming. This was Fieldwork 101 here. The community reacts to the presence of a stranger in a range of characteristic ways. The more often members of the group see the stranger, the more intense the reaction…

"…But I think you ought to know that I find you very attractive."

…and therefore… very often the anthropologist in the field will have to deal with a marriage proposal from a member of the native community. Maybe even two or three proposals.

At that point, I noticed that I had eight of these fried things in my mouth. I was reasonably certain that I don't look very attractive, at least in any objective sense.

Perhaps Christine wasn't feeling very objective that day.

A little over two hours later, she was snoring softly as I lay beside her, considering all the strange odors and textures of our lovemaking. My primary emotion was relief that I'd actually been able to perform the act. This was the first time I'd had sex without technological or telepathic enhancement. It was also rather odd doing it with just one person at a time.

But it wasn't too bad.

I looked around the interior of the molded aluminum room. It looked a little like the interior of a flying saucer from one of the science fiction films of that period.

Christine was quite a serious person, so I suspected that I would be leaving the YMCA (home to many newly arrived time travellers) and moving into the trailer park.

She'd probably insist that we get married as well.

Score one for the natives and I think I just flunked my fieldwork mid-term. But at least I'd get a better look at the Searchers who lived around here.

❋　　　❋　　　❋

Mrs. Bloomsbury held her services out-of-doors when the weather permitted it.

I grew up in environments were the distinctions between "inside" and "outside" or even "natural" and "manufactured" were quite blurred—so I found the whole idea of just walking through a doorway into non-mediated sunshine pretty disorienting.

I had to fight the urge to turn down the contrast on the sky.

But I found Mrs. Bloomsbury very reassuring in times of stress. With her I was able to find a way to enjoy sitting in the park bandstand with the rest of the Searchers.

We were listening to her.

Which is pretty much what we did most of the time.

"It's so terribly sad when what is best in ourselves is turned against us," Mrs. Bloomsbury said. She rests her hand on the shoulder of the Searcher seated next to her. It's Jamie, a young woman about 17 years old.

"If I was to ask Jamie, to tell us what she thought her best features where, she'd probably have some difficulty doing that."

Mrs. Bloomsbury looked at Jamie for a long time.

"Do you know why, Jamie?"

The young woman shook her head.

"Because you're a modest person with good manners."

Jamie's face bloomed with scarlet and she stared at the floorboards of the gazebo.

"But are you happy?"

The young woman shook her head again.

Mrs. Bloomsbury turned to face the group.

"The problem is that social humility can very often be twisted into very anti-social negativity. We become so habituated into denying our own self-worth that we start to believe that other people have no worth as well."

The Searchers were nodding, taking all of this in. I'm a little surprised; I didn't expect to find folk-psychotherapy within the culture of this group.

"Travel with me, friends." Mrs. Bloomsbury closed her eyes and laid her hands over her breast the way she always did before she proclaimed one of her revelations.

"If we are to ascend to the plane of Galactic Superculture of our Alien Gods, then we must purge our spiritual selves of this negativity."

I suddenly felt better. This kind of talk was more consistent with my classification system of religious doctrines.

I guess we're all looking for some sort of validation or other and Mrs. Bloomsbury could be reassuring at so many different levels.

She opened her eyes and held out her open hands to the Searchers.

"I would like us to go around the circle and have each one of us look at the person next to you... and then speaking only the truth... tell us what you admire the most about that person."

But I knew that I was going to hate this part.

The exercise took even longer than I expected and it was an extremely emotional experience. Lots of tears and hugging, people in the 20th Century really weren't used to hearing nice things about themselves.

As I feared, the discussion got awkward when we got to my part of the circle. I had no idea who Christine was talking about when she was looking at me. And I was truly pathetic in my response.

Guess I just wasn't used to telling the truth.

✱　　✱　　✱

Mrs. Bloomsbury defies description with standard life history formats.

Yes, I can tell you when she was born, where she went to school, when she got married, what happened to Mr. Bloomsbury, the date when she claimed that a purple beam of light first burned into her brain with a message from beyond the stars.

But that really doesn't tell you what's important about Mrs.

Bloomsbury.

She was the alpha and omega of all events in our little community. A classic charismatic leader with the power to inspire, comfort and spur. When I'm completely candid with myself I admit that I daydream about her in a variety of situations. My limited telepathic scans tell me that most of the Searchers feel the same way… whether they know it or not.

She's truly wonderful. And people like her have caused a lot of suffering and wars throughout history.

When our university's existential search engine twisted its way through the time-streams, they made one hell of a catch with Mrs. Bloomsbury.

Now, I just had to wait for events to unfold.

*   *   *

That afternoon she was giving a lecture on the nature of the universe.

Mrs. Bloomsbury placed the globe in her lap and sat in the middle of the living room floor while some of the younger and more agreeable Searchers were holding balls of various sizes and colours in different parts of the house.

Christine and I walked in through the front door.

Mrs. Bloomsbury smiled at me. "Hello! You're just in time to be the Planet Xorgon." Christine moved quickly and handed me a basketball.

"Over to the bathroom please!"

I complied with instructions.

"Now," Mrs. Bloomsbury said. "At its zenith, the Galactic Superculture extended to encompass almost all sentient life in the universe. But then, billions of years ago, there was some kind of dysfunction in the ethereal lines of communication…"

Mrs. Bloomsbury held the globe out for all of us to see. "And somehow, our world was cut off from all the others." Then she looked at my wife.

"Christine? Could you walk over to where I'm pointing?"

Christine walked over to the picture window.

"A great shadow then passed over whole quadrants of our galaxy. Vast tracts of interstellar civilization were isolated, this dark age extended from the far end of the dining room back to the hallway." Mrs. Bloomsbury smiled at Christine.

"Pull the curtains all the way shut, dear."

We all stood in semi-twilight, our little worlds in our hands.

"But the planets at the Galactic Core… over by the kitchen… are taking steps. They have already dispatched a giant mother ship to rescue those believers who are trapped in shadow."

If you didn't worry too much about internal consistency or scientific accuracy, Mrs. Bloomsbury's sermons were incredibly fun.

This entertainment factor may be an essential element in any successful religious movement.

❈   ❈   ❈

"I've got something to tell you." Christine looked across at me over another table on another day. But it was the same very serious tone.

If I was a better social scientist, or maybe if I was just a bit smarter I probably would have developed an analytic schema for predicting Christine's verbal behaviour. But that morning all I cared about was obtaining some pure, primitive coffee. Whatever else, monogamy had definitely changed me.

"There's going to be three of us by spring," Christine said. The rising sun was reflecting hard off those very thick lenses she had mounted over her nose. Her voice was very serious and her facial expression was impossible to read.

I wondered what I looked like as my emotions were rather mixed at that moment. The treatments for physical time travel had forever removed my ability to reproduce without the aid of advanced genetic technology. So if Christine really was pregnant then I certainly hadn't been her accomplice.

And from what I knew of her immediate time-stream, Christine wouldn't have the opportunity to enjoy her baby.

She leaned over the table; her eyes were magnified to gigantic proportions.

"Are you okay? Don't you have anything to say?"

I decided that it wouldn't look too good if I took a drink of coffee at that moment.

"It's incredible," I said finally. "Really incredible."

❈   ❈   ❈

I took a walk after work, still considering Christine's news. I decided that it really doesn't have any implications for the project but I still found the situation a little disturbing.

There's only one other person in the field behind the trailer park that evening. It's young Leo, hunched over a tiny metal tripod.

"Exploring the universe again?" I hoped my laugh sounded friendly. Leo has lots of things to deal with.

The teenager didn't look at me as he loaded a cardboard tube onto a thin rod extending from the tripod's base.

"I guess this must look pretty pathetic," he said. "Shooting off stupid little rockets when we know that there's giant starships hovering out there."

"I figured you were just impatient."

I did a telempathic analysis of Leo a few weeks back. He was in a difficult situation. Easily twice as intelligent than his family and school mates. I knew he was desperate for just about any kind of change in his life.

I watched him unwind a long line of copper wire to a Bakelite ignition switch ten yards away.

"Guess it's something to do while we're all waiting."

Leo's sexual orientation was also a problem in this era. I suspected that he was only just now coming to terms with his feelings. I doubted he even had words to describe himself.

He waved at me to step away from the tripod.

"Five… four… three… two…"

It probably made more sense for Leo to tell himself that he was probably some kind of star-lost alien progeny.

"…one… zero… *blast off*!"

Leo threw the switch and the little rocket spun upward riding a plume of blue gas. The cylinder disappeared from sight and a second later a tiny red cloth unfolded and started to drift earthward.

I was about to reveal more information than anyone in my role really should know, but I wanted to make poor Leo feel a little better.

"You're part of a great tradition," I said. "One of the first groups dedicated to the moral impact of extra-terrestrial life was called the Cosmic Circle back in the 1930s…"

"So it was quite a long time ago," Leo said looking a little irritated.

"They were a group of science fiction fans who were going to set up a commune in New Mexico, help themselves evolve into higher states of existence and make contact with other worlds."

Leo looked puzzled, my scans suggested he was wondering how such strange words were coming out of the mouth of Christine's big dumb husband.

"Model rocketry experiments were a big part of their belief system. They planned to do them every day."

"So what happened to them?" Leo asked suspiciously.

"Nobody's sure," I replied honestly. "They faded from the historical record."

"So they failed."

I walked over to the rocket and the parachute that had landed quite close to us.

"I don't know, maybe somebody picked up their signals," I shrugged. "Maybe they got a lift to somewhere further out than New Mexico."

Leo, of course, was far too cool to respond to this idea. He just took the rocket from me and started refolding the little parachute.

*   *   *

It's difficult to say which events preceded which that day. At the micro-level (where most of us live) temporal reconstruction tools aren't all that helpful.

Let's just say that it was a pretty intense time. Since I had a heads-up of over a thousand years, I was a *little* more prepared, but not by much. I just knew (for certain!) that this was going to be an interesting day.

Maybe it was worse for me because I saw it coming.

It began with Christine.

She sat on our largest piece of furniture (I'd folded it into a couch) and stared at me, gray-faced with vacant eyes.

"It's not going to happen."

A curl of dark blood unfolding in a stainless steel bowl.

The image from her recent memory shot through my consciousness.

No baby.

Now I picked up her emotions: pain, relief, despair, and confusion.

I knew it wasn't going to happen, a long time ago.

So I still couldn't explain my own shock.

Objectivity? Denial, probably, I decided. Then I wondered if I was as really as bad a scientist as I felt at that moment. At least I was a better scientist than a husband and that was an even more depressing realization.

I wondered if I ought to walk over there and put my arms around her, then my scan suggested that this was not a good idea.

Instead I said:

"There's a service today." I wish I'd said that out of compassion. "We should go," I said softly. I had to carry on with my work.

"Yeah." Christine sniffed and nodded her head.

Today was going to be an important day for data collection.

*   *   *

Mrs. Bloomsbury seemed to be distracted by something.

Her usual glow wasn't there, there was something missing in her greetings and blessings.

Mr. Cruthers also looked confused when she announced that tea was not ready and wouldn't be ready until after the service.

The preparation, distribution and consumption of tea was an essential bonding process in the services. Handling the tea was Mr. Cruthers' responsibility.

Now the poor old man had no idea what to do.

After a brief period of what can only be described as perfunctory meditation, Mrs. Bloomsbury stood up and walked over to the picture window.

"I didn't sleep last night," she said.

Neither did I. Because I had a reasonably good idea of what she was about to say.

"I experienced a new revelation."

Right on schedule.

"When we first spoke of living in these, the latter days..." Mrs. Bloomsbury pulled the curtains shut. "...we knew far more than we realized... but the emphasis has shifted to the days rather than the latter."

Mrs. Bloomsbury took Mr. Cruthers' hands and looked into the old man's eyes.

"It is the end," she said. "Our world will soon cease to be."

Then she let go and walked over to her chair and covered her face with her hands. We sat there in the darkness, looking at her, waiting for something to happen.

Finally, she looked up at us.

"Last night I was blinded by the flash and felt the fire."

Now all of us knew what was going to be said next. Christine took my hand and held on tight. She looked... content?

Perhaps I should have been able to predict that as well.

Mrs. Bloomsbury's face was streaked with tears.

"The atomic war is coming. Our lovely little planet will soon be burned into nothingness."

Most of the Searchers bowed their heads. My scan told me that their initial fear response was quickly over-shadowed by a sense of vindication:

They weren't crazy after all! It's all happening the way our prophet predicted!

Mrs. Bloomsbury smiled at us.

"But we must not despair. A rescue vessel is on its way to us. We must prepare for the great journey."

❋   ❋   ❋

Much later that night, Christine was driving us home.

For once she doesn't seem to care that we have such an old, uncomfortable car. I suppose I should be driving but even though I have mastered advanced time-travel technology, I'm not very good with internal combustion engines.

I turned on the radio and a news report started talking about a speech that President Kennedy gave about a naval blockage of the island of Cuba.

The announcer matter-of-factly mentioned that the United States of America and the Soviet Union are on the brink of a nuclear exchange.

Even with the crude devices of the far-distant past of 1961, this kind of conflict would pretty much kill everything on the planet.

Of course, after a few beers from this period, I could do the same thing with my field equipment!

❋   ❋   ❋

I saw a cluster of very serious looking mothers at the end of the road.

The Griffins, one of the four Searcher families in the trailer park were getting rather public in their preparations for the "great transition". At first it just looked like they were doing their spring cleaning early or holding a very late yard sale.

Boxes, more and more of them, labeled and carefully taped shut were stacked neatly on the freshly cut lawn. Steve Griffin, short, neat and dignified even at the end of the world had trimmed the hedges and pulled out the dandelions. Linda Griffin had cleaned all the windows on their trailer.

But potential shoppers were surprised when they examined the labels on the boxes. The contents were clearly identified but…

"Where's the price?"

"Whaddya want for this?"

Then silence and disbelief.

"It's free?"

Linda smiled and nodded.

"Please, just take what you need."

I walked over with Steve and watched him pay out the October rent earlier and explained to Mr. Cooprod, the owner of the park, that they could cut off the power and plumbing the day after tomorrow.

"You're leaving the A&P, Steve?" Mr. Cooprod dropped the end of his cigarette butt into a cold cup of his wife's coffee. "You buggering off on us, kid?"

Steve just grinned. So did I because this was all going to look absolutely fantastic in the ethnological record.

"Yes, we are moving. Quite some distance."

At first I was quite enjoying this but things got disruptive when Larry and Judy Griffin started giving away their possessions to the other children in the trailer park.

Larry, as careful and organized as his mother and father, gave his complete runs of his favourite comics to his best friend at school. He didn't want to, but Steve had given the Searcher lecture on weight allocations and the fact that even interstellar spacecraft had their technical limitations.

It was a lot worse when Judy gave away her Barbies to the girl in the trailer at the end of the road. Linda Griffin was famous throughout the park for her sewing skill. She made all of the clothes for Judy's Barbie and Skipper dolls and they were, of course, much nicer than anything you could get in the stores.

"Shelly can't accept these," her mother said. "It's just not right."

"Judy won't need them where we're going," Linda said happily.

None of the mothers were terribly satisfied with this response. My scans assured me that none of them had any idea of the Griffins' plans but almost everyone was nervous about what they were hearing on the news.

Weird behaviour from the people next door was the last thing people were interested in right now.

Eventually Jody's Barbie things ended up in a box, taped shut sitting on the lawn. I don't know if anybody ever took them away.

❈   ❈   ❈

Our broadcast and prayer vigil was less conspicuous but more intense.

A few of us were unable to free ourselves from mundane obligations even under these circumstances, but most of the Searchers had packed one bag and moved into Mrs. Bloomsbury's house.

There we sat in front of her radio and television and listened to news reports on the situation in Cuba. It seemed so quaint to me, so gentle and fragile, this process of quietly waiting for tiny little waves to flicker through the atmosphere only to be snared by jagged little wires sticking out of aluminum igloos and wooden huts.

Not like my time, where information is more a primal force—sort of like living in a smart tidal wave. It was overwhelming at times but there were some advantages: you were never really alone and if you didn't like your life conditions... well wait a nanosecond or two...

It was just past three in the morning and the only television station we could pick up had just gone off the air. Those of use who weren't sleepy were crouched on the floor listening to a radio.

What they referred to as "real news" in this era had finished over two hours ago and only had local programming. It was called "Night Owls" or "Night Talk" or "Dark Words" or something similar (I'd have to check my files) and was one of those shows where people would use telephones to call into a living person who was chairing this continent-spanning discussion.

These people could be so primitive.

Right now the threat of nuclear war was being assessed through stinging, bleary eyes of insomniacs, paranoids and the habitually unemployed.

"I don't know why the President is going to all this trouble," a tobacco-choked voice coughed out of the radio speaker.

"You mean the fact that the Russians have missiles less than 30 miles off the Florida coast isn't a problem?" The host replied, he sounded slightly amused.

Actually, I probably should have been paying more attention to this. But hell, I was exhausted. Taking these field recordings without looking too obvious was incredibly difficult. I was in the middle of an apocalyptic millennial group facing what really looked like an apocalypse. There was just so much phenomena you could take note of.

At that moment, I was slumped in an old and over-stuffed easy chair trying not to fall asleep. I had been activating my artificial stimulation system almost continually for the last two days and now my internal sensor was telling me that if I used it anymore the increase in my blood pressure would make my head explode.

So, I was trying to relax for a few minutes and my mind drifted off to more trivial matters, I idly wondered which of the fertile male members in my group was responsible for the impregnation of my "wife".

I decided that there was some potential value into looking into that. The elasticity of values and moral behaviour under conditions of community crisis and ideological transition. I might get a really good paper out of Christine.

But then I started to hear some really interesting things on the radio:

"Kennedy is wasting time," the caller growled. "He should just hit them right away."

"You mean attack Russia with our missiles first?" the host replied.

"And our planes, too! It's idiotic to even try to negotiate with soulless monsters. President Kennedy shouldn't mistake the Soviets for human beings."

The Searchers weren't the only people in this era with some odd theories.

*   *   *

The next day, the news got more and more serious and Mrs. Bloomsbury's living room became more and more crowded. Eventually, Mrs. Bloomsbury walked in, turned off Walter Cronkite and addressed all:

"Tonight."

So we all moved, sitting on a big hill by the river waiting for the saucer to arrive and rescue us from the atomic fires.

"Jesus wants me for a sunbeam…"

Some of the younger children started to sing the only religious song they knew by heart.

"…A sunbeam…"

I glanced over at Christine. I knew how her life was going to turn out. Alone, no children, dead in less than ten years. That's why I decided the marriage was actually a good research move. No danger of any paradox.

"…A sunbeam…"

Steve and Linda Griffin would move to nowhere in particular and never do anything of any particular importance. Their children and their children's children would follow the same pattern.

"…A sunbeam…"

Leo. He was sitting just next to the circle of singing children, looking happier than I'd ever seen him before.

"…A sunbeam…"

Leo would commit suicide a little more than two months from now.

That's why the Searchers were an excellent study sample. None of them were going to have any discernible impact on the unfolding of human history.

"I'll be a sunbeam for him!"

Mrs. Eleanor Bloomsbury. Less than eighteen months after Kennedy and Khrushchev pulled the world back from the brink of nuclear exchange, Mrs. Bloomsbury would be sent off for psychiatric evaluation. In less than five years she would be permanently institutionalized and chemically lobotomized by the crude psychoactive drugs of this era.

Mrs. Bloomsbury was going to leave this world but not in quite the way she had prophesied.

I really did have a lot of leeway with this group.

We continued our singing and our services. The communion with the cheezies ensued.

Sometime after 1:30 on October 25, 1961 Mrs. Bloomsbury asked us all to bow our heads and pray. I adjusted my equipment and folded my hands like everyone else.

Then, through the slits of my eyes I could just see a multicoloured field of light surround the hill and envelop the Searchers.

A choir of wondrous ethereal voices cried out in harmonious transcendence as we were all transported into the heart of the mother ship.

When we opened our eyes, Mrs. Bloomsbury pointed to a giant imaging curtain where we saw the Earth burn and fade to a scarred stone.

"Dear God!" we all said.

✳   ✳   ✳

One of the first things we did after we arrived was to change our name from "The Searchers" to "The Saved".

Then for the next few months (we had to use some kind of familiar system to explain the passage of time) we started planning different utopias. Deciding which ones would suit us best.

Christine's baby is due soon and she and Steve finally decided to have that frank and friendly chat they've been meaning to have with me. Linda's there too.

They explained that while they are operating an open-partnership marriage they still don't feel I'm suited to that kind of committed relationship.

Or any kind of relationship really.

It's a pretty accurate assessment.

"I guess it's silly to say I'm sorry," Christine smiled softly. "...In the midst of all this joy."

"But it is very polite," I replied.

Mrs. Bloomsbury has relinquished her leadership over the community and seems to be pursuing personal salvation through artistic expression. She spends most of her time recreating herself with various exotic media.

Leo tried to kiss me the other day and I'm not sure what I'm going to do about that.

Of course, there were a lot of objections when the Department discovered that I'd taken my research in a different direction. Showing up with over sixty people from the past and plugging them into an immersive simulated world is bound to make someone concerned.

Except perhaps for the people who are living in that simulated world.

They just think they're living on another planet and I intend to keep them there for the rest of their lives.

I did get some flack from my supervisor but even he had to give in. This was the first opportunity to study an apocalyptic community experiencing the consequences of their prophecy. So now I have enough material to last the rest of my academic career.

I'm happy.

They're happy.

We're all in heaven.

SEEKING BETTER PRODUCTION VALUES

I was having a sandwich with Laura Nordin, a very talented actor/writer/director, who set up a dramatic reading of a one-act version of my story, "The Progressive Apparatus," by Praxis Theatre.

A few months later, Laura and her creative collaborator, Emily Andrews, established the Film Co-op and in between teaching and acting gigs they oversee the production of short films and web-series episodes. They also host workshops and professional development seminars to support a growing body of media-makers.

I have been very impressed with a lot of their results. They even produced a short film based on a scene from my story, "Problem Project." It had broadcast quality acting and production values. I liked it a lot.

I've always been interested in dramatic writing and I often adapt my stories for stage, screen and, most often, radio. Thrift, Horatio! Thrift!

I love radio drama and think it is a near perfect medium for science fiction. The special effects are a lot cheaper and they almost always *look* perfect.

Since 2000, Shoestring Radio Theatre has performed adaptations of many of the stories in this collection as well as my original "made for audio" mini-series *Amazing Struggles, Astonishing Failures and Disappointing Success*. Founded and produced by Monica Sullivan and Steve Rubenstein, Shoestring is relentless and they are fearless. As with the Film Co-op, Shoestring Radio Theater is not (at least not yet) a major mainstream commercial enterprise. Much of what they do is for the love of the art and the need for free and uncompromised expression.

The same passion applies to Catherine Fitzsimmons, founder of Brain Lag Publishing, who made this very book, and my novel *Extreme Dentistry*, into something that you are able to hold in your hands and read.

Indie? Underground? Counterculture? I'm not sure exactly how to classify what these creative projects are. I rather miss the term counterculture because it has sometimes proved to be the breeding ground for some really fun and world-changing innovations.[10]

---

10 For example, *The Whole Earth Catalog*, first published in 1968, was a serious factor in the origins of personal computing. If you combine that with the domestication of the ARPANET, led by hacker activists, it is now possible for things like the Film Co-op, Shoestring Radio Theater and Brain Lag Publishing to even exist. A few other minor things, like the 21st century global economy and the complete transformation of human communication and culture, also happened.

(COPING WITH) NORM DEVIATION

Originally published in:
Tesseracts Eleven, 2007
Edited by Cory Doctorow and
Holly Phillips

*When I think back on all that crap I learned in high school, it's
a wonder I can think at all!*
- Paul Simon

That's a quote from a song. The title is *Kodachrome* and I mention
it because that particular film format is relevant to some things
that I did back in 1972 when I was in high school. Kodachrome, as
those of you who may remember when photography actually
involved non-digital materials, gave you really great colours with a
minimum of light.

In other words you could make some really good looking movies
on a limited budget and with relatively little equipment.

```
OPENING SHOT, EXTERIOR, MORNING


We  see  an  empty  highway  at  the  outskirts  of
town.  Suddenly  an  unmarked  black  van  rolls
past.

CUT TO:

INTERIOR SHOT, VAN.
```

A SOCIAL CONTROL OFFICER, wearing black leather, sits in the back of the van studying the readings on a glowing orange screen. The Officer sees a blip on the screen and speaks to the khaki-uniformed driver.

                    OFFICER
          I think we've got one.

CLOSE-UP

The driver looks grim and nods.

CUT TO:

EXTERIOR. BUS STOP. A FEW MINUTES LATER.

THE DEVIANT stands there. He holds a small stack of old paperbacks under one arm. Otherwise, the Deviant looks deceptively like an ordinary teenager: jeans, army jacket, T-shirt and running shoes. His hair is a little bit too long and pretty messy.

In the distance, the black van slowly comes to a stop. Since it is not the vehicle he's waiting for, the Deviant doesn't pay any attention.

ANOTHER ANGLE
The door of the van slides open and the Social Control Officer steps out. He now wears a helmet and his face is completely hidden by its mirrored visor.

CLOSE SHOT

The Deviant turns and watches the Officer walk towards him.

CLOSE-UP

The Officer stops and removes an ELECTRONIC GUN from his holster.

ANOTHER CLOSE-UP

At this point the Deviant looks alarmed.

EXTREME CLOSE-UP

There's a crackle of white-orange lightning as a bolt of electricity leaps from the gun barrel.

ANOTHER ANGLE

of the Deviant. He falls to the ground, unconscious.

The Officer, assisted by the driver, pick the Deviant up and drag him toward the van.

PAN TO CLOSE-UP

of the Deviant's books laying on the sidewalk. The CAMERA LINGERS on one of the covers. A woman is removing her heavy sweater revealing the undersides of rather full breasts. An astronaut fully covered in space armour stands in the distance. His leering face can be seen through the faceplate. Large yellow letters scream the book's cover: "SIN IN SPACE!"

Leo and I decided we were going to make a film. I wrote the script, Leo provided the equipment and would direct.

I quickly learned that it was a lot easier to write the words than to put them on film.

I met Leo Milgrom in my Grade 10 Visual Communications Class. I entered the course with great hopes of making exciting stuff, but I was definitely failing. For one thing I was trying to take videos of the daily and degrading lives of my fellow students—a subject nobody seemed too thrilled to help with. For another, I was using something that was ironically called a "portapack." It was a gigantic reel-to-reel videotape recorder unit that you strapped to your back and humped around while you pointed a camera about the size of a toaster oven at people and asked them not to notice you.

The problem was that I really wanted sound in the show, I wanted to get the voices of students talking about why it was important to smoke up and sit in the middle of the high way, why Black Sabbath is a great new band and why guys always lie about being virgins.

Even today, I still believe there was something of value to this project but I was facing certain disaster. I didn't have the technical and directorial skills to get decent footage and while I was staggering around the school with this massive gear there was the constant danger that I might trip and get trapped on my back like a doomed tortoise in the desert sun.

My teacher, Mr. Pozzi, a patient and essentially compassionate individual, assigned Leo to work with me. Leo immediately saw my narrative perspective as problematic.

"People hate seeing stuff like this about high school students," he said. "It scares them and makes them pissed off at us."

"It's supposed to spark a reaction," I replied, annoyed but grateful that he didn't mention how out of focus all my shots were.

"They'll never let you finish it."

"So what are you saying, I have to pull my punches here?" I'm sure I sounded totally shrill.

"You gotta balance it with something positive, and visually interesting. Then you can say whatever bad stuff you like—because it makes it look as though high school students are worth caring about."

He had a point there.

"And we need movement, lots of music, too," Leo seemed to be talking more to himself than me at this point. "So far all we've got is talking heads with zits."

We ended up taping a modern dance recital in the school and cutting in the interviews around that. We got an A-. Would have been an A+ if Leo had done all the camera work.

Leo also introduced his pride and joy to the project. A Bolex Super 8 camera with a beautiful zoom lens and a single-frame switch so you could do animation and superimposures. Leo had also rigged a shared remote switch that linked the camera to a cassette tape recorder. This was the first evidence of Leo's technical genius because this set up now gave us:

- Limited synchronized sound.
- Colour (video on portapaks was all black and white then).
- Mobility. The camera and tape recorder weighed less than five pounds, so we had the capacity to do some really cool camera movements.

This was the first summer of my parents' divorce and so it was the first year with no vacation trip. Having lots of time on my hands, I found myself standing with my bicycle in Leo's driveway. He had clipped his camera to the eyepiece of his uncle's reflector telescope and was filming the partial eclipse of the sun.

It was intimidating but too interesting to ride away from.

"Do you want to do another film?" Leo asked as he adjusted the focus.

"Really? Like on our own?" I felt like I'd just been invited to fly to Mars. "I mean school's out."

"That's the point, school would just limit us." Leo pressed the tiny disk at the end of an articulated cable and the little motor inside the camera started whirring. "We want to tell more complex and important stories."

"Yeah, right."

"That means we're going to need a script."

That's all I needed to hear. After a few minutes of not looking at the sun, I pedalled myself home, took the cover off my mom's IBM Selectric and went to work.

I was an early-model geek, so of course, it was a science fiction film. Of course, I saw myself as a serious writer so it was going to be set in a dystopian near future society.

Just after midnight, I had finished the first (and only) draft of a script called *NORM DEVIATION!* and it was always understood that I was going to star as the protagonist Norm D. This was partly because the story was doing to be a deeply personal statement but mostly because Leo had to be the guy at the other end of the camera.

I got up just after seven and my mom helped me with the

gestetner and I printed out half a dozen copies of the script. Then it was back on my bike to Leo's place. He chased his little brothers out of the kitchen and we read the script together over bowls of Captain Crunch and bottles of Orange Crush.

INTERIOR LABORATORY. CLOSE-UP

Norm D. opens his eyes and lifts up his head. He has been sleeping in his chair.

CLOSE SHOT. NORM D.'S POV.

A bowl and spoon have been placed on a tabletop in front of him. Next to the bowl is a completely white carton with the words "MILK" stencilled on one side. Behind the carton are three cereal boxes. There are no words on any of the cartons. One is red, the other green and the last one yellow.

ANOTHER ANGLE

Norm D. looks up at the clock. It reads: 6:55. Possibly it is morning.

ANOTHER ANGLE

Norm D. reaches out and picks up the yellow cereal box. There is a brief burst of orange energy. The young man howls and falls to the floor.

CUT TO:

INTERIOR OBSERVATION ROOM. A SECOND LATER.

BEHAVIOURAL SCIENTIST #1 AND #2 are watching Norm D on a black and white TV monitor. There is a shot of their subject writhing on the floor, clutching his hand. We see cathode rays flickering on the lenses of the scientists'

glasses as they make brief notes on their
clipboards.

Next to the shots with the Deviant Detector Van, this was one of the most complicated scenes we filmed. Which was kind of a surprise to me because when I wrote the script I thought it was just going to be some people sitting, standing and falling down in some rooms.

Of course it was all Leo's fault. He convinced me that we had to do this scene right. I just thought we should shoot the monitor from behind so we didn't actually didn't see Norm D. on the video screen.

Leo insisted that my approach was totally no good and that we had to see our poor hero on the screen. Video on film was pretty tricky to shoot back then because of the strobing effect you'd get on the final film. But Leo said it would end up looking really weird and cool and he was right.

The hard part was getting the shots of me rolling around on the floor on videotape. In a chain of unlikely events pretty much powered by constant nagging, I got my dad to let the building maintenance people make a tape with the lab security cameras and even use one of their monitors in the shots with the scientists.

And this looked way better than the 12 inch Sears portable from my bedroom.

So thank you Dad, Leo and building maintenance.

Dad also got us some labcoats for Margie and Rose to wear when they played the behavioural scientists. I suppose I could have just written them as "scientists" or "psychologists" but "behavioural scientists" sounded a lot more sinister.

It would have helped if the labcoats hadn't been four sizes too big but Leo shot Margie and Rose at angles that the bagginess didn't look too obvious. So that's Dad and Leo—always solving problems.

The big post-production project for that scene was the big burst of energy when Norm D. touches the wrong cereal box. We decided halfway through shooting to make the behavioural scientists try and condition Norm against the colour yellow.

We never got around to agreeing if the yellow-thing was just an arbitrary decision to test the power of their mind control techniques (in which case they could have decided to condition Mr. D. to fear umbrella stands) or if yellow was associated with some subversive future political movement (which also could have been represented by umbrella stands if you think about it).

Again, it was mostly Leo pushing the envelope again. I didn't think we needed any visuals at all when Norm D. touches the wrong box. We were talking about electricity here and under most conditions you wouldn't see the current.

"It's more realistic without the effect," I said.

"Reality looks boring on film sometimes," Leo replied. "Besides, it's too *Star Trek* last season."

Yeow! William Shatner grimacing and doubling over while he's attacked by yet another invisible (and cheap) energy field. Can't have that!

"We've got to have an effect," Leo said.

"Yeah." Yeah, he was right.

When we were editing, I was worried that when Leo was using a compass needle to scratch the emulsion, he would damage our only print.

"No worries," he said.

He was right. It was probably the best energy effect in the whole movie.

To our surprise, the cereal boxes and milk cartons were the most difficult bits of the whole scene. We wanted them to look like breakfast condiments from a depressing Orwellian future society so we wanted them to be uniform colours with just their contents stenciled on. No product placement here!

When I wrote this, I figured it would be no big deal to make them. I was mistaken about that.

I painted the boxes three times and Leo kept sending them back.

"Too streaky."

"The letters are on crooked."

"Now you're warping the boxes."

Leo knew that the camera can be pretty forgiving about the appearance of props so perfection in fabrication was not necessary. So this should give you some idea of just how bad those babies were.

My props were bad. *Mars Needs Women* bad.

After two days of unproductive manufacture, Leo called in Allison who he knew from his art class last spring. I'd seen her around but I hadn't taken art last semester and she was way too smart and pretty for me to come up with a credible reason for me to talk to her in any other context.

Of course, she had been friends with Leo for years.

Anyway, Allison shows up at my house and looks at my latest set of pathetic boxes (they were sitting on the basement floor, sagging in on themselves).

"What kind of paints are you using?"

My sister's tempera paints because they were left over from some fake stained glass windows she'd been making last December.

"Tempera's no good," Allison said. "It's very uneven on opaque surfaces and you have to use too much water for cardboard surfaces."

She said she had some acrylics she could use. "Not as good as an airbrush but it should look okay on screen."

I resisted the impulse to ask her what acrylics were, or an airbrush, as she picked up some unpainted cereal boxes and narrowed her eyes at them.

"What kind of bond is the paper you are using to cover the boxes before you paint them?"

Bond? Paper? Cover?

She gave me a smile that was incredibly condescending from someone so young.

"No wonder you were having so much trouble. You have to cover the boxes with paper before you paint. Otherwise you have to use tons of paint to hide the original illustrations on the box."

Oh.

Then in about 0.2 seconds, Allison undid the tabs on the boxes, folded them flat and packed them in her knapsack.

"I'll bring them back tomorrow."

Click. Whiz. Allison disappeared down the street on her ten-speed.

Next day she was back and there they were. Three perfect cereal boxes and a milk carton from a dystopian future.

I don't want to give you the impression that Allison was particularly stuck-up, or at least any more than she had right to be considering how clueless I was. Allison was just astonishingly competent and focused about certain things. Once you put her on a project, she was going to make sure that it was done right. And that was the way it was going to be.

I discovered this feature of Allison's character when she insisted on being there for the shoot when we were using her props. Make no mistake; they were *her* props now.

She wasn't disruptive or anything but she made sure that those boxes and the carton were photographed to their very best effect. Leo did the best he could and it was rather interesting that he didn't object when Allison told us that she was going to stick around and work on all the other props as well.

I didn't object because Allison was female and not a relation. And she was pretty interesting.

We had a third producer.

INTERIOR COMPLEX. TIME UNKNOWN. TRACKING SHOT, NORM D'S POV

He is being dragged down a seemingly endless corridor. The hallway is lined with strange hydraulic gauges and dull-coloured pipes. Wires and dome light fixtures are set along the ceiling—stretching out into the distance.

REVERSE ANGLE, CLOSE SHOT

of Norm D. He is handcuffed and held between the beefy arms of two leather clad Social Control Officers who drag him down the corridor. Norm's expression is slack and stupid; he has either just undergone some form of electroshock or has been injected with another sedative.

CONTINUOUS PAN, SWING TO ANOTHER TRACKING SHOT

We suddenly turn a corner, which changes the angle on Norm D. Just beyond the profile of his face, we see many, many locked steel doors.

Leo had some moments of true technical triumph. In the original draft, I just wrote: "Two social control officers drag Norm D. down a long hallway and throw him into a cell. D. puts up no resistance suggesting that he has been drugged." To the point, but not what we ended up shooting.

Leo was probably the only 16 year old in Saskatoon in 1972 who knew all about Orson Welles' famous tracking shot in *Touch of Evil* which was probably one of the reasons that he was looking for opportunities to "open up" our movie.

"Come on!" he would say whenever I'd complain about how complicated this was getting. "Are we creating cinema, or are we just writing a book?"

Just? I'd suppress my immediate reaction, then I'd look over at that Bolex of his and then I'd just shrug and let him get on with it.

Anyway, it was really my Dad's fault.

When I went to see him at his lab one day, no doubt to beg for an advance on my allowance to buy some new film, I brought Leo along with me to explain that I wasn't going to use the money to buy cigarettes, booze or dope. Somehow I knew that Leo would radiate the aura of "pure cinema" that would erase any of my Dad's doubts. I was right, two minutes into the conversation, Dad reached into his wallet and gave us 50 bucks. That was a lot of money in 1972. Then he took us out to lunch.

Maybe it was because we were such weird looking kids, or maybe Dad was getting into our SF mindset—but instead of taking us through the main lobby of the building, he took us down through the sub-basement and along the connector corridor between the labs and the university cafeteria. My thoughts were essentially gustatory lust, i.e. anticipation of the gravy and French fries that I knew would be waiting for us. Leo, on the other hand, was completely gob-smacked by the industrial design of that hallway.

"This is Douglas Trumbull!" Leo cried. "*Silent Running!*"

Silent Running was a pretty strange film by today's standards. It was directed by Douglas Trumbull who was one of Stanley Kubrick's special effects people on *2001* and consequently one of Leo's cinematic heroes. Stanley Kubrick was one of Leo's other heroes. *Silent Running* had lots of cool models and optical special effects (which you hardly ever see these days) but the locations were what Leo was talking about. Trumbull had doctored up the Valley Forge, a real aircraft carrier, to use as the interiors of a giant spacecraft. It was pretty convincing. The corridor between my Dad's lab and the cafeteria reminded Leo of what Mr. Trumbull did in that movie. So Leo become obsessed with the idea of using it in *Norm Deviation!*

The line of my script: "Two social control officers drag Norm D. down a long hallway and throw him into a cell" was where Leo could inject his cinematic magic.

When Reg and his big brother Bob showed up in their black leather jackets and evil biker helmets, Leo turned up with something that I wasn't expecting: a) Allison (who was always welcome and not entirely unexpected) and b) a circular wooden platform with four small wheels bolted onto the bottom. The platform was about four inches off the ground and Leo could sit cross-legged on it and point his camera in any direction he liked.

To me, he looked like a thin mobile Buddha down there but that was how he got those great tracking shots in the corridor.

While they were dragging me down the corridor, big brother Bob was using his other hand to haul Leo along on his rolling platform. The angle change, when we turned the corner, was really an accident. Bob's grip loosened a little and the platform rolled over to one side. Leo—the embryonic professional—smoothly adjusted the angle of the camera to match the speed of his drift and stay in focus.

Leo said that the shot worked because of exacting craftsmanship behind the Bolex lens and the incredibly forgiving properties of Kodachrome film. Possibly those were factors, but he was just being modest. It was the best shot in the movie and he pulled it off.

INTERIOR TESTING CHAMBER. LONG SHOT

of Norm D. strapped onto an examination table. Wires extend from electrodes pasted on his head and chest.

The two behavioural scientists stand in the distance. They are busy adjusting a bank of electronic instruments.

CLOSE-UP

of an ECG monitor. D's heartbeat bounces steadily along an illuminated checkerboard.

                    BEHAVIOURAL SCIENTIST #1
          His cardio-sino rhythms appear almost
          normal.

                    BEHAVIOURAL SCIENTIST #2
          Almost deceptively so.

Her finger traces the pattern of the steady
green curve.

                    BEHAVIOURAL SCIENTIST #2
          It's just outside the range of true
          human parameters.

CLOSE SHOT

of behavioural scientists #1 and #2. They look
at each other intently.

                    BEHAVIOURAL SCIENTIST #1
          Do you think this is more evidence of a
          genetically engineered organism?

                    BEHAVIOURAL SCIENTIST #2
          We will need more tissue samples to
          tell.

CLOSE-UP

Norm D., still groggy from medication, looks
down in the direction of his feet. His eyes
widen in alarm.

ANOTHER CLOSE-UP, NORM D'S POV

A thick articulated tube headed with an evil-
looking suction nozzle gradually snakes its way
up one of his legs.

Okay, a lot of films have their unintentionally funny moments and
Norm Deviation! was no exception. When you think about it, really
it was astonishing that we had so few. But the tissue-sampling
scene was pretty hysterical.

   It wasn't my fault this time. When I originally wrote the scene, the baddie behavioural scientists just used a needle to extract some blood. Fast, painful, plausible and good on camera.

But not according to Leo.

"Too subtle. Besides, blood effects are hard to do."

Then Sheila, who played Behavioural Scientist #2, suggested we go for a sperm sample instead. On reflection, I think Sheila had something of an obsession with sperm samples.

Back in Grade Seven when the curriculum in Health Class was covering the masturbation chapters in the human sexuality textbook, Sheila came up to me and said something.

What she said was that our teacher Mrs. Day (who was beautiful, had an amazing rack, and was the object of every boy in the class' fantasy) wanted me to demonstrate this self-pleasuring process in front of everyone.

For a second I believed her and I was both horrified and fascinated at the prospect. Then, of course, my face must have turned about 300 different shades of red. Then, Sheila laughed at me and went off to do some giggling with her friends.

I stood there and wondered what kind of a mind would think of a joke like that.

I lost touch with Sheila after we finished the movie but I do remember that she went on to become incredibly popular during the last two years of high school.

Leo didn't need a lot of convincing. Doing the "jack-off machine" as he so delicately put it immediately became a priority.

"It's edgy," he'd mutter. "Real edgy."

It was also a chance for him to experiment with more SFX tech. He decided that he was going to use some clear fishing line to make it look as though the hose was floating towards my penis. If anybody watching this scene can stop laughing long enough to look, they will realize that we actually pulled off the effect.

I'm very thankful that we didn't go with Sheila's suggestion. She thought we actually needed to see my penis being menaced as the nozzle moved up my leg.

"You could shoot it in stop motion animation," she said to Leo.

Which would have been pretty horrifying, it would have involved me laying there with my dork out for two days while every cast and crewmember could wander in and gawk at me.

Leo really liked any opportunity to use the single-frame feature of his camera so I don't hold it against him that he actually seriously considered Sheila's idea for a minute. Then his shook his head.

"No, Kodak would never develop films of somebody's weiner."

We shot some of that scene at the Phys-Ed Department at the University. The sets and props looked incredibly complicated and realistic but most of the shoot was pretty easy. Some grad students had gotten a grant from the Saskatchewan Research Council to study the effects of cannabis consumption on the brain and physiological structure of teenagers. I'd heard my dad telling one of his colleagues over lunch that so far the grad students hadn't signed up a single volunteer so that they were smoking up all day and using the equipment to measure themselves.

I can neither confirm nor deny this report, but I can say that when I called these guys up to ask if we could use their lab for a day, they said yes and giggled a lot.

The evening that we shot those scenes was the same night that the local CBC station broadcast *Night Gallery*. Leo and I went over to watch it at Allison's place because she was the only person we knew with a colour TV.

Leo liked *Night Gallery* a lot because he said it had great lighting—at least for something produced for American network television. He had a point; most shows back then had lousy lighting.

I liked *Night Gallery* because I was interested in anything weird or spooky and I was fascinated by Rod Serling. There was something mysterious and tragic about that little man with the deep rumbling voice. I knew him as the voice that took me to aquatic wonders when he narrated the Jacques Cousteau documentaries. I loved those shows because they made me feel like I was exploring another planet.

I was a little too young to remember Serling from *The Twilight Zone* series and much too young to know about stuff like his social realist teleplays like *Requiem for a Heavyweight* or *Patterns*—but I had read somewhere that he was once considered a pretty serious and important writer and that his reputation was now in some doubt.

Night Gallery was an uneven show at best and you could tell from watching his introductions, that Serling was bothered about this. When the segment was dumb, he looked a little sad and more than a little embarrassed. When it was a good show (usually something he'd written) his craggy, tight-skinned face looked pleased, even a little hopeful.

For some reason he reminded me of myself.

That night, *Night Gallery* had two segments. The first one was about a fisherman who used a magic potion to try and consummate his love for a mermaid with unfortunate results (dumb). The second segment was about a boy who has the ability to predict earthquakes and other future occurrences with REALLY unfortunate results (good).

"Nice side lighting," Leo pronounced as the credits ran over the strange Gil Mellé theme. Then he got out of his chair. "I gotta go."

Allison said that he should stay. The late movie was *When Worlds Collide* and she remembered that Leo said he wanted to see it.

"Can't," Leo replied. "My mom told me that we just got the first reels back from the developers."

"Hey!" Both Allison and I were pretty excited.

"I want to run them through the editor right away."

Of course we asked if we could come along.

"Not until the rough cut is ready."

Sometimes Leo was a team player. Other times he was such a bloody auteur.

Allison knew Leo even better than me, so she knew that there was no point in arguing with him. "You can stay for the movie," she said to me. Since I didn't have anywhere else in particular to be I was happy to do so.

My main impression of *When Worlds Collide* was, like all the other Technicolor films of the 1940s and 1950s, that somehow the brilliant and completely artificial colours made all that bad acting and terrible dialogue a lot more interesting.

Not necessarily better but different and somehow able to hold your attention. Strange effect that.

My memories of Allison that night were even more vivid but far more natural.

About halfway through the movie, when the scientist hero decides to tell his girlfriend that the planet Earth is essentially destined to become space toast, Allison was sitting very close to me on the couch and I became aware.

Aware of her.

Aware of me.

I kept noticing the lines of her bra underneath her T-shirt. I noticed the angled contour of her back. No spare flesh there but it looked strong.

Her hair was messy and a little oily, it hung in strands over her ears and the back of her slightly tanned neck. Her hair was much more interesting than anything in Technicolor.

Kodachrome might suit her better.

I noticed the sides of her small breasts. Even though I was miles away from touching them, they seemed somehow warm. I wondered if it would be okay with Allison if I did touch her breasts.

I glanced over at the TV screen. More close ups of people talking and looking concerned about astronomical events.

I looked back at Allison and noticed that she was watching me from the corner of her eye. At that point, I still wasn't sure about her breasts but it seemed definitely okay if I kissed her just then.

"Allison…"

Then something happened. One switch in my head clicked in and another one shut down. It wasn't that I was scared or even particularly nervous. I just suddenly knew that nothing was going to happen that night.

It wasn't that there was anything wrong with me. There certainly wasn't anything wrong with Allison; she was absolutely perfect. She probably still is.

No, I just knew that this was not the time for her and me to be doing such things.

So we went into the kitchen and found another bag of potato chips and watched the rest of movie. A little over an hour later we had killed an entire carton of colas while we watched the dawn on a new cartoon-ish planet and heard the voices of the Martian Tabernacle Choir swell as the end titles asked the profound question:

"The End?!"

"Or the Beginning?!"

Music swells. Fade to black.

End credits.

And there I was, riding my bike home in the early morning darkness.

Wondering when it would be my time for such things.

INTERIOR CONTAINMENT CELL. NORM D'S POV

The door opens and three figures walk in: THE

POLITICAL OFFICER, BEHAVIOURAL SCIENTIST #1 and a SOCIAL CONTROL OFFICER. The three are dressed in a khaki zippered jumpsuit, a labcoat and black leather respectively.

ANOTHER ANGLE

Norm D sits in the corner. He wears a gray T-shirt and pants and no shoes. His head has been shaved and there are red circles on his scalp where electrodes have been fastened. D looks pretty terrible.

CLOSE SHOT, NORM D'S POV

The Political Officer removes a computer punch card from his shirt pocket. He looks at the card, then looks at D with great contempt and starts to read from the card.

> POLITICAL OFFICER
> I have been authorized to inform you that after undergoing all legally mandated medical tests, you have been diagnosed as "Deviant Category No.1" according to all political and biological criteria.

CLOSE-UP

Of D. He seems to be struggling to understand what the Political Officer is saying.

CLOSE-UP, REVERSE ANGLE

of the Political Officer. He smirks as he continues to read from the card.

> POLITICAL OFFICER
> You have therefore been sentenced to vaporization without appeal. This

> action is necessary for the protection
> of the Greater Social Entity and will
> be carried out within the next 24
> hours.

ANOTHER ANGLE

The Political Officer drops the card in front
of D.

> POLITICAL OFFICER
> As a citizen it is, of course, your
> right to examine the scientific data
> and test scores used to arrive at this
> determination.

The Political Officer smiles, while the
scientist and Social Control Officer remain
expressionless. The Social Control Officer
opens the door and the three leave.

CLOSE UP

of D. After the echo of the slamming door
fades, he picks up the computer card and looks
at it carefully. He then runs his fingers along
the tiny punch holes as if the cryptic punch
holes might be some kind of machine-Braille.
Then the he tosses the card aside and puts his
head in his hands.

SLOW FADE

to an opaque wash of hazy blue. We hear D's
laboured breathing.

The easy part was the computer punch card. It was what
Saskatchewan Power was using to calculate your electricity bill.
Nobody knew what they said but it looked very technical and
official.

    Most of that scene was pretty tough to do.

It started one morning when Leo came up to me and announced: "We're fucked."

Very helpful information, I thought. I decided to further explore this realm of discourse.

"Uh, why are we fucked?"

"We don't have enough money," Leo replied. "My mom says that I've got to get a part-time job and pay for my own film from now on."

Get a job?!

We were indeed fucked.

Even with a divorced parent cold war in place with my folks I doubted that I could squeeze any more good will or charity out of them. Well, maybe there was some good will and charity but definitely no more cash.

No more money. No more film.

And we still had some key scenes to shoot.

Our deliverance came from an unexpected source.

I wanted to use the locker room at our school as the scene for D's confinement cell, so I asked Mr. Pozzi, my visual communications teacher, if he could help us get the necessary permissions. The fact that we students had Mr. Pozzi's home phone and the fact that he was taking calls over the summer vacation is some indicator of what kind of a teacher he was.

Mr. Pozzi set things up for us and much to my surprise with a lot of enthusiasm (I hadn't been all that great a student). So I felt badly when I had to call him up again and tell him that we would have to cancel the shoot because we had run out of film and funds.

Mr. Pozzi would have none of it.

"Don't worry about it," he said. "I've got tons of film stock left over from last semester. It's past its expiratory date but it should be just fine."

"Really?! Holy sh—I mean, thank you Mr. Pozzi!"

Getting them to unlock the school doors was tougher to arrange. Eventually we had to cast Gordon Thomas, who as the son of the Vice-Principal and was elected student council president for next year, to help grease the wheels.

It was typecasting but Gordon gave us a great performance as the Political Officer.

Looked like we only had solutions here.

Leo didn't agree. We had more than enough film now but the

stock we got from Mr. Pozzi was Ectachrome.
    Not Kodachrome.

*   *   *

1972 was a pretty uneven year. A few aesthetic and interpersonal highs. Some very pronounced lows.

1972 was the year I discovered (admittedly crude) cinematography and books. It was the year that my father left my mother and me. It was the same year that the same man gave me copies of Deutsche Grammophon recordings of Holt's *The Planets*, all six *Brandenburg Concertos* and *Also Sprach Zarathustra*, which were the seeds of my lifelong love of classical music. Can't get enough of the stuff and now at age forty-plus I can actually play a little piano.

I took to classical music fast which was one of the few things my mother had reason to be grateful to my father for. Whatever grief I was giving her back then, at least she didn't have to put up with poundingly bad electric guitars vibrating the house off its foundations.

1972 was the year I found God and stopped going to church. It was the year that I grew up and asserted my independence and hurt my mother almost as much as my father had done.

INTERIOR CONTAINMENT CELL. LATER THAT NIGHT.

FADE IN UNTIL THE CELL IS FLOODED WITH STRANGE BLUE LIGHT.

Norm D. lays on the floor, apparently asleep, the computer card still next to him. He stirs, slowly awakened by an eerie buzzing sound. Eventually D. sits up and looks in the direction of the light.

CLOSE UP

D. is truly astonished by what he sees.

NORM D.'S POV

A turquoise coloured alien stands there. The being is over six feet tall with incredibly thin limbs and body. It has a large oval head with two enormous jeweled compound eyes and a thin lipless mouth.

The buzzing rises and falls in pitch—as if the alien was trying to communicate with D.

CLOSE-UP

D shakes his head. He does not understand.

NORM D.'S POV

The alien moves toward him. The being walks with an odd flowing motion as it were using some kind of force field to protect it from higher gravity.

CLOSE-UP

The alien points at the computer printout card. The thick paper starts to curl and smoke and finally burns away into a pile of ash.

CLOSE SHOT

The alien uses both of its hands to hold D.'s face. It pulls D.'s face closer and gives him a long, lingering kiss.

The blue light gets incredibly bright until the screen WHITES OUT.

CUT TO:

INTERIOR CONTAINMENT CELL. SOMETIME LATER.

Norm D. stands there. He is alone.

```
D.'S POV

The door to his cell is open.
```

Okay, the summer of 1972 was the time of my great artistic and intellectual awakening. It was also the summer that I got kissed by a puppet.

By the time we got to film that moment, I was happy and relieved to do so. Honest!

Leo was constantly complaining about how hard the remaining scenes were going to shoot with Ectachrome and there was no way we had enough lights to shoot any interiors with that f-stop and colour balance. He announced that unless I could do a re-write with all exteriors we couldn't finish.

Leo could be really stubborn sometimes.

"How about we just kill D.?" Leo said this over a plate of fries at our favourite fish and chips place. "The SCOs march him out in front of a wall, shoot him with some electrical guns and them dump him in a mass grave with a few hundred other dead deviants."

"Very cheerful," I replied. I ate some of Leo's fries and thought about that narrative possibility for a moment.

"We could shoot the scene over by the concrete quarry," Leo continued.

This was getting risky, when Leo was doing logistics, he usually had pretty much made up his mind. So I swallowed and shook my head.

"Only as a last resort. It's just too much of a change in the tone of the film."

Leo grimaced. "As opposed to the feel-good-movie of the summer that you had originally conceived?"

Leo had progressed from being difficult to being cranky. I really did not feel like having this kind of a conversation with him.

"Besides," I said. "Where are we going to get all those dead deviants? We don't have that many friends."

Leo was quiet for a moment. I had raised a legitimate technical problem. We ate his food and stopped talking about the project for a while. The next day we discovered that Mr. Pozzi had anticipated the photographic challenges of the new film format and lent us four banks of floodlights. Now we could shoot all the interiors we liked.

Still Leo wasn't completely satisfied. "The film grain and the colour balance is going to be completely different," he complained.

"You'll make it work," I replied.

The look he gave me!

There were two other problems associated with shooting that scene: Allison and the Alien.

Allison had pretty much vanished after the *When Worlds Collide* viewing. I was worried that she noticed that I had been staring at her breasts and had decided that I was a real-life deviant and was now hanging out with nicer people who were genuine artists.

Either Leo didn't know where she was, or didn't feel like telling me.

Never mind, I had an alien to worry about. Originally we were going to get Reg to play the creature. Leo had ordered a mutant monster mask from a *Famous Monsters* magazine. Easy, right?

Like many simple solutions, it turned out not to be a solution at all. When Reg put the mask on he looked like a big teenager with an old lady's ass stuck onto the back of his head.

Not quite the sense of awe and wonder we were hoping to invoke.

"How about something more conceptual?" I suggested.

"Conceptual?"

"Symbolic. Maybe the alien isn't something that we'd recognize as any sort of a life form at all. Like a big prism or crystal or something."

Leo looked thoughtful.

I continued, sensing that I might have something here: "Or we could paint the door black and shoot it from a low angle, looking up, so that it looks like—"

"A monolith?"

I'm pretty sure I looked very embarrassed.

"You know," Leo said with a certain amount of justifiable disdain. "There's a difference between doing an homage and just being pathetic."

Allison reappeared and she had a brilliant solution to our alien problem.

The puppet.

The fucking beautiful alien puppet.

She had made this fantastic marionette, taller than she was, and made it of lightweight balsa wood. Allison had shellacked it with green varnish that somehow looked turquoise on film. The eyes were made of mirrored beads, plastic "gem" stones and bits off old charm bracelets.

Allison had locked herself in her basement all week, building this amazing thing.

To hold it up we used the same fishing line we had used to operate the nozzle of the jack-off machine. Allison then lay on top of a row of lockers and pulled on the wires to make the puppet move its arms and legs.

Getting kissed by the alien was Allison's idea. I wasn't crazy about it but after she'd put in all that work, what could I say?

Leo put a blue filter on the lens turned on every one of our flood lights while we were shooting. The end result anticipated all those close encounter scenes that Spielberg and Cameron would be showing us for the next 30 years.

Homage, indeed.

INTERIOR BASEMENT CORRIDOR.

D. steps out of his cell. He looks around.

LONG SHOT, D. 'S POV

D. sees the body of a Social Control Officer laying on the floor.

ANOTHER ANGLE

D. half-runs, half-staggers toward the officer.

CLOSE SHOT

D. bends over and removes the officer's helmet. The fallen man is breathing—very, very slowly.

EXTREME LONG SHOT. PAN DOWN

to reveal D. running up the labyrinth of stairs leading up from the sub-basement of the Complex.

CUT TO:

NEXT LEVEL OF THE COMPLEX. LONG SHOT, D.'S POV

The two Behavioural Scientists are laying on the floor. Their arms and legs are splayed wide open and they are surrounded by loose pages from their clipboards. Whatever hit them, did so very suddenly.

ANOTHER ANGLE

D. stands there for a moment, studying the bodies. He turns and runs down the corridor.

CUT TO:

GROUND FLOOR LOBBY

D. pushes open a big set of double doors and stops to catch his breath for a moment. His eyes widen in surprise at what he sees.

CLOSE-UP, D.'S POV

It is the Political Officer. He is also laying on the floor but his face is bruised and his head is twisted at an odd angle. A pool of dark arterial blood has pooled on the floor around his head. The P.O. is not asleep.

CLOSE SHOT

D. looks up

TILT TO LONG SHOT, D.'S POV

of the top of the Complex's atrium. Presumably the P.O. was leaning on one of the upper rails when he fell asleep.

CLOSE-UP

of D. His expression is impassive.

CUT TO:

EXTERIOR COMPLEX, MAIN ENTRANCE. DAY

D. throws these doors open and races down the stairs.

CLOSE SHOT, D.'S POV

He sees a row of bicycles parked next to the building.

CLOSE-UP

of D. He smiles.

CUT TO:

MONTAGE OF SHOTS. D. riding a bicycle at high speed. He leaves the Complex Campus, then past the gray government buildings of the downtown district. There is no traffic or pedestrians— the sleep seems to have affected the entire city. Next D. rides past wider suburban streets, then finally he pedals down a seemingly endless ribbon of prairie highway.

There isn't much to say here that isn't another re-telling of the earlier production stories I've been telling you. Like true novices we were actually shooting most of the scenes in the order of the script but we were learning all the time and at this point we were actually pretty experienced. What we were getting out of the process was the solid joy of quietly doing the right things well.

A couple of things of note at this stage:

1. The Ectachrome stock did indeed look very different from the

footage we had in Kodachrome. But this worked to our advantage: it was a subtle thing—today we might call it "subtextual"—where it looked like the very nature of reality changed after the manifestation of the alien. Now I didn't write it that way and Leo certainly didn't direct it that way but it was really quite powerful. I'm pretty sure a lot of what we think of as genius is actually the ability to take advantage of these happy artistic accidents.

2. Okay, so Leo was completely surprised by how great the change in film stock made the end of the film—but the tracking shots from the bicycle montage was one of the greatest examples of Leo's technical skill and courage. He made a small L-clip out of metal and used it to attach his Bolex to the front wheel of his ten-speed.

At the time I was shocked that he would risk his most treasured creative tool in such a way—but the resulting footage was fantastic.

It is interesting to note that while I'm seen riding the bike at the beginning and end of the scene—it was Leo doing the driving during the montage itself.

It wasn't that I was such an unreliable cyclist but knowing Leo I think that he worried that if the camera did have an accident he didn't want to blame anyone but himself.

```
EXTERIOR PRAIRIE FIELD.  MORNING

D.  brakes  the  bicycle  to  a  stop.  He  looks  to
the sky.

LONG SHOT

D.  and  his  bike  are  dwarfed  by  the  shining
silver and crimson hull of a huge SAUCER SHAPED
SPACECRAFT.  There  is  a  LOW  RUMBLING  SHOUND  as
the  ship  descends  to  the  ground  and  a  GANTRY
WAY swings down.

CLOSE-UP
```

of D.'s face. He looks surprisingly calm. After
a moment he nods his head slightly.

LONG SHOT

D. wheels his bike inside the saucer. The
gantry way swings up and the rumbling sound
resumes.

ANOTHER ANGLE - GROUND LEVEL, LOOKING UP

There is another sound—A HIGH-PITCHED WHINE—as
the saucer starts to spin and hurtles into the
sky.

CUT TO:

SPACE. LONG SHOT.

The saucer, still spinning at high speed,
coasts past the sun.

PAN

The camera follows the saucer as it recedes
into the distance and disappears into the star-
sprinkled void.

FADE

TO CREDITS

Doing the shoot out in the field was pretty easy and I was
impressed with how Leo was able to manipulate the focus so it
looked like I was walking into a gigantic spacecraft when in fact he
was holding one of his little brother's toys very close to the lens
while I was walking very far away from the camera.

The rest of the film was essentially post-production work and
that made Leo very happy because it gave him a chance to play
around with the Bolex's stop-frame animation feature. It also got
the rest of us out of his hair for a while.

He used one of the floodlights with a black construction paper background to re-create the sun and Allison sprinkled icing sugar on more black paper to generate our starscape.

I never saw that set up. The project really didn't need me to be there all the time and my life was insisting on moving on.

The next few years were not going to be the easiest for me. Thinking about it now, I understand that making *Norm Deviation!* was my way of delaying dealing with those inevitabilities—at least for one summer.

My parents' breakup had entered an ugly stage. Mom divided most of her time between crying and trying to sell the house.

"Too many memories," she'd say. "Too many memories."

Things were getting too tense for me to just go over and hang out at my Dad's lab any more. It looked like disloyalty to Mom. So I'd see Dad on those legally mandated visits and sometimes we'd actually take in a good movie. My favourite was when he decided we should go see *The Godfather* because he'd heard that *The French Connection* was too violent! Unfortunately it wasn't the same kind of quality time that we'd had when Leo and I were shooting the film. Probably because Dad was so distracted with all the wedding arrangements.

It was awkward and it was starting to weigh pretty heavily on me. When we got back into school in September it was pretty apparent that my grades were going down (and they weren't spectacular in the first place), my teachers didn't like my attitude (understandable as I had become a very sullen and sarcastic kid) and was getting punched out on a fairly regular basis by members of our Provincial championship football team (not surprising given the fact that I was pretty cute back then and they had lots of unresolved homo-erotic issues).

By early October the summer of creative magic was most definitely over. I had gone from making a film about an oppressive future called *Norm Deviation!* to living the life of a norm deviation in an oppressive now.

There was a brief interlude around Hallowe'en when I got to re-live that summer for just one evening.

Leo had finished all the editing and post-production work and was ready to premiere the film. The gala was staged in the family room in the basement of his house and he wired the Bell and Howell projector to his Sony cassette player for the synchronized sound. And in another display of early seventies technological prowess, he had connected the tape player to the amps and speakers of their eight-track stereo.

"Simulated Surround Sound," he explained.

It sounded great. Mostly, I'm glad I kept my dialogue to a minimum.

The audience consisted of cast members, bored siblings, proud and bemused parents (not mine) and Mr. Pozzi. Some of the kids were on their way to a costume party (not me) and were in costume (also not me, I had gotten way too self-conscious at this point). Allison was dressed up as a magical fairy. She wore a ballet costume with a frilly tutu and she had these amazing and beautiful delicate butterfly wings made from coat hangers and coloured Kleenex.

Reg was dressed up in his Social Control Officer outfit; on reflection I think we had started what looked like an unnatural attachment to things leather. There were also a few aliens and astronauts in the audience as well. In 1972 these were NOT particularly cool themes so we should have been honoured by the tribute.

The film. The film?

Pretty much as I've written it out here.

The one thing that I haven't been able to express was the musical score. In complete violation of international copyright laws, Leo had mixed in music by a band called Syrinx. They were pretty unconventional for the 1970s, consisting of a percussionist, saxophone player and—get this—a synthesizer artist. Very new age and long before we even had the concept.

The music was perfect for our movie, particularly the ending with the bicycle escape and the ascent into the flying saucer. While we were filming I imagined the music would be something a little more traditionally associated with science fiction/outer spacey stuff—like the theremin and orchestra composition that Bernard Herrmann wrote for *The Day The Earth Stood Still*.

At one point I almost suggested we go with classical music a la Stanley Kubrick then I remembered Leo's monolith remark and decided to keep quiet.

Leo was such a fucking genius, not just a great technician but someone with incredible artistic sensibilities. For the ending scene he used a Syrinx piece called *December Angel*. Very haunting, gentle and ethereal music. Not only did it pull at your heartstrings as you watched poor lonely D. disappear into the saucer it was a great accompaniment for people working with sprocket and glue technology.

Looking at Allison and admiring how the light from the screen flickered on her face and those tissue-paper wings. I wished that I could have written her and those wings into the movie somehow.

And just over 30 minutes later, the show was over. I honestly don't remember the specifics of what people said or did later that night. Mr. Pozzi did corner me and told us that we should submit the film for course credit. Leo and Allison did just that. I didn't because I was feeling too bummed out by some stupid thing or other.

Over the next weekend Leo and Allison and I got together and talked about making a sequel to *Norm Deviation!* where we see what happens when Norm reaches his destination somewhere on a distant planet. Leo envisioned it as a special effects extravagancy where he could really do some animation with the Bolex.

"We could populate the world with alien robot hybrids," suggested Allison. "I could do some model cities for them."

"Something with winged beings," I added looking at Allison through the corner of my eye.

"I bet I could even do a couple of matte shots," Leo said excitedly.

I guess that was a big deal.

Somehow the sequel never happened. Maybe the scope of the project was just beyond us at the time. The Monday morning after our meeting made me feel like just about everything was beyond me at the time.

First period, my science teacher was reading excerpts from my latest assignment out to the class, and not in a good way.

Next it was off to the Vice Principal's office to discuss my latest beating. "What is it that you're doing that provokes them so much?" he asked me.

Then just before lunch I got my latest Algebra test back.

"That's the lowest score in the class," Mrs. Newton told me.

Inspiration was in rather short supply those days.

About six months later, Mom sold the house and we moved to another city. This was essentially the end of my first cinematic collaboration.

Leo and Allison went on to creative careers. He went into film (of course!). Allison did a lot of different things but ultimately ended up as a reasonably well respected painter and sculptor.

We kept in touch, more or less, over the years and even used to visit each other in our various resident communities. Leo and Allison even dated on and off for almost ten years but it didn't become anything permanent. I finally lost track of Allison by the early nineties. Perhaps she put on those fairy wings and flew off to be with more interesting people.

Leo never did become the next Stanley Kubrick. However after *Eyes Wide Shut*, I'll bet that Leo doesn't feel too badly about that.

I guess I should talk about what happened to me between 1972 and now. Well, things got better, things got worse, better, worse, you see the pattern, right? Besides, it's just a little too involved to get into right now.

You could say that I'm coping.

~

ASTONISHING FAILURES

Your imagination and art must go where they have to and there's usually a lot of cross-pollination when you're telling and re-imagining stories that you care about.

Speculative fiction by its very nature is a strange yet potent mix of grass-roots movement and global media manifestation. *Star Trek* (which begat *Star Wars* which then begat almost everything) only returned from cancellation limbo because of the continued popular culture activism of generations of fans. Most of the classic American SF writers came from buzzing cliques of mimeograph zine printers. Even H.G. Wells—the inventor of many of SF's central paradigms[11]—came from a very humble lower-class background.

I can understand why SF has something verging on an obsession when it comes to checking credentials (Pro? Semi-pro? Fan?). In such a continually shifting landscape it can be difficult to acknowledge artistic achievement. Also, the potential risk of embarrassing yourself can be enormous.

Risk.

The risk of being misunderstood. The risk of not having the experience or creative skills to say what you need to. The risk of being ignored. Of being laughed at.

When you're writing, failure is definitely an option.

However, I submit that interesting failures—particularly those that lead you to try new things or see things in different ways—can be much more valuable than conventional success.

It is foolish to try and make a Hollywood feature film with old-fashioned home movie equipment and your best friends as actors. It just won't happen. Maybe it is silly to devote time writing for and performing in such an increasingly invisible media as radio drama.

---

11 The alien invasion story (*The War of the Worlds*), the time travel story (*The Time Machine*), the space exploration story (*The First Men in the Moon*), the scientific monster story (*The Island of Doctor Moreau* and *The Invisible Man*), the future war story (*The War in the Air*), the dystopia story (*When the Sleeper Wakes*) and so on. As a youngster, Wells even published his own zine of sorts—his editorial voice apparently fueled by the large personal library of his mother's employer and a family love of cartoons and jokes.

Who's going to hear you? Very possibly, writing about UFOs and sick robots and the world ending multiple times is a harebrained enterprise. Who's going to care?

As a reader you decide whether you care about these stories or not. That's part of the risk.

And I won't stop taking it.[12]

---

12 I did fail to become a major film-maker (darn). But "(Coping with) Norm Deviation" was very much informed by my early attempts at movie making, and it received an honorable mention in the 2007 *Year's Best Science Fiction* anthology and received a very nice review in *Locus* magazine. That felt like success.

Hugh A. D. Spencer completed graduate studies at the University of Toronto and McMaster University where he conducted anthropological studies into the origins of religious movements in science fiction fandom.

Twice nominated for Canada's Aurora Award, Hugh's science fiction has been published in *On Spec*, *Tesseracts 8*, *11* and *6*, *Interzone*, *Descant* and *New Writings in the Fantastic*. Many of his short stories have been dramatized by Shoestring Radio Theatre for the Satellite Network of National Public Radio. His most recent short stories are "Five Stories About Alan" which was published in *Dandelions of Mars: A Tribute to Ray Bradbury* and "John, Paul, Xavier, Ironside & George (but not Vincent)" which was published in the *Ominous Realities* anthology. Hugh's first novel, *Extreme Dentistry*, was released by Brain Lag in 2014.

Hugh is also President and Senior Consultant of the cultural consulting company Museum Planning Partners. He worked on the Ontario Prehistory and Canadian Ethnology galleries at the Royal Ontario Museum and has travelled to Asia, Europe, Australia and throughout North America on assignment for many different museum, art gallery, science centre and world's fair projects. Even with all this travel, he always happy to return to his home in the aging suburbs of Toronto which he shares with his family, friends and two dogs.

www.ingramcontent.com/pod-product-compliance
Lightning Source LLC
Chambersburg PA
CBHW032222050726

47591CB00001B/223